# TIMEWYRM: GENESYS

# DOCTOR WHO – NEW ADVENTURES

Also available:

TIMEWYRM: GENESYS by John Peel
TIMEWYRM: EXODUS by Terrance Dicks
TIMEWYRM: APOCALYPSE by Nigel Robinson
TIMEWYRM: REVELATION by Paul Cornell

CAT'S CRADLE: TIME'S CRUCIBLE by Marc Platt
CAT'S CRADLE: WARHEAD by Andrew Cartmel
CAT'S CRADLE: WITCH MARK by Andrew Hunt

NIGHTSHADE by Mark Gatiss
LOVE AND WAR by Paul Cornell
TRANSIT by Ben Aaronovitch
THE HIGHEST SCIENCE by Gareth Roberts
THE PIT by Neil Penswick
DECEIT by Peter Darvill-Evans

# TIMEWYRM: GENESYS

John Peel

Foreword by Sophie Aldred

First published in Great Britain in 1991
by Doctor Who Books
an imprint of Virgin Publishing
332 Ladbroke Grove
London W10 5AH

Reprinted 1993

Copyright © John Peel 1991
Foreword copyright © Sophie Aldred 1991
'Doctor Who' television series copyright © British
Broadcasting Corporation 1991

Cover illustration by Andrew Skilleter

Typeset by Type Out, London SW16
Printed and bound in Great Britain by
Cox & Wyman Ltd, Reading, Berks.

ISBN 0 426 20355 0

This book is sold subject to the condition that it shall not, by way of trade or otherwise, be lent, resold, hired out, or otherwise circulated without the publisher's prior consent in any form of binding or cover other than that in which it is published and without a similar condition including this condition being imposed on the subsequent purchaser.

# Preface

Here is an introductory word about *Doctor Who — The New Adventures:* continuity.

Our objectives in publishing this series of novels are: to continue the time and space peregrinations of the Doctor and Ace from the point at which we last saw them on television, at the end of the story *Survival*; to continue the Doctor Who traditions of exciting science fiction stories laced with humour, drama and terror; and to continue the trend of recent seasons of television stories towards complex, challenging plots with serious themes.

Within these objectives there is room for a universe of types of story and styles of writing, and I've encouraged the authors of *The New Adventures* to take full advantage of the scope offered by the medium of the novel. In *Timewyrm: Genesys* John Peel has produced a two-fisted, sword-wielding, action-packed adventure that doesn't pause for breath between the first and last pages. Each subsequent book in the Timewyrm series — *Exodus* by Terrance Dicks, *Apocalypse* by Nigel Robinson, and *Revelation* by Paul Cornell — has its own style; all, however, share the common Doctor Who heritage. A second series, of three novels, is in preparation.

Creating a new series of original Doctor Who novels is a considerable undertaking — I can vouch for the fact that the TARDIS is a tricky craft to pilot — and thanks are due to all who made it possible: Chris Weller of BBC Books, for letting us do it; John Nathan-Turner, for supporting the project right up to the end of his Producership; Andrew Cartmel, Marc Platt, Ben Aaronovitch, John Peel, Ian Briggs, and Jean-Marc Lofficier, for providing the plot and characterization details out of which I have tried to create a consistent background for the series; Andrew Skilleter, for stepping into the void to illustrate the covers; Sylvester McCoy and Sophie Aldred, for providing such vivid characterisations of the Doctor and Ace, for allowing us to use their faces on our book covers, for supporting Doctor Who in general and *The New Adventures* in particular, and thanks especially to Sophie for her generosity in writing a foreword for this novel; Ríona MacNamara, my assistant, without whom I simply couldn't have done it; and every single one of the people who have submitted proposals for stories.

The Doctor continues — unregenerated, but with a new lease of life.

Peter Darvill-Evans, Series Editor
February 1991

# Foreword

The legend of Gilgamesh and Enkidu takes me back to wet Thursday afternoons in the history room at school, doodling in my rough book and half listening to a droning voice at the front of the class. And when John Peel mentioned that his new book in some way encompassed that age-old story, my heart sank and I remembered a very bad essay that I'd once written about Mesopotamia. 'Oh, great: that's fantastic,' I muttered, summoning up a false grin. Imagine my delight when John sent me his first draft which I started reading and couldn't put down. Why hadn't my history teacher described these characters as though they existed and shaped a real world, *our* world, all those thousands of years ago? Well, I suppose she can be forgiven, for she had no TARDIS, no Time Lord and no Ace to help her relate something so far back in time to our modern lives.

No Doctor, no Ace. That's something we all feared would happen at one point. I was heartbroken to say farewell to such a dynamic, interesting character, one who was such a good foil to Sylvester's irascible, quirky, utterly lovable Doctor, a character to whom even strangers could relate and use as a role model, a real life companion who reflected our society and especially the young woman's role at the end of 1980s.

And now all is not lost! Ace continues to live on the printed page, as bolshy, as aggravating and just as much a headache for the 'professor' as she was on the small screen.

I'm very honoured to have been asked to write the foreword for what marks an exciting journey ahead for *Doctor Who*. I wish the writers good luck and happy hunting, for there are an infinite number of stories yet to be told.

And you, the reader, will ensure that his strangely wonderful man will continue to inspire the imaginations of millions of people all over the globe, with his twinkling eye and his unquenchable thirst for knowledge and truth whenever or wherever he pops his head out the door of that battered old police box.

Finally my thanks go to all those who have welcomed me so warmly into the *Doctor Who* family. I have this strange feeling that it's one I shall never leave.

Sophie Aldred
February 1991

# TIMEWYRM: GENESYS

For Jeremy and Paula Bentham
and it's about time

People of Eridu, hear me!
You who shop in the market place, listen.
You who tend the vines by the Great River, stop your work.
You who guard the flocks from wolves and lions, give heed.
Mighty are the deeds of Gilgamesh, king of men!
Strong is the arm of Enkidu, brother to the beast!
Mysterious are the paths of Ea, god of wisdom.
Bright the promises by Aya, goddess of the dawn.
You who would know their story, listen!

When the gods make war, the Earth trembles.
Stars fall from their fixed abodes and rain death upon the world.
Glorious and featful Ishtar came among us
Ancient and cunning, Utnapishtim made his path known to us.
If we did not have Gilgamesh to watch over us, where should we be?
If the arm of Enkidu was not raised in our defence, should we not fall?
If the wisdom of Ea had not spoken in our ears, would we still live?
If the brightness of Aya had not been granted us, how could we see?
Listen then, and hear their tale, people of Eridu.
You who dwell between the waters, give me ear.
I am Avram, the songsmith. What I saw, I tell.

# Prologue

The starship shuddered. Another bolt lashed through the ether and ripped at the ship's exposed flank. Somewhere a klaxon sounded, unheeded and unceasing. Smoke drifted through the darkened corridors. In the blood-red emergency lighting the creeping smoke was surreal, a living creature crawling towards the remnant of the crew.

Hissing to herself in fury, she surveyed the scene in the control room through the dying eyes of the pilot. Struggling to obey her and to stay alive, he fought back the clutching fingers of death. The pain in his chest subsided, and he tried to reach the screens with his right hand. In a haze, he realized that he no longer had a right hand. Using his left he finally managed to hit the controls.

'You cannot die yet!' Her command thundered through his fading brain. 'Focus on the readings! Focus, damn you!'

He finally forced his head to turn far enough to see the figures on the screen. Dimly, he knew that they meant that the shields about most of the craft had collapsed. Several sections had been gutted, and whoever had been in them had been either fried or sucked into the void. Their attacker had finished this pass, and was returning to make another. It would undoubtedly be the final one. Already the crippled starship was hanging together almost entirely through the force of her mind.

'Imbeciles!' she screamed, and within their minds they all felt her contempt and fury — those that were still alive. She could sense no more than a dozen left to her now. In a spasm of rage she wrenched her mind away from the pilot, and felt him die. Normally she would have hovered nearby, licking mentally at his death-throes. Now there was no time to enjoy herself. In moments she, too, might be dead.

She slipped into the mind of the navigator. He was still almost whole and began the scans that she had ordered. This far out from the hub of Mutters spiral there were very few possible havens for her. The figures scrolled upwards. Only one planet that could sustain humanoid life in the small sun system ahead of them. Not that she needed such an environment to live in, but her slaves would. The other worlds showed up as totally unsuitable for her purposes. No life of any kind. As for the third planet...

She cursed at the results. Life, yes — but no intelligence! No radio waves, no radioactivity, no sign of industrialization! Useless, completely useless!

The captain's panicked thoughts broke through her waves of fury, and she burrowed into his mind. He was once again becoming frantic with fear as their attacker swung about to begin the final assault — the barrage that they could never survive.

She forced herself to become calm. Well, this third world would have to do. Without technology she would be trapped there, but if there was life, then she could feed and survive. In time, what she needed might become available — if she managed to escape this attack.

Enclosed within her life-pod, she started the launch sequence. But she would need to camouflage her escape. If they knew she was baling out, the others would hunt her down. She had to do this very carefully indeed...

She reinforced her grip on the navigator's mind, and made him change the ship's heading. Dropping the remaining, useless shields, she had the hands she controlled start the overload sequence on the reactor core. The count-down began. Her thought turned to the captain, and she made him manoeuvre the ship about. Then she triggered the drive units — and propelled her dying ship directly into the path of the oncoming aggressor. *Taste this!* she screamed mentally, in defiance, at her old foes. One of her slender talons hovered over the trigger. There was just one final act to perform...

The last eleven crewmembers were barely clinging to their

foolish lives. Well, there was still something that they could do for her. They could die. She sent the command, feeding off their final energies, feeling her own mind grow slightly stronger with each death. There was no time to savour the feasting, so she was forced to rush. She had no idea when she might be able to feed again.

When they were dead, she hit the release.

Space surrounded her. She barely had time to register the bulk of her tattered ship rushing past her before it exploded, showering slivers of debris across her field of vision. The explosion would have blanked her attackers' sensors long enough for them to have missed her escape. She switched from *drive* to *standard*, slipping back into normal space-time. The wreckage faded from about her tiny craft. With luck the blast would have damaged the attacking ship.

The third planet hung below her. It was half-lit by the light of its sun, and gleamed blue and white. It was almost like home. She began a closer scan, and cursed as each of the indications confirmed what she had read from the main ship. No concentrations of electro-magnetic power; no emissions of exhaust gases; no transport systems; no communication signals. Whatever life was here was so primitive as to be totally useless to her. She needed intelligence, not simply animal life. She couldn't feed from uncomprehending beasts. Without minds to plunder, she would die. That pretty little globe below would become her tomb.

Abruptly, an alarm sounded. Glancing at the screens again, she saw that the pod had been damaged. She had left her escape too late. The thrusters were almost empty of fuel, and she was losing control of the small vessel. Gravity was pulling her into the planet's embrace.

She found herself enjoying the irony of the situation. Having escaped, and taken control of the starship, and fled across space, she was going to die in this barren, lifeless wasteland. It would all end here... Was it better to die in the flames of planetary entry or later, alone and starving for the only food she could eat? After all of her efforts — to die like this, in solitude, in this wretched spot, this wasteland planet of blue and white and green...

# 1: Serpent In The Garden

'Gilgamesh!'

The voice was a whisper on the breeze, but Gilgamesh heard it clearly. Frowning, he glanced about the wooded slopes. Now there was no sign of the strange white antelope he had followed from the plains below. That idiot calling his name had scared it away before he had been able to find a clear shot with his spear.

'Gilgamesh!'

There is was again, and louder this time 'O fool, shut up!' hissed the hunter, annoyed. Shielding his eyes from the glare of the sun, Gilgamesh darted his gaze about the copse. It was most strange — he had seen the white deer enter this grove, and yet there were no tracks on the ground, and no movements in the bushes. And, now that he thought of it, no sign of the owner of that mysterious voice.

'Gilgamesh,' the voice called again. 'This way, O man.'

Gilgamesh flung his spear down in disgust. He might as well try and fight a fly in the market-place as hunt a deer with that idiot yelling. Then, thinking better of it, he retrieved the spear. There were still brigands in these border hills, and it was best to be safe, although he was carrying no valuables and it was unlikely that any common robber would recognize him as the king of Uruk. He looked nothing like a king at the moment — all he wore for the hunt was a knotted loincloth, a pair of sandals, and a couple of armbands. He had reluctantly left his regal clothing in the palace of Uruk before he had embarked on this spying mission.

It hadn't been his idea, initially. He hated spying. Dirty, underhanded and devious, those were the ways of the spy. Gilgamesh preferred honest, open warfare — the thrust of the spear, the well-aimed arrow from the bow, the war-club crushing the skull of some opponent. Those were deeds of which men could sing. But to skulk about, prying and spying — gods, it set his teeth on edge. But his advisers had insisted that more information was needed before any warfare could be considered. Gilgamesh had bowed to their collective wisdom when his trusted friend Enkidu had agreed with them.

The strain of silent slinking had soon proved too much for Gilgamesh. Having left the plains of his own kingdom to venture into the realm of the ruler of Kish, he had rapidly lost all patience with his mission. The flight of the white deer ahead of him into the hills had been all the excuse he had needed to leave the rest of the patrol in Enkidu's capable — if hairy — hands, and to make his way up the slopes in pursuit of the fleeing hart.

His leather sandals made no noise as he crept toward the source of that irritating voice. His bronze skin, burnt by the eternal sun, rippled over his muscles. His huge fist held the spear, his only weapon. For a fleeting moment he wondered if it had been a wise move to leave the patrol and his friends to hunt this weird deer alone. Then he buried the thought; was he not Gilgamesh, mightiest of the sons of men? Was he to be shamed into running by some perplexing voice?

He broke through the ring of trees and halted in amazement. When he had led a hunt through this spot barely two seasons ago trees had filled the crown of the hill. Now the branches lay burnt and broken. In the centre of the space was a pit. The evidence suggested it had been recently dug. But who would dig a pit up here, on a hill that no one normally visited? And for what purpose?

Gilgamesh moved forward, cautiously. Again, the voice called his name, and this time he could tell that the owner of the voice must be within the pit.

Perhaps someone had fallen into the pit and needed his help to climb out? Hardly likely — for who could not see such a large hole in the earth? Except perhaps at night — but the voice was not calling for help, but for *him*... If it were someone trapped within the pit, how could they know that it was Gilgamesh passing by, and not some other man?

Standing on the lip of the pit, his spear held firmly before him, Gilgamesh stared down into the depths.

It was like the mountain of the gods down there! Smoke rose from the blackness, fading as it curled into the sunlight. Gilgamesh could not imagine what might have caused this. Then he recalled — two nights ago, during the feast of Shamash, one of the priests had seen a star falling from the sky! Gilgamesh had assumed that the priest had taken a little too much of the new beer, but what if the man had indeed told the truth? Could this be where the star had fallen?

The idea appealed to him. No one in human knowledge had ever found a fallen star. It was well known that stars changed into common rock when they fell from their appointed places in the sky. Yet Gilgamesh could see the brightness of something that lay within the pit. If he could be the first man to bring back to Uruk a star still burning, it would be yet another triumph for them to add to the songs about him! With hope growing, but still with care, he started down the slope into the pit.

Once out of the glare of the sun, he could see more clearly, and he paused yet again. Jagged pieces of something that glinted littered the walls of the pit. He bent to touch his spear to a piece of it. The object rang when struck, as copper would. But this was certainly not copper. Carefully, he picked up the object. It felt like copper, but it looked a little like dull silver. It was hard and polished like metal, but what could it be?

'Gilgamesh!' The voice was back, whispering from ahead of him. 'Do not be afraid.'

'I am not afraid, O voice,' he said, annoyed. 'No man calls Gilgamesh afraid.'

'I am sorry, Gilgamesh,' the voice murmured, but it sounded more amused than ashamed. 'But I am no man, as you will see if you come further forward.'

Warily, Gilgamesh stood his ground. 'Well, O voice that belongs to no man, why should I come forward? I am the king of this hill. I think that you should come to me, not me to you.'

'Ahhh.' It was a long, drawn-out sigh. 'If I could come to you, I should. But I am not able to move that far.'

'What are you, then, that can sound like a man, but not move like one?'

'Come and see,' the voice suggested. Although it was still the same as he had been hearing all along, it now seemed to have taken on further qualities. Now it sounded definitely female. Gilgamesh knew that he had nothing to fear from any woman, and moved further into the pit.

He saw where the jagged pieces of the not-metal he had found had come from. In the heart of the pit lay a large shape, something like that of the immense ziggurat that was at the heart of Uruk itself. But this ziggurat's shape was broken, the perfect pyramid form marred by shattered holes. It was from these holes that the spirals of smoke and steam were issuing, in slow, hissing spurts. One hole, more regular than the rest, looked almost like a normal door — but who would build a ziggurat with a door like that? And, who would build a ziggurat of this size and then hide it in a pit on the top of a hill in the wilderness?

Gilgamesh could see within the regular-shaped hole the creature that had been calling him. Whatever it was, it had told the truth: it was no man.

It was about the size of a man, and about the shape of a man. But instead of skin it was covered in the same shining non-metal as the ziggurat itself. Instead of eyes it had twin golden fires that burned without consuming any fuel. It had arms and legs, too, and a body. But it had neither hair nor clothing. Yet it was not naked, as a man would be naked. Nor was it shaped like a woman.

It moved slightly. It had been sitting in the hole, leaning against something as if it was tired. Now it hunched forward, and raised a hand toward him.

'Come to me, Gilgamesh,' the female voice urged.

'No,' he replied, slowly. 'I am not some fool, to do the bidding of a stranger. What are you called, and where are you from?'

A hissing noise escaped the creature, and Gilgamesh could see what appeared to be a mouth of sorts, under the burning eyes. 'I am called... Ishtar.'

'Ishtar?' he echoed. Could this creature be telling the truth? 'Ishtar is the goddess of love and battles, stranger.' He gestured with his spear. 'Your form doesn't look suited to love, nor are you armed for battle.'

'My form is what I wished it to be, Gilgamesh,' Ishtar replied. 'I can change it to suit the needs of the moment.'

'Then if I were you, Ishtar, I should alter it to be able to walk. Then you could come to me. If you came as a woman, we might make love. If as a man, we could fight. As you are, your form seems ill-suited to anything.'

Another long sigh escaped from the creature. 'You are wrong, Gilgamesh. My form is suited to many things — not the least of which is descending from the heavens to the earth.'

'Indeed?' he said, and laughed loudly. 'You are from the heavens, are you? And if you can step down from the skies, how is it that you cannot step over here? Ishtar, if you are a goddess, you seem to be one of lies and trickery, not honest love or war.'

'Foolish man!' Her voice trembled. 'I did not walk down from the skies.' She gestured weakly at the ziggurat about her. 'I came in this.'

'Ah.' He grinned. 'Your house walked, then, not you. Still, it seems to have been a hard journey down from the sky — as well it might be. I see that you've lost a few bricks here and there. I would think that their loss would make it a lighter task for what remains to walk about.'

'You persist in your foolishness,' Ishtar hissed. 'But I can show you the truth in what I say. I called you here from the plains of Eridu to commune with me.'

Gilgamesh scratched at his oiled ringlets, and grinned once again. 'I followed a white hart here, Ishtar, not your voice.'

'This white deer, O man?' she asked, pointing.

Gilgamesh gazed, then stiffened. His quarry stood, docile, on the slope of the pit. It stared at him, unafraid. Quickly, the hunter raised his spear and threw.

It passed into the deer's pale body without breaking the skin, and then through it, to bury itself in the earthen wall of the pit.

Slowly the deer faded away.

For the first time Gilgamesh felt his confidence begin to slip. This stank of magic, not of honest guile or simple trickery. Perhaps this strange creature was indeed telling the truth — however odd that truth sounded to his ears.

'Come to me, Gilgamesh,' Ishtar called. 'Come, and you will not be disappointed.' As she spoke, her form shimmered, like the haze that rose from the southern desert sands, and changed. Now the non-metal skin was flesh, and she was like a woman — and yet like no woman that he had ever seen. Her skin was light, her hair dark and loose, her arms open and inviting. 'Come to me, Gilgamesh, strong in war and love.'

'Lady,' he said, with a hint of respect in his voice, 'it may be that I have wronged you in thinking that you lied. But if you are indeed Ishtar, and a goddess, then I dare not come to you.'

'So,' she said, and he winced at the mockery in her voice, 'the mighty hero, Gilgamesh, is afraid of the embrace of a woman.'

'Not so,' he argued. 'Many woman have felt my embrace, and all have enjoyed their time. But to be the paramour of a goddess is a risky thing at best. I have heard how Ishtar serves those she loves. Her love consumes them, it is said, in tongues of fire. She takes their strength in one embrace, leaving them dead, and forgotten by all who knew them. No, Ishtar, it is not fear that makes me turn you down, but wisdom. What a fool I should be to exchange my years for one embrace from you.'

'Gilgamesh, obey me and come to me!' The pleading, beguiling tone had vanished, and in its place was only harsh determination. 'I swear that if you do not, then I shall seek you out and crush you.'

'Ah, now we get to the truth of it,' he said, his poise returning. 'Nay, lady — if you cannot move to get me while I stand before you in this pit, then you will not be able to get me when I am feasting in my palace in Uruk. I thank you for the strange hunt you've led me on, but no more. Fare you well, lady — and fare well apart from me.' With a final salute he turned and strode away.

'Fool!' Ishtar yelled after his retreating back. 'You have

turned me down, Gilgamesh, but you will regret it. I shall indeed come to you soon enough — and when I do, not one stone of Uruk will be left to tell the world where Gilgamesh once was king!'

Her strength failing, Ishtar fell back. No sense in wasting energy cursing that sly, suspicious humanoid now. Ah, but he would pay — he would pay dearly for this rejection!

She checked her power reserves again. Enough, if she carefully eked them out, for another six of this planet's days. There would be another human along by then. And it was doubtful that he would be as crafty as Gilgamesh. To conserve energy she disconnected her image reproducer and allowed the disguise she wore to fade and slide into the familiar shape of her once-powerful body.

She crept into the ruined escape pod and shuddered as she felt the mind of Gilgamesh slipping from her senses. He would have been such a delightful feast. Such life, such power, such pride. She hadn't tasted a vigorous soul in all the months she had spent in space. Her power levels were low, and her need for a mind to devour was all-encompassing.

One must come along soon! Then she would feed — then she would grow — and then she would utterly destroy this miserable little world...

Still trying to make sense of his hilltop encounter, Gilgamesh almost ran into the captain of his own patrol. His reflexes took over when he saw the figure of a soldier, but he managed to restrain his spear-arm when he recognized the man.

'Lord,' the captain said, falling to his knees. 'Is something amiss?'

'Nothing,' he replied. 'I have had... a vision. A vision of a most perplexing kind.' Abruptly, he grinned, and clapped the man on the shoulders, sending him sprawling. 'Still, let's not let that disturb us, eh? We've got a job to do. It's time we were off again. Kish won't wait on us forever. Come on!'

'Yes, Lord,' the captain said, brushing dust from his legs.

Gilgamesh was deep in thought for the rest of the journey,

virtually ignoring Enkidu's attempts to draw him out. He was torn between telling the story for the praise it might bring him and keeping silent in case he was secretly ridiculed. Had he won a victory over Ishtar? Or had he been the victim of a trick? Naturally, his subjects would believe his story — he'd have them executed if they showed the slightest scepticism — but did it really enhance his reputation? Or could he change the tale, improve it? He wished he were a better inventor of stories. If he had a court musician, he mused, he might be able to set the man to work on this germ of an idea and have it developed into a real tale that men would remember.

He made a mental note of two points: first, to keep the story to himself until he could find a better ending for it; second, to hire himself a good court composer.

Ta-Nin languidly examined her reflection in the polished mirror. It was a good body, perhaps the finest in all Uruk. Gilgamesh had complimented her on it many times, before and during their lovemaking. *The body of a queen*? she wondered. Perhaps, when he returned, Gilgamesh would take her as his bride this time, instead of merely his concubine... There would be plenty of hearts broken, she knew, by such an action. Many of the women of Uruk hoped to move from Gilgamesh's bed to his throne-room.

She applied her oils carefully, choosing only the most fragrant. To lure a king, one must be seen to resemble a queen... She dressed in her finest spun gown, fastened at her shapely, bare neck by a golden brooch in the shape of a leopard's head. Her servant girl completed the effect with her elaborate coiffuring arts. Ta-Nin hung round her throat a simple necklace of lapis lazuli, and examined her reflection one final time.

She had to smile. Never had she looked more brautiful. This time, surely she would win the king's heart, and share in his power. She half-turned, and admired the curve of her bare back. How could he resist her? She looked exactly like a queen.

A servant arrived with the message that the feast was beginning. Gilgamesh had commanded her to attend. She exulted. Tonight she would triumph over her snickering, manipulative rivals.

The feast-hall of the palace was becoming crowded as the guests arrived for the banquet. All the talk was of the spying mission from which the king had just returned. She noted several barely-disguised scowls, and knew that there were many of the nobles who would have preferred it had their king been caught and killed by the troops of King Agga of Kish. Petty jealousies, that was all. Didn't every man in Uruk wish he had merely a portion of the powers of Gilgamesh — either in feats of war, or of love?

Ta-Nin looked about, but Gilgamesh had not yet made his entrance. He enjoyed making a show of it, drinking in the applause and adoration that he knew were his due. But now Ta-Nin did not know where she should sit. To go straight to the head table and claim her place by the king's side might seem presumptuous. But to take another seat would be beneath her dignity...

The main doors were thrown open, and Gilgamesh entered with a wide grin on his face. All of his guests jumped to their feet, pounding on the tables and yelling his name. The king waved for the applause to die down. Naturally, it did not — no one there was stupid enough to believe that he meant this gesture for a moment. Finally, he roared for silence, and instantly the room fell quiet.

Gilgamesh made his way to the head table and dropped onto the cushions beside it. At this signal, the others could also take their places. Ta-Nin remained standing with her gaze demurely lowered, waiting for Gilgamesh to see her and call her to join him. After what seemed an eternity she heard him call her name, and looked up. She froze.

There was another woman with him. Her mind seemed paralyzed as she saw the king fondling this other creature. Why, it was the daughter of that inept Gudea, wasn't it? That little slut, barely thirteen, barely marriable. And here she was, pretending to be a grown woman, putting herself on public display to have her body pawed by that egotistic lecher. The girl giggled as Gilgamesh slipped a hand down her front and tweaked.

Crimson, Ta-Nin glared at them both. 'Ta-Nin,' Gilgamesh repeated, a little louder this time, 'don't you think you'd better sit down?'' He gestured to the second table. 'Your husband is over there.' He smiled, and gave her a friendly wave with his free hand.

Burning with anger and hurt, she remembered to bow — not as much as she was supposed to, but Gilgamesh overlooked this, as he was trying to lap up the wine he had deliberately spilled onto the girl's breasts. Overcome by the humiliation, Ta-Nin scurried across the hall to join her spouse, who was trying to look as if he hadn't noticed his wife's embarrassment.

She ignored him and turned her furious eyes on Gilgamesh. She had been publicly humiliated. Those harpies of the town knew she had been sharing his bed. She had ordered new robes for her regal status. How their tongues would wag at this. Thrown over, for this... this stupid little whore!

How could Gilgamesh do this to her?

Oblivious to the jealousies of his noblemen and their wives, the king finished lapping up his drink and lay back on his pillows. The girl — he wished he could remember her name, he could never remember their names — giggled again, and wiggled most pleasingly. Now, this was what a woman was for. He grabbed a roast pheasant with one hand and her backside with the other.

'My Lord!' she tittered, trying to pull her skirt back down. 'Can't you wait... at least a while?'

'I've waited long enough,' he told her between mouthfuls of bird. 'And now this silly spying stuff is over, I can get down to important things.' He squeezed the firm buttock again.

'And was your adventure dreadfully boring?' she asked, making a show of fighting him off.

'No,' he told her. 'There was one interesting bit.' Then he grinned down at her. 'But wait till this feast is over...' he promised. 'Then we'll have more interesting bits than you've ever imagined, my girl.'

# 2: Memories Are Made Of...

She awoke in the darkness, worried.

About what?

She lay still, feeling the bedsheets rise and fall as she breathed. Nothing came to mind. Nothing, save that she was worried.

*All right*, she decided. *Start from what I know. I'm in bed, and it's night.* Then she became really worried.

She couldn't think of anything else to add to those facts.

Fighting back the panic that was threatening to erupt inside her, she sat up quickly.

The lights came on gradually, as though someone or something had taken note of her movement. When her eyes adjusted to the light she looked around, hoping for some clues.

She was in a large bed; the frame was of polished brass. Beside the bed, a small cabinet supported a Tiffany-style table lamp, and a glass of what looked like water. Carefully, she sipped. It was water. Score one to her. Replacing the glass, she continued to scan the room. A chair, a mirror on a stand, a small dresser, and two doors in the wall. Then a small table, and a ghetto blaster perched on the table, a tape in the deck and ready to go.

Momentarily, she felt relieved. Her mind was working; it could recognize and label everything in the room. So why didn't she know where the room was? A house? Weren't rooms usually in houses? Or maybe in a hotel? A boarding house by the sea, maybe?

She looked at the walls. No pictures at all. And funny kind of walls, come to think of it. There was a regular pattern of inlaid circles, each cut about six inches into the wall itself. Did they make houses with walls like that? She didn't think so; there was something vaguely fluttering in the back of her mind that told her walls were usually covered in wallpaper, and pictures of cottages or people walking by the sea.

Funny sort of room. Oh, well, she was here, now. Start from that. A room in a house. Or maybe a hotel? She listened very carefully. No sound of people in the hallway. Nor was there a smell of salt in the air, or anything that could help her to decide. She could hear a sort of low, throbbing, humming sound, right at the threshold of her hearing. Machinery of some kind, obviously. The air was crisp and fresh, with no smell of any kind at all that she could make out.

Where else might she be, if not in a building? A boat, maybe, or an aeroplane? No, there would be a sense of motion, and the bed was as steady as a rock. She'd learnt as much as she could in the bed. The only way to find out more was to get up.

Tossing back the covers, she swung her feet to the floor. They hit something, and she glanced down. A pile of clothing. It didn't look familiar, but she guessed that it must be hers, since there wasn't anyone else to claim it. Of course: she was stark naked, so it made sense that they'd be her clothes. Only... Did she really like this kind of stuff?

She bent down and picked up a garment. Her fuzzy memory finally identified it as a tee shirt — worn over the top half of the body. She studied it carefully. it was a dirty pinkish colour. Did she really dress like this? She assumed she did, but it rang no bells with her. Maybe there was something else to wear instead? There was a thought that came to her — clean clothes.

Right! These must be the clothes she'd worn yesterday, whenever that was. Today, she could choose some clean clothes. Eyeing the tee shirt again, she decided she'd try to pick something with a bit more class.

But where did she keep clean clothes?

The dresser was the first thing that came to mind. In the drawers, that's where people usually keep clean clothes. She started towards it, and then stopped as she passed the mirror and caught sight of herself.

Was that what she looked like?

Medium height; a bit gawky, maybe? Not exactly elegant, anyway. Dark hair, right now in something of a mess from being slept on all night. A good, swift brushing would sort that out. Nice enough face, she guessed, friendly and young and interested, though she couldn't recall any other faces at the moment to compare to hers. Body — well, it looked kind of useful. Muscular, but still obviously feminine. Well, at least she could remember how to tell the difference. She smiled, then frowned. She wished she knew more about who she was.

She wished she knew anything about who she was.

Moving closer to the mirror, she examined her reflection carefully. She saw herself reflected in her large dark eyes. Who did that face belong to? People had names, didn't they? Surely she had one, then? And didn't people normally wake up knowing things like their own names?

What had happened to her? Well, maybe she'd find out when she found out who she was. She shook her head at the mirror, and the reflected person that she didn't recognize shook hers back. 'Hello,' she said softly to the mirror. Silently, it spoke with her.

This was daft! A horrible thought snaked into her mind, and wouldn't go away. Maybe she was mad — crazy. Maybe she had been locked away in an asylum or something. What if she didn't remember anything because there was nothing to remember? If she was crazy, she might wake up like this every morning, having forgotten all about her life. She vaguely felt she'd heard something about cases like that. People who had short-term memories, but no long-term ones. Was that the sort of person she was? She didn't think so — she could recall all kind of stuff. It was just that none of it was in any way personal. She stared into the eyes of the image in the mirror. They didn't look like a mad person's eyes. Clear, bright and intelligent, that's how they looked. So why was she in such a fog?

Dragging her eyes away from the mirror, she walked resolutely to the dresser. She pulled open the top two drawers and saw that her earlier guess was right: they were crammed with clothes. Well, that was a start, anyway. Check them out...

Now, what did she normally wear? Again, she drew a blank. Abandon that line of thought, then. Try identifying the clothing, instead.

A piece of cloth, with three holes in it. One large, two small. *Knickers*! she thought, triumphantly. That's what they were. And they were worn on the lower half of the body. She was getting somewhere. But she knew that they weren't worn alone. Other clothing went with them ... Jeans, maybe a shirt. Right! But which went on top, and which went underneath? Right, knickers first, the other stuff over it. She was getting the hang of this!

Slowly, hesistantly, she managed to get dressed. It took her a while to sort out the bra, but finally it was fastened and fairly comfy. Then jeans ... In the cupboard! She went to the two doors. By chance, the first she tried was the right one. Inside was a smaller room, with a selection of clothes. After a moment or two, she found a battered pair of Levis that seemed to be right. Buttoning them up, she went back to the main room and picked out one of the clean tee shirts. She struggled into it.

Was that all?

She looked around the room again. On the back of the chair was a jacket of some sort. It looked well-used, with a couple of burn marks and several places where the fabric had been gashed and then repaired. And tons of badges on it. None of them made any sense at all to her — but what did, right now? With a shrug she pulled it on, then examined her reflection again.

God, what a mess! Did she normally dress like this? No matter how hard she tried, she couldn't remember a thing about herself. It was odd — all the general information was there, and she could name anything she saw that made sense. But nothing at all that related to herself. She spotted a hairbrush on the dresser, and knew what it was for. But she didn't know if she normally used it. Or how she usually wore her shoulder-length hair.

Weird! She could remember things about human beings, but nothing at all about herself.

No matter how hard she concentrated, she didn't even know her name. Or where she was. Or how she had got here.

Furiously, she brushed out the kinks and knots in her hair, as though with each stroke of the brush she might knock something back into her head. She brushed until she had tears in her eyes, but still nothing at all in her memory.

What had happened to her? Well, maybe when she knew *who* she was, she'd know what had happened. But how could she discover who she was?

When in doubt, look about. The other door had to lead somewhere, didn't it?

Unless she was a prisoner.

She felt like screaming in frustration. She didn't *think* she as a prisoner — but what did that prove? She didn't have any idea who she was. Still, hanging about here wouldn't help — the only possible route to self-discovery led through that door. If it was locked, then at least she'd know one thing: she was a prisoner.

It opened readily enough at her touch, into a corridor. The walls all had those indented circle patterns in them. It seemed to be the style throughout wherever-she-was, rather than just in her room. It didn't mean anything, but at least it was a fact. File it away for future reference. Now — which way? The corridor led to both the left and right.

Toss a coin? Guess? Try a bit of logical thinking?

The background humming sound seemed a little louder out here. It also seemed to be slightly stronger in her left ear. Okay, assume that there's someone about — that hum meant machinery, and machinery meant people.

Or... There was a ticking doubt in the back of her mind that refused to come out and let her look at it. People, that was the key word. Maybe whoever or whatever was here with her (assuming it was anyone else at all) wasn't a person? Was something else? Once again, she really didn't know. It was so frustrating!

'Oi!' she yelled, at the top of her voice. 'Anyone home?'

After a moment or two, it was quite clear that no one was going to answer. Maybe no one was home, or maybe whoever was home simply couldn't hear her. Or simply couldn't reply, for one reason or another.

Was there danger waiting ahead? Maybe it had been stupid to shout aloud and announce her presence! How could she tell?

Thrusting her doubts and questions to the back of her mind, she set off grimly down the corridor. Around the corner, it split into two. Following the noise of the humming, she continued on her way, resisting all urges to examine the closed doors she was passing. One of them might contain information about herself, but it would be a complete waste of time even to start looking. If there was someone about, it would make the whole task a lot faster.

Wherever she was, it was a large place. She seemed to be walking for a long time without anything looking appreciably different. Finally, though, the corridor ended in a pair of large doors. The humming was a constant background sound now, and the source probably lay behind the door.

Steeling herself, gathering her courage, she threw the doors open.

It was a single, large room, about thirty feet or so across, and almost fifteen feet high. In the centre of the room was a hexagonal unit that looked like a large, technological mushroom, and in the centre of the unit was a glass cylinder that was rhythmically rising and falling, pulsing with light as it did so. On the mushroom were several panels filled with levers, lights, dials and other equipment. Around the room were scattered various untidy pieces of furniture: a hat stand by another, larger, set of doors; a wooden high-backed chair; a small chest and mirror.

And, finally, another person! She stared in amazement at the figure.

He was seated on the floor in a lotus position: legs crossed, hands together, fingertip to fingertip, his chin resting on the pinnacle thus formed. His eyes were screwed tightly shut, and he appeared to be fast asleep.

If she had thought her taste in clothing was questionable, his definitely looked objectionable. Scruffy shoes that didn't seem to have seen polish for at least a decade; baggy trousers; a floppy coat of some unsavoury brown hue; a paisley tie, badly knotted; and a sweater adorned with question marks. Thrown over the chair that was close to him was a battered tan hat and a paisley scarf almost as appalling as his tie. An umbrella was hung over the back of the chair.

She peered at the man, studying his features. A broad face, with plenty of laughter-lines. Sort of ageless, really. If only it looked familiar to her! But she couldn't even remember having seen him before.

Still, at least he might have a few answers that could help her out. Reaching out a hand she gripped one of his wrists, and shook him. 'Oi, wake up!' When there was no immediate response, she shook him again, harder.

He seemed to unfold in a second, rolling backwards out of her grasp, and leaping to his feet in a fighting crouch, eyes bright and expression ferocious. Then, seeing her, he visibly relaxed.

'Didn't I tell you not to do that?' he snapped, crossly. 'You could have permanently damaged my psyche, breaking the trance like that.' He peered at her, somewhat myopically. 'Done something with your hair, haven't you? Don't like it.' He turned away from her, and bent to study the readings on the central panel.

'I don't know what you're talking about,' she told him.

With his back to her, he said: 'Well, you normally wear your hair sort of gathered — '

'Not about my hair,' she snapped. 'About *anything*.'

That got his attention. He twisted about to stare thoughtfully at her. 'Can you explain that?'

'I can't explain anything,' she told him, miserably. 'I don't know anything. Who I am. Who *you* are. Do I know you?'

'Oh dear . . .' He began to nibble nervously at his thumbnail. 'No memory at all?' She shook her head. 'But you can speak English — and get dressed.'

'I can remember all sorts of generic stuff,' she told him. 'It's just when I try and remember anything at all about myself that I draw a blank.'

He turned back to the controls again, scuttling about the console. Stopping in front of one set of instruments, he slammed his hand down, hard. 'Bother! I had a suspicion it would be a mistake. I should have listened to myself — but I never do, do I?'

'How should I know?' she asked, crossly. 'All I want to know is who I am and what's going on.'

'It's not so much *going on* as *going out*,' he told her, cryptically. 'I've been editing a few of my useless memories, and I seem to have set the field a bit too high. It didn't just erase my brain patterns, but all of yours as well.'

A lot of that didn't make much sense, but she managed to gather one thing from what he had said. 'You mean that *you* caused me to forget everything?'

'I'm afraid so, yes,' he apologized. 'Purely by accident, of course.'

She wasn't sure whether she should be furious at this point. Would a person get angry because their memories had been stolen? It seemed reasonable, and she certainly felt annoyed. 'You stupid idiot!' she yelled. 'What have you done to me?'

He hopped nervously from foot to foot. 'Well, hopefully, nothing that I can't reverse,' he answered. 'All your memories must still be in the TARDIS's telepathic circuits, so all I have to do is to —' He smacked the controls, hard, with his clenched fist.

Abruptly, another person materialized by the panel. This one was tall and imposing. A long burgundy-coloured coat and a long, red scarf hung over the thin frame. A burgundy-coloured hat perched atop a mass of curly brown hair. The newcomer's facebroke into a hearty, toothy grin.

'Hello, Doctor!' he said.

'Oh no!' Her companion started at the intruder almost in despair.

'Who's that?' she demanded, startled.

'Me...'

# 3: When You Wish Upon Ishtar

'Will you stop that pacing!'

Pausing in mid-step, Gudea guiltily wiped his sweating palms on the sides of his robe, then carefully set his foot on the limestone floor. He glanced nervously at Ennatum, who was slumped casually in his gold-inlaid chair as though he had no worries in the world. Gudea knew he would never match the poise — or arrogance — of his co-conspirator's facade.

'Aren't you at all worried?' he asked, fingering his beard.

'Why should I be?' Ennatum growled. 'You're worrying enough for a small army. Why don't you simply sit down and wait for the others?'

'I don't have your nerves,' Gudea admitted. 'I have to walk off some of my fears.'

'By Enlil, man,' Ennatum complained, 'when a man plots treason against his king, it's unfortunate that he cannot choose his fellow conspirators as he'd like. If Gilgamesh were to appear now and so much as look you at you, you'd die.'

Glancing nervously around the council chamber, Gudea wrung his hands together. 'You don't think there's any chance? Of Gilgamesh coming back, I mean?'

Ennatum laughed, a short, sharp bark like a jackal's. 'I doubt it. That posturing braggart talked himself right into this suicide mission. I was all set to call upon a dozen reasons why we should have another spying mission to test Kish's defences, and the moron didn't even wait to hear them.' He put on an affectation of Gilgamesh's bass tones. 'We need a look at Kish's walls? Right, Enkidu, let's be off.' In his normal voice, Ennatum spat:

'Gods, but the man must be as soft in the head as he is hard in the muscles.'

Unappeased, Gudea strode to the table that lay opposite the door. It contained a small supply of food and drink that the servants had prepared. He helped himself to a jar of the barley beer. Sipping nervously at it, he said timidly: 'But Gilgamesh has survived suicide missions before. He survived that spying trip to Kish only a matter of weeks ago.'

'You needn't tell me that,' Ennatum replied. 'The man has the luck of the gods, that's all. But even luck can run out.'

'Not his.' Gudea sighed. 'I wish I had half his prowess.'

'If you did, you'd be ten times the man you are,' the other snapped back. 'Or maybe twenty. As it is Gilgamesh is already doing his best to replace you in your bed.'

'He raped my wife,' Gudea retorted, almost aggressively — for him. 'Several times.'

'Of course he did,' Ennatum laughed, cruelly. 'And that pretty daughter of yours, too, of course. But that's not what *they* called it.' Gudea had to be the only person in the city not to know of his wife's infatuation with the king. And there were even stories about the daughter joining the two of them. Only someone as gullible and self-deceiving as Gudea would think that pair of harpies could be innocent.

Hotly, Gudea explained: 'You can't accuse the king of rapine, like any normal man. Of course they claim they were willing; it's more than their lives or mine is worth to say otherwise. But I abhor Gilgamesh's libertine manners. That's why I agreed to help you in this plan to get him killed. To save my family from further degradation at his hands.'

'Or other parts of his anatomy, eh?' Ennatum said crudely. 'Stay!' He held up his hand. 'A poor jest, I agree. But I trust you didn't tell you wife what we have planned for Gilgamesh? She might have — ah — accidentally passed on the information the last time she was — assaulted.'

'I've told no one,' Gudea said glumly, finishing the beer and pouring himself another. 'But I do wish we could be certain that Gilgamesh will die this time.'

Sighing, Ennatum rose from the chair, and strode over to

Gudea. He placed an arm about Gudea's shoulder and smiled. 'Well, if it will set your mind at ease, my friend,' he purred, 'I will let you in on the secret. This time we can be sure Gilgamesh will die. You see, to make absolutely certain that he's caught, I took the liberty of sending a man to Dumuzi, the high priest of Ishtar in Kish. By now, the Kishites know of Gilgamesh's every intent. This time, Gudea, he will die.'

The double doors at the end of the meeting room were flung open. Two spear-wielding guards entered, heralding the arrival of the other nobles of Uruk. Ennatum tapped his companion's shoulder. 'Carefully,' he hissed. 'We'll keep that little tidbit of information from the High Council, shall we?'

Nervously, Gudea nodded, and pattered off to his seat at the conference table. Shaking his head, Ennatum followed. Gudea was the one weak link in all of this plotting, but a necessary one — for now.

The temple of Ishtar in the city of Kish was not the largest of the young metropolis's temples. That honour belonged to the ziggurat of Zababa, patron god of the city. But Ishtar's temple was by far the busiest of them all. The smoke of sacrifice rose constantly from the several altars within. Once, Dumuzi had taken great pleasure in the smell of the burning wood and the scorching entrails. Now, however, he took pleasure in very little. Many who had known the high priest believed that he had changed — for the worse over recent months. Ever since the enthronement of the goddess Ishtar in her temple, in fact.

Dumuzi himself thought little of this. Dumuzi thought little of *anything*. The brilliant mind of the priest was now almost permanently clouded by the Touch of Ishtar.

He tried to concentrate on the message that this stupid little man had brought him, but he couldn't quite focus his mind. These days it was getting harder and harder for him to gather his scattered wits. He winced and frowned with the effort.

*Stop struggling, Dumuzi!* The voice of Ishtar echoed in his mind, bringing lancing pain. *You exist only to fulfil my desires, to think my thoughts, and to do my bidding. Do not try to have a life apart from me.*

With Dumuzi's rebellion subdued Ishtar's mind focused through the eyes of her priest and ransacked his memories for what she needed. Ah yes. The grovelling worm at his feet was a messenger, claiming to be an emissary of the lord Ennatum of the neighbouring pathetic little native village of Uruk. Ishtar's will played with Dumuzi's vocal chords.

'Tell me again, O man, the message you bear to me.'

'Mighty Dumuzi, High Priest of Ishtar,' the servant said again, prostrating himself once more, 'I am to tell you that the King of Uruk, Gilgamesh the Mighty, is even now on his way to spy on the inhabitants of Kish. He is planning to lead a war on Kish, and seeks such information as will best help him in this plan. He will approach your city from the south towards evening, and can be captured or killed with ease. There are with him only five men and his fighting companion Enkidu.'

'So you say,' Ishtar replied with Dumuzi's voice. 'But why do you come to me with this tale? Are you not sworn to obey your king?'

'I am the bondsman of Ennatum, Lord,' the man said, nervously. All priests were mysterious and imposing, but there was something even more unsettling about this one. 'It is at his bidding that I bring this message.'

'I see.' Puzzled, Ishtar allowed Dumuzi to regain some control of his mind. *Why should this Lord Ennatum wish to see his king captured or killed?* she demanded of her priest.

'Gilgamesh is a mighty warrior, my lady,' Dumuzi said aloud — though there was no need for words: Ishtar could read his thoughts as easily as he could scan the clay tablets of the temple records. The indentations of the cuneiform-writing stylus were like chicken scratchings to most people, and Dumuzi prided himself on his ability to both read and write. It was not a common feat, but Ishtar had dismissed his achievement with contempt. She took what she wanted directly from his mind, without need for either talk or writing. 'But he is arrogant, too,' Dumuzi continued, 'and has an almost insatiable appetite for the young women of Uruk. The nobles of that city would dearly love him dead — but none of them dare confront him in person.'

Ishtar's delighted peals of laughter rang through Dumuzi's

mind. *You humans are such foolish creatures, priest! I am tempted to allow Gilgamesh to come and go unmolested — just to terrify these pusillanimous plotters. But I, too, have a score to settle with Gilgamesh the mighty warrior.*

'You, lady?'

She could read the amazement in the priest's mind. *Yes, Dumuzi.* The memory still rankled within her, burning in her soul. *Gilgamesh once rejected me. I offered him the peace and power that I later offered you, yet he spurned my embrace. But you O loyal one, did not. My Touch has brought freedom and peace to your mind, has it not?*

He could not deny it: she did not allow him the will to contradict her. That would have been wasteful. Encompassing further portions of his mind, she used his eyes to star down at the trembling messenger.

'Can we trust this man?' she wondered aloud. 'Perhaps he is sent not to inform us, but to trick us?'

'No, Lord, I swear it,' the peasant insisted. 'I tell you the truth.'

'You have no need to assure me, O man,' Dumuzi told him. He stumbled over the words as he felt Ishtar's grip loosen inside his head. 'Follow me — you will swear to Ishtar herself that you bring only the truth.'

Eagerly, the man scrambled to his feet. Dumuzi turned, and led the way out of his priestly quarters and into the temple. The servant expected that he would be required to take an oath at the main altar. Dumuzi could feel Ishtar's pleasure as she allowed him the luxury of that naivety for the moment, her anticipation that it would make the end result so much more rewarding.

The temple was an impressive building even in the grand city of Kish. This, the main portion of the construction, was two hundred and fifty feet long and fifty wide. The roof was almost twenty feet above their heads. Stone pillars held up the ceiling, and triangular windows cut into the walls allowed in light. The walls had been covered with mud brick into which small cones of clay had been pressed. The end of each cone was painted, either in black, or white, or red, and the walls bore zigzag patterns of markings on them.

Worshippers of Ishtar moved throughout the building. Some brought sacrifices, others coins to buy time with the sacred harlots that waited in the numerous chambers at the sides of the great hall. The temple was never a quiet place, but a reverent silence seemed to gather in the air as Dumuzi led the spy after him.

At the far end of the temple was the altar. Teams of priests worked here, some taking the animals offered for sacrifice and slaughtering them, others accepting the grain offerings and sending them to the granaries to be stored for the winter months. The slaughtered beasts would be separated: the livers were used for divination, the entrails for the sacrificial flames, and the meat would be roasted and stored for the meals of the temple staff.

Beyond the main altar was the area private to Ishtar. Dumuzi held aside the curtaining, and the messenger nervously passed through. The room beyond was hidden in darkness, and it was obvious that the man was afraid of a knife in the back as a reward for betraying his king.

'Move on, O man,' Dumuzi's voice laughed. 'Come and feel the Touch of Ishtar herself. She will know if you speak the truth to me.'

The messenger moved slowly forward, hesitating until his eyes could become accustomed to the lack of light.

His caution was futile: within the room were two of the handmaidens of Ishtar. Blank-eyed, they gripped the man's arms with a ferocious strength that owed little to their humanity. The man cried aloud, and tried to wriggle free. Their hands cut into his flesh, holding him on his knees by the doorway.

'My Lord!' he screamed, trying to twist his head about to see Dumuzi. 'I swear, I tell you the truth!'

'Do not swear to him, O man,' Ishtar said in her own voice from the black depths of the room. 'He does not care whether you speak the truth or a lie. But I care. Feel my Touch, and know my peace.'

She moved into the half-light. The messenger gazed, open-mouthed and silent. He knew he was in the presence of a true goddess. Never had he seen such perfection: such a graceful form, taller than a man; such skin, so pale that it seemed to shine; such a beautiful face, surrounded by floating hair.

The man screamed again as she began to change. He writhed madly in the iron grip of the unmoving priestesses. Ishtar's eyes, burning red, descended towards him. She held out her arms in a mocking embrace, and enfolded him. His scream was choked off as her metal palms touched the sides of his temples. A soft *whirr* followed, and he went limp.

She withdrew her hands, smiling as she saw the reddened area on his left temple where she had inserted her link. The two handmaidens released him, and he remained on his knees, swaying, eyes closed.

Ishtar loosened her thoughts, sending them through the link into the man's mind. It was pitifully small and tasteless, like those of so many of these humans. She noted almost casually that he had been telling Dumuzi the truth: Gilgamesh was indeed on his way here on a spying mission. What a fool! She would see to it that he would not be lonely... But he must not die — yet. She wanted vengeance, she wanted to taste his fear, before she allowed him the luxury of death.

What to do with this peasant, meanwhile? His mind wasn't worth feeding on, nor would he make a good slave. He lacked talent, and she had no inclination to have him trained. She didn't need another mind just yet... With a mental sigh, she allowed the man the only release he would ever know. She didn't even hear the rattle of death as he collapsed backwards, grotesquely huddled on the floor. The handmaidens would clean it away.

One of the priest that she controlled seemed disturbed. Using his eyes, she saw the reason why: Agga was in the temple and striding towards her quarters.

The King of Kish? Interesting. He didn't much care for Dumuzi, she knew — as she knew all that Dumuzi knew. Agga was a devotee mainly of the city-god, Zababa — but he was not foolish enough to ignore the visit of a living goddess, and he had met her several times. Each time she had sensed his distrust, and it had amused her, knowing that he could do nothing to fight against her. She had been tempted to add him to her collection — his felt like a mind well worth a taste: a sharp brain, a keen insight, a commanding personality. But she still lacked the strength she needed to run every alleyway in this pitiful dung-heap of a city. While she was still accumulating power it was best to allow Agga a certain measure of freedom. Her puppets were very talented, but they lacked the fire and creativity that independence normally gave them. She shivered with delight as she felt her shape change again.

Agga pushed aside the curtain and waited. His body was strong and muscular, with a slight inclination towards fat. His beard was full and curled, strong with the scent of the oils used. His clothing was restrained, but the robe was clearly expensive. About his neck he wore the cylindrical seal that ratified the orders of the king. His only other jewellery was a golden chain inlaid with amber that hung across his chest.

His eyes, growing used to the lower levels of light that Ishtar preferred, took in the dead body on the floor. His powerful body went rigid with controlled anger as he glared at Ishtar's insolently-turned back.

'Another human sacrifice?' he growled. 'It seems to me that your arrival in our city, Ishtar, has not heralded the benevolent reign of the gods, but the predations of Nergal, father of death and pestilence.'

'Have a care with that tongue of yours, Agga,' she murmured. She turned, and Agga could not restrain the sharp intake of breath that betrayed his inevitable response to her beauty. 'I bear a lot of abuse from you,' she said, smiling, 'because it suits me to allow you to be the king of this wretched city — for now. But if you provoke me enough, perhaps even you shall feel the Touch of Ishtar.' She held up her right hand, and he thought he saw something metallic flash in her palm. 'Or, perhaps,' she mused, 'that pretty little daughter of yours — Ninani? She'd make a delightful addition to my retinue, don't you think?'

'If you try to Touch my daughter, Ishtar,' Agga growled, 'then I shall certainly see to it that this temple of yours is destroyed while you and your priests are inside it. It might be interesting to see if a mere man can destroy a goddess.'

'Such a futile temper,' she mocked gently. 'However, as long as you do my bidding, I hardly care what you may think, O king. But for now that precious child of yours shall be free. Meanwhile, would you be good enough to despatch a few of your best troops to that well at the south of the town? I have it on —' she smiled down at the corpse on the floor '— good authority that Gilgamesh will be there towards evening. Instruct your men to take him alive. Warn them that if he is killed, they will pay for it. And if he escapes, they will answer to me.'

'Gilgamesh?' The news surprised Agga. The king of Uruk had long coveted the lands of Kish, he knew, but he thought that even the hot-headed Gilgamesh had more sense than to try to slip into this city. 'Capturing him alive will not be simple.'

'Nevertheless, I want it done!' For the first time anger crept into her voice. 'He has a debt to pay me, Agga, one that I shall take great pleasure in extracting from him inch by excruciating inch... Perhaps I shall let you watch, to see what happens to those who incur my wrath. It might be — educational.' Then, burying her lust for the blood of the man who had rejected her, she returned to matters in hand. 'But why did you come here? Aside from another of your complaints about the — litter I cause?'

Agga wrenched his attention from the litter on the floor. 'We need more copper if we are to continue the lining of the walls with those new patterns that you have laid out.'

'So,' she said agreeably, turning away to indicate that the audience was over. 'Well, Dumuzi will see that the temple vaults are opened for your artisans. The artistic nature of my work demands a good deal of copper.'

Agga nodded. 'Ishtar,' he said, softly, 'I do not believe you have a single ounce of love within you for any kind of art. The patterns you designed, and that my men are making on the walls, are for some other purpose, are they not?'

Smiling, Ishtar turned back to face him. Not for the first time, the sheer perfection of her beauty seemed to him suddenly hard, almost grotesque. Hers was a face shaped by a divine craftsman out of living metal. Even her hair was reproduced in silvery strands. But the beauty could not at these moments entirely disguise the cruelty in her heart.

'Perceptive,' she murmured. 'Yes, indeed, there is much more to my plan than an appreciation of art, O king.'

'What?'

'That you will discover when I choose to tell you. Until then, simply ensure that my wishes are translated into stone and metal.' She again turned her back on him. 'Now go. I have much thinking to do.' She could almost feel the mind of Gilgamesh writhing in her taste buds as she stripped it apart, layer by lingering layer...

Agga turned also, but paused, watching the goddess glide back into her lair at the heart of the temple he had once loved to enter. Now its darkness was more than physical. His city had indeed fallen on terrible times since the arrival of Ishtar. But what could he do to stave off the desires of a divinity? With her powers, she could raze the city on a whim. No, for now he must placate her and conceal his true thoughts. But one day...

# 4: Past Lives

She stared in increasing bewilderment at the two men in front of her. So far, she had discovered exactly two things about her surroundings. First, she was in something called a TARDIS, whatever one of those might be. Second, the man she had met was called Doctor.

No, both men she'd met were called Doctor.

'I don't get it,' she said. 'How can he be you? You don't even look alike.'

'How many times do I have to explain?' the first of the Doctors asked. 'Oh yes, I forgot — you've forgotten everything, haven't you?' Shrugging, he ignored her and stared at the other man. 'I'm not a human being,' he said off-handedly, over his shoulder. 'I'm a Time Lord. We're not limited to the tiny portion of time that your lives span. When we age and tire, we change, we regenerate. And I used to look like that —' he indicated the other man '— quite some time ago.'

The other man was standing perfectly still, the smile frozen on his cheerful face. She inched forwards, examining him. 'He's not much of a talker, is he?'

'I've got him on pause,' the Doctor told her. 'Strictly speaking, he's not really here. It's a recording of some kind that I seem to have triggered.'

She tried to reach out and touch the eccentric figure. Her hand passed straight through it. With a jerk, she pulled back. 'You mean, like a tape recording?'

'Something like that' the Doctor said airily. 'But infinitely more sophisticated. It's a temporal projection, programmed into the TARDIS's telepathic circuits. And designed to manifest itself right now, for some peculiar reason.'

'Programmed?' she repeated. 'By who?'

'By whom,' he corrected her, absently. 'By me, of course. I wonder why I did it?'

'Don't you know?'

'Of course I don't know. If I knew, I wouldn't have to do this to jog my memory. It must be very important. I just wish I knew *why*.'

'Why not ask him?' she said, gesturing towards the frozen figure. 'Presumably he'll be able to tell you.'

'You're always so impatient, Ace,' he chided. He hated to be rushed into anything.

'Ace?' she asked, eagerly. 'Is that my name?'

'Yes.'

She mulled it over, while he stared at the person he'd once been. 'Funny sort of name,' she decided, finally.

'It's not your given one,' he added. 'But you preferred Ace to Dorothy.'

'I did?' When he nodded, she shook her head. 'I wish I knew why.'

'I'll see about getting your memory back in a minute.' He gestured at the frozen projection of the former Doctor. 'Right now, I'm more concerned about him.'

'Thanks a lot,' Ace muttered, gloomily.

'Your time will come,' he told her, cryptically. Then he keyed in a sequence on the central console. The other Doctor came back to life again.

'I haven't got much time,' he said. 'I've been in the Matrix — but I'm sure you'll remember all about that. What's vanishing fast is a piece of information that I picked up there. Beware the Timewyrm.'

'What's a Timewyrm?' Ace asked.

'It's no good asking him,' the Doctor told her. 'He's just a trans-temporal projection. He can't see or hear us.' Before she could say anything, he added: 'And it's no good asking me, because I haven't the foggiest notion what I'm warning myself about.'

'Timewyrm,' the recording repeated. 'At the core of the Matrix. Oldest input, from Ancient Gallifrey. A sort of future myth, end of the Universe, very apocalyptic. You'll have to do something about, I'm afraid. A unique creature noted for its ability to... to...' The figure faltered, and looked uncertainly at the console. 'Why am I talking to myself? Leela? Leela? Where is that girl... Oh. Yes.' His insubstantial finger reached out to a control, and vanished.

'Well,' Ace said, after a moment. 'What was all that about?'

'I've no idea,' replied the Doctor, a worried frown creasing his features.

'But it sounded important,' she insisted.

'It was,' he agreed. 'Vitally. But it still doesn't make any sense to me. I've never heard of a Timewyrm.' Shaking his head, he started to play with the controls. A small screen lit up, with information scrolling across it. 'And neither has the TARDIS,' he announced, finally.

'But *he* knew about it,' she objected. 'Surely you know what he knows, if he's how you used to be?'

'It's not that simple,' the Doctor snapped. 'Life never is. Look, he — I — was once linked to the Matrix back on Gallifrey. And before you ask, Gallifrey is the world I come from, where the vast majority of the Time Lords live. And the Matrix is a sort of data storage bank for almost every piece of information that has existed or will exist. It scans the reaches of time and space, and accumulates a vast amount of knowledge. Most of it's completely trivial and worthless, of course, but sometimes bits of it are very useful. And I must have come across a bit of it back then, and needed to warn me now about it.'

'But he seemed to forget what he was doing while he was doing it,' Ace pointed out.

'It's a safeguard,' the Doctor explained. 'My people, the Time Lords, don't like to interfere in the affairs of other worlds. And the Matrix gives a person access to enough information to allow someone to meddle rather effectively. So whenever anyone uses the Matrix to get any specific piece of information, anything else that they might accidentally stumble across is wiped from their minds. He — me — had to enter the Matrix when Gallifrey was invaded by the Sontarans. But my memory of what I found there was completely wiped out, at least theoretically. So the warning about the Timewyrm must be pretty urgent, for me to have been able to keep it in my memory long enough to get back to the TARDIS and warn myself about it.' He sighed. 'I just wish I had remembered enough to make it worthwhile.'

'And what's a Leela?' Ace asked.

'Who, not what. She was a travelling companion of mine. You didn't imagine you were the first person I ever took along with me, did you?'

'I hardly know what to think,' she snapped back. 'You stole my memories, remember?'

'Of course I remember,' he scowled. 'You're the one with the slate-clean mind, not me. Try to concentrate. This Timewyrm must be something very important. I wish I knew what I wanted me to do.'

Ace shrugged. 'You'll just have to be very careful if we run into a Timewyrm.'

'That's rather obvious,' the Doctor said. 'I could have worked that out for myself.' He stared at her, and shrugged. 'Let's see about getting you your memory back, shall we?'

'That would be nice,' she said, sarcastically. 'How did you manage to wipe my mind, anyway?'

'I was clearing up some of the clutter in my forebrain,' he explained, hovering over the telepathic circuitry. Decisively, he stabbed at a pattern of controls. 'As I said, I'm a Time Lord. We live for a vast length of years by your standards. And in that time, we get an atticful of useless memories. Every few thousand years, we like to clean them out, so to speak. Edit out what we don't need, and leave plenty of room for new stuff as we go along.'

'And what happens to the used memories?' she asked with interest. This was like nothing she'd ever heard about before — at least, as far as she could recall. 'Do you write a book? *My Lives and Times*?'

'Don't be absurd.' He was trying to concentrate on his programming. 'The TARDIS stores the important data. The rest are wiped. Pfft. Gone.'

With sudden panic, she stared at the panel he was playing with. It seemed full of red lights. Her generalized knowledge told her that red lights were used as warning signs. 'Is that what you've done with me?' she asked, gripping his arm and pointing at the console. 'Have you *pffted* me out of there?'

Shaking her free, he stared haughtily at her. 'Of course not. There's plenty of room in the TARDIS's memory banks for the contents of that small mind of yours. It's just a matter of accessing it and — aha!' Grinning in triumph, he pointed at the little screen again. Ace peered at it: whatever language it was written in, she couldn't recall knowing it.

'I can't read that,' she complained.

'Of course you can't,' he agreed, infuriatingly. 'It's in ancient High Gallifreyan. All the best computer programs are. But that's you, right there.'

'But I want to be me right here.' She tapped the side of her head.

'I'm getting to that. Come over here and put both hands palm down on these two metal plates.' He gestured to the base of the telepathic circuits.

Warily, she held her hands almost in position. 'Why?' she asked. She couldn't remember if she trusted him or not, and preferred to play it safe, given what she knew about his actions so far. A man — a Time Lord, she corrected herself — who erased everything you ever knew purely by accident was not someone to trust implicitly.

'You've got to make contact with the circuits, or I can't transfer those memories back.'

'Well, you drained them out, and I was nowhere near this panel,' she objected.

'You were asleep,' he explained, with all the patience he could muster. 'And the telepathic matrix somehow overlapped your mind. Your defences were down, and you were relaxed. Now your defences are up, and you're very tense. So I need a good, clean contact pathway between your brain and the circuits. Do as you're told.'

'When I get my memories back,' she asked, annoyed by his attitude, 'do I like you?'

'Everybody likes me,' he told her. 'Well, almost everybody.' When she gingerly placed her hands in position, he nodded, and tapped in the final codes.

Ace felt like she'd been kicked in the brain by a bad-tempered Cyberman. She tried to scream and draw free, but she was rooted to the spot, frozen. Through the pain, she could feel her mind expanding. Memories were flooding back, she supposed, but it just felt like she was being grilled over mental coals.

After an eternity, the agony was over, and she was free.

With a stifled sob, she collapsed to the floor.

'Bit of a strain, I expect,' the Doctor said, without any obvious sympathy. 'Need a rest.'

'What I need,' she told him from the floor, 'is a loaded submachine-gun and a target painted on your back. Or a can of nitro-nine. You can have a fifty yard start.'

'Ah,' he grinned, entirely unmoved by her anger. 'So you remember who you are now?'

She considered it. Reaching into her mind, she discovered that she did know: *Dorothy — God, how she hated that name! And she and the Doctor had taken off a while ago in the TARDIS —*

*— TARDIS: Time And Relative Dimension In Space. A sophisticated machine that looks like a dilapidated London Police Telephone Box on the outside. Inside, its dimensions are vastly larger, and it is capable of traversing all the known boundaries of time and space by passage through the Vortex —*

*— they had taken off in the TARDIS from near her home. Perivale, West London. Not much of a home. They had fought the Master (image of a sneering, bearded face, elegant clothing and fangs) on the planet of the Cheetah people (smell of blood, pounding of feet, the thrill of the hunt, the...)*

'Yes,' she said, unable to conceal the smile in her voice. 'I'm Ace.'

'Well, that's an improvement,' he said.

Climbing unsteadily to her feet, she leaned on the console for support. 'Doctor, how could you possibly be so stupid?' she demanded wearily. 'What if I hadn't got my memories back?'

'You'd have found some new ones,' he told her blithely.

'You're young and adaptable.'

'You what?' Ace could hardly trust herself to speak. 'This is important, Doctor. You have to know who you really are.'

The Doctor made no reply. A shadow crossed his face, and he looked lost and alone. Ace decided to change the subject. 'Well, I prefer knowing, all right? Anyhow, how do I know I've got all my memories back?'

'We'll do a spot check, Where did you first meet me?'

'Iceworld,' she said, promptly. 'I was a waitress. Tedium City. Boring job, boring people, I was dead chuffed when you turned up — a bit of excitement at last. And...' She broke off. 'Then there's something about Fenric ... He planned the whole thing. I was at school, in the lab, mixing up a batch of nitro, and there was this mega explosion... and I was on Iceworld. But it was Fenric who made it all happen, wasn't it?'

'Yes,' the Doctor told her, grimly. 'It was Fenric.'

'Have you been mucking about with my mind?' she asked, aggressively. 'Changing things about in there? Did you edit out some bits of it?'

'If I had,' the Doctor replied, 'I'd have made you a lot less rude than you are. No, you've got back whatever the TARDIS took from you. You're all you again — for better or worse..'

'Thanks a heap,' she muttered. 'I don't think I'll ever be able to go to sleep again in peace.'

'I can put a few buffers into the circuits. Stop it from happening again. In fact —'

He broke off as a low, booming sound filled the room. After a second, it was repeated.

Nothing in her memory gave any clue as to what the noise was. Ace turned to the Doctor, who looked almost ashen. 'What was that?'

'The Cloister Bell,' he told her, grimly.

She couldn't remember any cloisters in the TARDIS. 'Well, why's it ringing?'

'I don't know,' he answered. 'It's not sounded since — since the Logopolis affair. When I died — the me you saw in that recording, that is. It only rings in the direst of emergencies.'

That wasn't exactly reassuring. 'Like what?' Why was he

always so frustratingly tight-mouthed with information that might be crucial?

'Oh, the end of the Universe. Imminent death and destruction on a colossal scale. A regeneration crisis of painful proportions. That sort of thing.'

Ace thought about it for a moment. Not good, clearly. But then with the Doctor so few things ever were. She realized that in one way having regained her memory was not so marvellous — it made her painfully aware of all her previous adventures with this strange traveller. 'Then what could it be signalling now?'

'How should I know?' He examined the controls. 'We're still in the Vortex, and there's nothing outside the ship. I don't know why it's sounding.'

'You don't know much, and that's a fact,' Ace told him in disgust.

'The Duchess in *Alice's Adventures In Wonderland*,' he told her, after a moment's thought. 'I know where you stole that quotation from.'

An idea occurred to her. 'Do you think this Cloiser Bell thingy is connected with whatever it was you were warning yourself about a few minutes ago?'

*Boom...*

The Doctor started at the sound, and stared into nothingness thoughtfully. 'It would appear so, yes. The Timewyrm.'

*Booommm...*

Worried, Ace glanced around. 'It's... it's responding to what we say.'

'Of course it is,' he told her. 'It's the TARDIS, trying to communicate with us.'

'Can't it do better than this? Or are we expected to play twenty questions to find out what the problem is?'

The Doctor glared impatiently at her. 'The TARDIS can't speak directly to us. Its intelligence is of a vastly different order to yours — or even mine. It's doing the best it can. Whatever is happening must be very drastic indeed. The Cloister Bell is a sort of warning signal it sounds to get my attention.'

'Well, it's certainly got mine. Then what?'

He stared at the panel. A light was blinking, steadily. The scanner control... He glanced up at the screen set into the far wall, and it burst into life.

Ace jumped, and then stared at the face she saw there. 'It's the Brig!' she exclaimed. The military bearing, the clipped moustache, the calm and efficient air were all familiar to her — Brigadier Alastair Lethbridge-Stewart, once head of the United Nations Intelligence Taskforce in Britain. But he looked younger here, and he wore his UNIT uniform over a much trimmer body than when she had met him.

'Doctor,' the Brigadier said, in his precise, measured tones, 'I need your help. Doctor?' Then the picture faded away into nothingness.

'A cosmic distress signal?' she asked him. 'Did the Brigadier get your number from interstellar directory enquiries?'

'Very funny,' the Doctor snapped. He tried fiddling with the controls, but nothing happened. 'No, there isn't any way that he could have done this. But why...'

The screen lit up again. This time, it showed a frightened young girl. She had long brown hair and was dressed in a Victorian-looking gown. 'Doctor!' she called. 'Doctor! Where are you? Help me! Help me!' The girl glanced over her shoulder and screamed. Then she, too, vanished.

'What's going on?' Ace demanded. 'Who was that?'

'Victoria,' the Doctor replied tartly. 'A much quieter and less obstreperous travelling companion than you are. And she didn't ask as many pointless questions.' He rapped his knuckles hard on his forehead. 'Come on Doctor, think. Think!'

Again, the screen lit up. This time, it showed a young man with long, wild hair, dressed in a kilt and wielding a claymore. 'Doctor!' he yelled, in thick Scottish tones. 'I canna see ye! Help me! Doctor!' Then, in his turn, he faded out to the white screen.

'Jamie McCrimmon,' the Doctor said hastily, fending off the obvious question. 'Another person who travelled with me for a while.' He snapped his fingers. 'Got it! Those are all events that happened in the past! The TARDIS is using my own memories, projecting them onto the screen...'

'But why?' Ace asked, frustrated. The more she learned, the less she knew.

'I don't know... yet. But there's got to be a reason for it all,' he assured her. 'The TARDIS never acts without a very solid reason.' Ace snorted in disbelief.

The screen lit up again. This time, it showed a young girl of about Ace's age, with an elfin face, and thick, dark hair. She wore a loose-flowing gown, and stared out of the screen with a trusting expression on her face.

'Your temple travels through many times, Doctor,' she said. 'Truly, it is a wondrous thing you do.'

'Katarina,' he said swiftly. For a moment, Ace thought she saw a tear hovering on the edge of his eye, but then it was gone.' She's dead, now.'

'Temple,' Katarina's image repeated. 'Temple. Temple.' Then the screen flashed a brilliant white. The blinding expanse was punctuated by a series of coordinates that looked familiar to Ace.

'Here!' she exclaimed. 'That's the code you always set to get us to Earth!'

The Doctor nodded. As they watched, the numbers began to dissolve, flowing and vanishing as they did so. Eventually, the screen was pure white again. Obviously, it was over.

Ace glanced uncertainly at the Doctor. 'What was all that about?' she asked.

He turned a haunted face towards her. 'Well,' he said, slowly, 'unless I've very much misinterpreted the warning, I'd say that the TARDIS was telling us that deep in the Earth's past is something that could change the whole course of human history rather drastically.'

'Drastically? *How* drastically?'

'Drastically as in — BOOM. No more Earth...'

# 5: Ambush

'I've got a very bad feeling about this.'

Gilgamesh decided he couldn't ignore the comment this time. He paused and looked back at his friend, a resigned expression on his face. Enkidu took a little getting used to.

Not merely his mood swings, but even his appearance. He was tall, brooding and muscular, but hardly from the same stock as Gilgamesh and his men. Instead of the long, oiled beards of the men of Uruk, Enkidu had long, dark hair all over the exposed portions of his body. The bony ridges above his eyes projected forwards, his chin jutted out equally savagely. Mysterious black eyes lay almost hidden in his face. Had he been somehow catapulted five thousand years into his own future, Enkidu would have been hailed with glee by archaeologists and anthropologists as a prime specimen of a Neanderthal Man, supposedly long-dead by this point in history.

'Stop grumbling, and come on,' Gilgamesh told him. 'We'll never get our work done if you hang back and complain all the time.'

'It's too quiet,' Enkidu said.

'I'm sorry, but I couldn't persuade any musicians to accompany us on a dangerous spying raid,' Gilgamesh retorted. 'Will you come on?'

Warily, Enkidu moved up to join his king. He continued to scan the depths of the grove of date palms through which they were passing. The seven-man patrol was now well within the boundaries of the land ruled by Kish, but there had been no signs of travellers or even workers yet. Enkidu mentioned this.

Sighing, Gilgamesh paused. 'So, they finished work early. Who cares? It'll be sunset in a couple of hours, and I'd like to be inside the gates of Kish by then. They still have lions in this area, you know. And while I'm always fond of a good lion hunt, I don't want to get side-tracked from our mission.'

'I suppose so,'' agreed Enkidu, looking as worried as ever. He took his duties as guardian of the king very seriously — too seriously, Gilgamesh sometimes thought. But at least he did pick up his pace somewhat.

Leaving the protection of the grove of trees the patrol made its way into the fields. Barley and rice were both being grown, and the crops looked healthy. Irrigation ditches, very like those of their own Uruk, watered the plants. Kish was clearly prospering, and heading for a well-stocked winter. Shielding his eyes with his hand, Gilgamesh scanned the horizon.

Kish was visible in the distance — at least, its large stone walls were, and the occasional tower or roof jutting above the level of the walls. He was puzzled by an odd, orange gleam on the stones. On his last trip here, the walls had not looked like that ... Something noteworthy certainly seemed to be happening here. Perhaps this trip wouldn't be a complete waste of time.

Just ahead of them in the fields was a cluster of palms about a small pool. Gilgamesh nudged his friend. 'Cool water, eh?'

'And welcome,' Enkidu agreed. He shifted his bow and quiver uncomfortably. 'I'm parched.'

Leading his men in that direction, Gilgamesh glanced up at the sun. They had plenty of time for a short rest and drink. Then they would head for Kish, and slip into the city before the nightly curfew. A friendly inn, a flask or two of barley beer, and maybe a willing wench ...

They were jumped just inside the circle of trees. Soldiers of Kish had been waiting for them. As the patrol passed between the closely-growing trunks of the palms, the ambushers attacked.

Unable to draw their weapons or use their bows, Gilgamesh's men tried to fall back and gain time to unsheath their swords and battle-axes. But more men rose from the irrigation ditches, throwing off the shields covered with soil that had hidden them.

Gilgamesh and his men were surrounded.

Ace looked at the Doctor, appalled. 'Aren't you overreacting a bit?' she asked hopefully.

'I never overreact,' he replied grimly, ignoring Ace's outraged exclamation. 'There's something very unwholesome going on somewhere in the Earth's past. And if we don't stop it, then there might not be an Earth as you know it. It'll just be dust blowing in the cosmic winds.'

As he fiddled with the controls, Ace tried to take it in. 'But — I'm from the Earth, Professor,' she objected. 'If it's destroyed in the past ...'

'You may very well cease to exist,' he agreed, concentrating on the settings. 'Or your Earth will be confined to a sliver of the Universe, cut off from the rest. So we'll have a sort of barometer to see if what we're doing will work. If you vanish, we've made a mistake.'

'Somehow that's not very comforting, Professor.'

He glared at her again. 'Must you address me like that, Ace? I knew I should have edited that out of your memory while I had the chance.' He sighed. 'Ace, there are times when there is no comfort in time travel. This may be one of them. We seem to be heading for a crisis of unimaginable proportions here — something that could unravel the fabric of the Universe.'

'But ... but how could something change the past?' Ace persisted. 'I mean, it's already happened, hasn't it? Didn't you once tell me that we can't change the way history's written?'

'You can't change your past,' he agreed, mulling over his settings. 'But a Time Lord could. As far as I'm concerned it hasn't happened yet, and Time Lords have much more power to call on than any human being. And so do some other races. Any being powerful enough to alter the course of human history is a force to be reckoned with indeed.'

'You're giving me the shivers,' Ace complained in a quiet voice.

'I'm giving myself the shivers,' he replied. As he watched, all of his settings began to change. Ace stared at the controls. 'The TARDIS is taking over the flight plan herself,' he informed her. 'She knows what she's doing.' He patted the console, and smiled thinly. 'Let's only hope that we know what we're doing when we arrive.'

Ace couldn't make much sense of the readings beyond the basic code for the Earth. 'Any idea where we're going to turn up?'

'Oh, yes: Mesopotamia, 2700 BC.' He looked thoughtful. 'A crucial point in human history, Ace. The first walled cities were being built. Irrigation was transforming your people from nomadic gatherers and hunters into city-dwellers. Writing had just been invented, and the system of a warrior aristocracy. An exciting period of time, and a very vulnerable one. If this experiment had failed, the human race might have remained in a state of primitive savagery for thousands more years.'

'Is that what we've got to prevent?' Ace asked.

The Doctor shook his head. 'I doubt it. I have a feeling it's something much worse than that ...'

Ace stared at the time rotor as it rose and fell. 'Great ...' she muttered, without much conviction.

'I told you I had a bad feeling about this,' Enkidu complained. Grabbing one of the attackers by the throat, he used the hapless man as a living shield to fend off the sword-blows aimed at him.

'Oh, shut up,' was the best Gilgamesh could manage. He ducked the first blows aimed at him, and then succeeded in getting his hands on his axe. There wasn't room for much of a swing, but he managed well enough to spill the guts of the next man that came at him. Screaming and clutching at his stomach, the soldier fell backwards into the path of his companions.

With this brief respite Enkidu managed to grasp his war club. He swung out at the nearest attacker. A solid *thunk* stove in the man's brains, and he collapsed soundlessly to the ground.

Enkidu glanced around. Three of the men from his patrol were already dead, their blood irrigating the earth. The fourth and fifth men were injured. Only he and Gilgamesh remained unscathed as yet, and there were at least twenty Kishites about them. In the open, that would be good odds, but here there wasn't room to swing a solid blow.

The captain of the attackers gestured with his sword. 'At them!' he yelled. 'Gilgamesh is to be taken alive, remember, but the ape can be slaughtered.'

'Ape?' Enkidu yelled, furious. 'Come here and repeat that!' He made his club whistle above his head.

'You're too touchy,' Gilgamesh laughed. he was puzzled by the order to take him alive, but he had no intention of being taken at all. The problem was that the advantages were all with their attackers. This time, he couldn't see a way out.

'Lugulbanda,' he grunted in prayer to his personal god, 'This would be a pretty good time to get off your backside and do something for a change.'

There was a moment of eerie silence. Swords were stilled in mid-air, spears halted in mid-thrust. Then, growing like a roll of thunder, an ear-splitting roaring sound filled the air. It sounded almost like an elephant hunt — the sound the dying behemoth made when it was being slaughtered. Rising and falling, the noise seemed to be coming from the air itself, because there was certainly nothing visible.

Enkidu seized his opportunity. With a fierce roar of his own, he jumped into battle with the closest of their foes. Gilgamesh was right behind him. The noise that had shocked everyone stopped, and then there was a tall, blue box standing in the circle of trees. On its top, a small fire burned without consuming anything.

Enkidu laughed in pleasure as his club shattered another skull. Flinging the dead man from him, he paused long enough to see a young woman walk out of the box. He blinked and shook his head. From the expression on her face, she had not been expecting to step into the middle of a battle.

There was no time for further gawping. Another soldier thrust at him, but Enkidu twisted aside. The sword passed by his left arm, narrowly missing him. Enkidu smashed down on the arm that held the sword, and heard the pleasing sound of shattering bone. The attacker screamed, and dropped his sword. Enkidu smashed the man's face and kicked the body backwards.

Gilgamesh was likewise in the midst of his battle frenzy. His war-axe whirled, clearing men from about him rapidly — they either moved back or died.

The captain of the Kishite soldiers didn't like the way the tide had turned. He nodded to two of his archers. 'Kill the ape, but only wound Gilgamesh,' he ordered. The men dropped to their knees, and aimed past their companions.

Ace wasn't sure which side she should be supporting, but she couldn't simply wait for one or other side to win. Apart from the fact that there was no telling how they'd react to her, it simply wasn't in her nature to back out of a fight. Feeling in the backpack she'd slung over her shoulder on leaving the TARDIS, she grabbed a can of her invaluable nitro-nine. She primed it, tossed it into the air, and threw herself to the ground.

For the fighters it was as if a new sun had suddenly appeared in the sky. With a terrible roar of sound, flames lit the entire oasis. The archers, taking careful aim, were blinded by the sudden light and then knocked flying by the blast. The men standing were thrown aside like leaves in a gale and slammed into trees. Gilgamesh and Enkidu, too, felt the explosion above them, as if mighty hands were pressing them down to the ground.

With their ears ringing and their eyes seeing flashing lights, the two warriors of Uruk gathered their wits and weapons, but the attack was broken. The remaining soldiers were picking themselves up and fleeing back to Kish. It was bad enough fighting the king of Uruk, but this new event had shattered their hearing and their confidence alike. With satisfaction, Gilgamesh noted that less than half of the attackers were crawling home, and none of them uninjured. Staggering back to his feet, he looked around the corpse-strewn pond. Of his patrol, only he and Enkidu remained alive. Both had nicks and scratches, but no real wounds.

His eyes lit on the strange girl, who stood staring back defiantly at him. So this was the answer to his irreverent prayer! Well, if Lugulbanda was going to answer this promptly in the future, maybe it was time he got a little more of that old religious feeling back! He looked over the girl with a professional eye.

A bit on the skinny side, and very pale, but otherwise a healthy-looking wench. But — was she a human being or a god?

'Who are you?' he asked her, with respect, just in case.

'Ace.' Ace in her turn stared at the half-naked man facing her. His chest was heaving, his muscles dripping sweat. His hairy face wasn't unhandsome, but she wasn't certain she like the look of that calculated gleam in his eye.

'Aya?' he repeated. The goddess of the dawn herself? Well, that would explain the bright light and the noise she had somehow created. True, the gods weren't much noted for walking amongst men, but he had, after all, seen Ishtar herself only a few weeks ago. There seemed to be a veritable plague of gods hereabouts!

The door of the strange box opened again, and another figure came out. This was a man, obviously, but like none that he had ever seen before. He was dressed in strange clothes, and carried something in his hand that was certainly not a formidable club.

'And I'm the Doctor,' this newcomer said brightly. 'I do hope we've not dropped in at an inconvenient time?'

Enkidu's wits had come back to him now, and he looked from the Doctor to Ace in stupefaction. 'Where did you come from?' he asked.

Gilgamesh laughed. 'Enkidu, you fool, these are gods! I prayed to Lugulbanda, and the old reprobate actually answered me for once. The pretty one is Aya, goddess of the dawn. And the weird one must be Shamash, the god of the sun. Though he hardly looks the part of a warrior god, to be honest.'

'I'm not a warrior of any kind, really,' the Doctor said, quickly. 'I'm a student, a scholar, a man of learning.'

'Ah!' Gilgamesh grinned at this. 'Ea! God of wisdom. By the holies, Lugulbanda really answered my prayers, didn't he? You two are just what I need to complete my mission. Light and knowledge!'

'What are you —' Ace began, but the Doctor nudged her in the ribs, and stepped forwards.

'Well,' he said, cautiously, 'If you were to tell us a little bit more about your mission, maybe we might be able to help you.'

Enkidu had had enough of the talking, and he set about

49

salvaging whatever was useful from the bodies lying around the oasis. Gilgamesh laughed, and clapped an arm in comradely fashion about the Doctor's shoulders. The Doctor tried not to wince in pain.

'My companion in arms Enkidu and I were just off into Kish to check out the state of things. We've heard some disturbing stories of strange happenings there of late.'

'Strange happenings?' the Doctor echoed, with wide-eyed innocence. 'Really? Well, I happen to be a bit of an expert in the realm of strange happenings. Maybe Ace and I will pop into Kish with you for a little look, eh?' He lowered his voice in conspiratorial tones. 'There wouldn't happen to be a temple in this city, would there?'

'There are many temples, Ea,' Gilgamesh replied. 'Did you want to check on your servants there? I have to admit that I'm not certain where your temple would be.'

'No... More on anything out of the ordinary.'

Ace tugged on his sleeve. 'What's this sudden interest in a temple, Professor?'

'You remember that Katarina's image laid great stress on the word.' He tapped his nose with the handle of his umbrella. 'I have a sneaky suspicion that we'll find a few of the answers inside one of the temples in Kish.'

# 6: Spying Tonight

Agga's palace was close to the temple of Zababa, patron god of the city of Kish. The palace was a large building, made mostly from stone and brick, and decorated by the omnipresent coloured clay cones. Some of the walls had been whitewashed, and paintings of gods and mortals mingled on this canvas. Statues lined the corridors and rooms, giving stone life to figures of men and beasts. Returning from another round of futile prayers to Zababa to unclench the fist of Ishtar from around the throats of the Kishites, Agga collapsed wearily onto his throne, ignoring the fawning ministrations of the nobles and servants that surrounded him. One hand rested on the leopard-headed arm of his throne; the other supported his own tired head.

One voice cut through the babble of the attendants, and Agga opened his bloodshot eyes to see his daughter staring sympathetically up at him.

Ninani was fourteen, and a woman in the eyes of the laws. But Agga saw only the image of his long-dead favourite wife in Ninani's exquisite features. In the normal course of events, Ninani would have been married off by now, but Agga had not been able to bear the thought of losing her to some other city. Now that Kish had been blessed with the arrival of Ishtar, Ninani was his one refuge from the nightmares about him. Hers was a gentle and kindly soul, and a fragile beauty that he had always done his best to protect — and always would.

Gesturing slightly, he allowed her to approach him. Her dark eyes burned into his own, and she shook her head in despair.

'You've been to her temple again, haven't you, father?' she

asked.

'Is it so obvious?' he growled, simultaneously grateful and annoyed that she could read him so well.

'It always is.' Ninani said, simply. She sat at his feet, and began gently to rub his left hand. 'You're always so tense, so haunted.' She shook her head. 'I had always imagined that to be visited by one of the gods would be such a blessing. Yet — forgive me — there seems to have been little for us from Ishtar's visit but a curse!'

Agga's eyes darted across the faces of the nobles and servants. Was one of them in *her* service? Could she see and hear through them? Did she even now know what Ninani had said? There was no way to tell, no way to be certain he could protect his daughter. 'You shouldn't say such things,' he chided her. 'Mortals must endure whatever the gods visit upon us.'

'Endure?' Ninani echoed. 'Father, you're suffering, not enduring. And our people are suffering. I used to enjoy visiting the temple of Ishtar — it was always happy and —' her lips twitched slightly as she remembered the sacred priestesses and their noisy duties '— educational. But now there's more merriment in a field of unburied corpses than in the temple of Ishtar.'

'Do not say such things,' Agga insisted. 'It is not wise to talk about the goddess so.' He wished that he could tell her the truth, but she was too sensitive. It would hurt her to be so blunt. No, better that she have the protection of ignorance. Better to pretend.

Ninani held her beautiful head high, arrogantly. 'I am not afraid of Ishtar,' she snapped.

'That is because you are still young and foolish,' Agga told her. 'If you were wise, you would be very afraid of her. She can kill. Or...' He shook his head, not wanting to think about it. 'There are worse things than death. The gods know them all. Stay away from Ishtar's temple. And do not criticize the gods.'

'You speak as if you expect to be betrayed to her,' Ninani said, perceptively. She gestured about the court. 'None of these citizens or servants would willingly betray you, father.'

'I know, my daughter,' he replied. 'But the gods have ways to possess a man or woman, and to make them spies whether they will it or not. Ishtar can cloud their minds, and shackle their spirits. If she wants to know what we do or say, then she will discover it. The nurse at whose breasts you suckled may be Ishtar's spy if Ishtar wishes it. Any one of my wives might be my assassin if Ishtar tells them to slay. The gods know best. While Ishtar is with us, we have security and peace.' He stroked her hair thinking: *I know peace only when you are with me.*

Ninani refused to be put off, and glared angrily at him. 'Peace? You call this peace? Let us face her down!' she exclaimed. 'It is not right that you, above all people, should live in this fear. I shall take a spear and slay her — or die trying!'

'You will not!' he thundered, rising to his feet, furious at last. One look at his face cowed Ninani completely. She had obviously gone too far. Throwing herself to the stone floor, she kissed his feet. She had rarely seen her father so furious, and never at anything she had said or done. The throne room was expectantly silent.

'Forgive me,' she whispered.

'Of course I forgive you,' he said coldly, reaching down with his staff of office. Relieved, she climbed to her feet again. Princess she may be, and daughter of his loins — but if he had not publicly forgiven her, she would have been stoned to death for angering him. 'But,' he added, pointing his staff at her, 'you are not to go to the temple of Ishtar, for any reason. Do you understand me?' He hated to force this upon her, but it was for her own protection.

'Yes, father,' she agreed, meekly. 'And if she should send for me?'

*If she should send for you*, he thought, *then I shall forget my worries and tear the temple down about her ears*. 'Did you not hear me?' he said. 'You are not to go anywhere near her temple or her servants there. That is all I shall say on the subject.' He sighed, and signalled for his chief steward. 'Now, I am tired and hungry, and will eat. Leave me, daughter.'

Ninani bowed, and walked backwards out from the throne room. Even for the king's daughter, to turn her back on his divine presence would be to invite death.

In the corridor Ninani paused thoughtfully. Her maid, Puabi, hurried over. She was a good maid, but something of a gossip. That was what Ninani valued most about her. Ninani had to remain in the palace for days on end, and Puabi was her eyes and ears for everything taking place outside the palace compounds. A plump, middle-aged woman of peasant stock, Puabi made it her business to know everything that was happening within earshot of the city.

'Puabi,' she asked, carefully, 'do you know any of the sacred harlots?'

'Ishtar's harpies?' her maid replied, opening her eyes in surprise. 'One or two, though not too well.' She was trying to work out why her mistress should ask. The only logical answer came to her, and she grinned. 'What, has your father agreed to marry you off at last, and you need some advice on how to please a man?' She nudged Ninani in the ribs. 'That I can tell you, believe you me. Keep your mouth shut and your legs —'

Ninani glared at the maid. 'I find it hard to believe that you ever keep your mouth shut,' she retorted, drily. 'But that's not what interests me. I simply want to talk with one of the younger girls there. One who can be trusted to keep her mouth shut when she returns to her place.'

Shrugging, Puabi thought for a moment. 'One of my nieces works in the temple. Bright girl, name of En-Gula. She knows when to keep her peace.' Then she winked, and nudged Ninani broadly in the ribs. 'And I hear she's just the girl to talk to about those other matters that you're not yet interested in. From all accounts, she's got a few effective methods of giving pleasure to a man —'

'I would like to see her *today*,' the princess said, pointedly.

Throwing up her hands in mock despair, Puabi marched off, muttering to herself: 'I don't know what the world's coming to today. When I was in my prime, the men were lining up for...'
Thankfully, a corner in the corridor cut off whatever else she was saying. Sighing, Ninani shook her head. A good maid in many ways, but a little too forward in others...

As she walked back to her own quarters in the palace, Ninani mused over the events of the past few weeks. Since the arrival of Ishtar and her enthronement in the temple, Kish had changed — for the worse. There was that mysterious work that was being done to the walls, for one thing. Ninani was not allowed to leave the palace compound at all now — for her own safety, her father had insisted — but Puabi had told her all about the massive building project that seemed to involve strips of pure copper being laid over certain of the stones. Even her father had no idea why the goddess wanted this done.

Her father... He had changed the most. His old cheerful self had been changed into a grim, tired soul. His eyes held a haunted fear in them that sometimes, as earlier, erupted to the surface. Though he would never say it, she knew that he had grown to hate Ishtar. He was spending longer and longer hours in the temple of Kish's city-god, Zababa, praying that she would leave. These prayers, it would seem, were so far unanswered.

She knew how much these events must be preying upon him. Normally the kindest and wisest of men, he was now so harried and tired. He was too tired, or too frightened, to lift a finger against Ishtar. Well, whatever he said, she was the daughter of a king, and someone had to do something. She knew that he thought she was too tender to be capable of anything, but she would show him.

Though he had warned her off, Ninani couldn't simply stand aside and let his terrors gnaw away at his entrails. She would find a way to do something — anything — to help. Perhaps this acolyte of Ishtar's would be able to offer some advice.

The sacred prostitutes of Ishtar were an old order of the priesthood. Through the rituals that they performed, and the offerings that they gave and accepted in their bodies, the goddess was pleased to grant fertility and peace to the city. But of late, it seemed that fewer men went to the temple to participate in the rites, and there were stories going about the palace that many of the men who went to the temple came back changed...

In her room, Ninani threw herself onto her small couch. Catching sight of herself in the polished bronze of her mirror, she sighed. She picked up the tortoiseshell comb from her table and began to tidy her long, black hair. At least the rhythm of brushing kept her occupied for a while. She could forget, for a brief moment, the uncertainties and fears that she felt, and lose herself in the simple actions.

Her relationship with her father had always been her most precious joy. She knew that few kings valued their daughters as anything more than pawns to be married off to cement alliances. Yet her father had never treated her this way. On the contrary, he generally sought and listened to her opinions, and allowed her to cheer him out of bleak moods. He had always been gentle and loving with her — until the arrival of Ishtar. Now everything had changed. Ninani was grimly determined to restore their old relationship, even if it meant risking her life.

But would she be able to do anything? Could any mortal plot against a goddess — and live?

'What is that?'

Wide-eyed and innocent, the Doctor followed Gilgamesh's disgusted gaze. 'This?' He held up the offending object, a long, red cloak, and assorted items of clothing. 'It's a disguise.'

'A what?'

'A disguise,' the Doctor repeated. 'They're all the rage this year. You wear one to get into Kish without being spotted. The Kishites will think you are a merchant.'

Curling his lip, Gilgamesh shook his head, firmly. 'I will not hide myself behind the scraps and rags of a peasant tradesman. The king of Uruk will not play charades.'

Ace cursed their luck. Why was the Doctor so frequently forced to work with idiots and buffoons? Even a simple matter such as a disguise was causing the hackles to rise in this king of Uruk. Patiently, the Doctor tried once again. 'These guards were waiting for you here, Gilgamesh. They are expecting you in the city, obviously.'

'Let them.' The king tapped his battle-axe. 'I could use the exercise.'

Enkidu put his hand on his friend's arm. 'Listen to Ea,' he urged. 'The god of wisdon has a plan, clearly. And he is right, you know.' He gestured at Gilgamesh's biceps. 'You know what will happen when you arrive at the city gates? The guards will take one look at you and say: "Who could this be? Such mighty muscles, such a fighting stance — they could belong only to Gilgamesh, King of Men!" '

A smile played across the king's lips as he imagined the scene. 'There is truth in what you say,' he conceded. Then he looked at the garments again, and wrinkled his nose in disgust. 'But to wear the rags of a common peasant — Enkidu, it offends my dignity.'

Ace had had more than enough of this posturing. The Doctor rarely saw the need for them to wear local clothing, but he had insisted in this case. She had already been forced to don a cloak, and a winding cloth to cover her long hair. If she was stuck with it, then she saw no reason why Gilgamesh shouldn't suffer likewise. 'Besides,' she told him, 'all good spies wear disguises. It's a mark of their cunning and skill.'

'Really?' he asked. She could see he was beginning to warm to the idea. Vanity was clearly his biggest weakness. That and his tendency to try to touch her up whenever they were close.

'Yeah,' she assured him. 'James Bond, John Steed, Mickey Mouse — they're all doing it.'

Gilgamesh mulled over the names, unwilling to admit that he'd never heard of them. 'Shamash Bond?' he echoed. Well, if an aspect of the glorious sun god Shamash could wear a disguise, who was he to complain? 'Very well,' he told the Doctor. 'I will wear the clothing.'

'Great,' Ace said, grinning. 'I'll bet you look a lot better than Mickey Mouse.'

The Doctor scowled at her as he helped Gilgamesh get ready. 'Enjoy your little jokes while you can,' he muttered to her.

Blithely, she smiled back. 'I will,' she assured him. She was quietly transferring cans of nitro-nine to the pockets of her jacket. The Doctor had insisted that she leave her bag behind, not wishing to have her transporting explosives into the city. She was equally unwilling to go on without them, and saw no need to mention that her bag was empty as she threw it into the TARDIS.

Finally, even Gilgamesh was ready. The Doctor had raided

the TARDIS's wardrobes for all the clothing that would pass muster in Mesopotamia. They looked a little odd, but he was certain that the city guards would let them through, taking them for simple tradesmen. At least, he added to himself, they would if it proved possible to keep Gilgamesh in line.

'Right,' he said, with as much enthusiasm as he could summon, 'time to be off. Now, remember, let me do the talking.'

'It'll be impossible to stop you,' Ace muttered, falling in step behind him. Swinging his brolly, the Doctor flashed her a look but said nothing. Enkidu fell into step beside Ace, and Gilgamesh somewhat reluctantly brought up the rear. He had agreed to hold his position because Enkidu had managed to convince him that he would be able to get a better swing from there if a fight broke out.

Ace studied Enkidu with undisguised interest. He reminded her uncannily of Nimrod... Her mind flashed back to the terrifying experiences she had had in nineteenth-century Perivale, in the haunted house called Gabriel Chase. The Victorian mansion had been the disguised home of the strange, alien entity known as Light, collector and cataloguer of species. Light had selected Nimrod as his representative of Neanderthal Man. And now, here she was, walking alongside another member of the supposedly extinct species. Rumours of their death, she thought to herself, were clearly exaggerated.

Enkidu caught her gaze, and misinterpreted it. 'I'm sorry if my appearance offends you, lady.'

Snorting, Ace assured him: 'It doesn't worry me, chum. I was just thinking about an old mate of mine you remind me of.'

'Mate?' he echoed. 'Ah! You took one of my kind as a lover once in the past?'

Flushing, Ace shook her head. 'No, I meant mate as in friend. It's a sort of — um — affectionate term.'

'Oh. Pardon my ignorance of the heavenly languages.' Enkidu smiled, his canine teeth flashing slightly. 'You do not find me repulsive, then?'

Ace grinned. 'Compared to some people I've met, you're positively gorgeous,' she assured him. This Enkidu was all right.

A regular guy. Nodding her head backwards, she added: 'On the other hand, Gilgamesh is a right royal pain in the arse. How do you put up with him?'

Enkidu looked shocked. 'He is my master. It's not a question of putting up with him. I am honour bound to do whatever he wishes me to do.' Then, breaking the mood, he added: 'But, as you suggest, he is a trifle overbearing at times.' He considered for a moment, 'But he is a good king, and he makes Uruk strong. And if he is at times a little rough, well — that's just his manner.'

'Lack of manners, I call it,' Ace said, ruefully. 'Has he always had trouble with wandering hands?'

Enkidu smiled. 'I gather he has quite a reputation among the noblewomen of Uruk. I take it you do not like his attentions?' He glanced at the Doctor's back. 'Perhaps you are already spoken for?'

Following his gaze Ace laughed, and shook her head. 'Not by him,' she assured the Neanderthal. 'We're just travelling companions. And sometimes we're even friends. But that's all.' She eyed him mischievously. 'We're not even of the same species.'

'Ah.' Though he obviously couldn't follow this, Enkidu politely didn't probe. 'Then why do you travel with him?'

Ace shrugged. 'Life's always exciting with him. And he generally fights for what both of us believe in.'

'Much the same reasons I stay with Gilgamesh, then,' he told her. 'We are very alike.' He held up a hairy hand. 'Despite our obvious differences.'

'When you've quite finished socializing, Ace,' the Doctor broke in, loudly, 'take a look at those.' He gestured with his umbrella towards the walls of Kish. Standing almost twenty feet tall, and built of heavy stone, they stretched about the city. The tops of the walls were wide enough for four men to march abreast about the entire town. Guard towers rose from the battlements at regular intervals. There were several gates visible, each of them guarded by armed men.

'Wicked,' Ace said. 'Could be a problem getting in.'

'Is that all you can see?' he asked.

She shrugged. 'That, and the copper strips they're putting

all over the place.' It was impossible to miss the gleam of the orange-coloured metal in the slowly dying sunlight.

'What do they teach youngsters in school nowadays?' the Doctor sighed.

'School?' Gilgamesh rumbled. 'What's that?'

'A divine institution,' the Doctor informed him, 'to give young people knowledge and instruction in life.'

'Right,' Ace said, sarcastically. 'Positively heavenly. And it's centuries since you were in one, Professor.'

Ignoring the jibe, the Doctor asked her: 'And what colour is copper?'

Chemistry was one of her specialities. There was plenty of scope for doing interesting things — like blowing up schools... 'Orange,' she answered. Then, remembering the copper-topped domes of the London skyline, she added: 'Except when you leave it out in the rain. Then it oxidizes green...' Her voice trailed away as she realized what the Doctor was getting at. The copper on the walls of Kish was brightly-polished. 'Well, maybe it doesn't rain much in Mesopotamia?'

'I'm sure it doesn't,' he agreed. 'But the use of non-tarnishing copper is out of line with this civilization, Ace. They have to alloy it into bronze to stop corrosion.'

Staring at the walls, Ace felt a chill pass through her. 'Then what's that stuff doing there?'

'It's what it's not doing that worries me. It's not corroding...' He tapped the side of his nose with his umbrella. 'There's something fishy in Kish.' Then he grinned. 'Spying tonight!' he announced, and led the way towards the main gate.

# 7: Talking Union

'Escaped?' hissed Ishtar, furiously. 'Escaped? You call that a report?'

The terrified captain of the guards shook his head — the rest of his body was shaking without any conscious effort on his part. 'There was...' he began, hardly knowing what to say. 'We almost had Gilgamesh, but then something happened...'

Ishtar seemed to slide towards him from the depths of her sanctum, her pale skin shimmering in the gloom that she preferred. 'What happened,' she whispered dangerously, 'is that you were incompetent fools, and you failed me!'

'No!' the guardsman insisted. 'There was some kind of divine intervention that saved him!'

'Then you had better pray for some divine intervention of your own,' Ishtar warned him. 'I will not tolerate fools and failure!'

'I swear it!' the unfortunate man cried, then screamed as Ishtar's hands gripped his head. He could see nothing but the silver sheen of her flesh as he felt his neck begin to twist. 'Mercy!' he croaked.

'This *is* mercy,' she hissed in his ear. 'Had I the time, then you would die much more painfully...' The pleasing sound of the snapping of bones made her smile, and the man ceased struggling.

She released the corpse, and let it fall to the stone floor. Paying it no more attention, she glared at Dumuzi. 'My priest,' she purred, 'he was a poor choice for the mission. Perhaps Agga deliberately chose him, knowing that he would fail and thus anger me?'

Dumuzi, gathering what individual thoughts he still retained, shook his head. 'No, goddess, I doubt it. Would he run the risk of angering you? Especially with your threat against his daughter so fresh in his mind?'

'True,' Ishtar said. 'Then why was Gilgamesh not captured?'

'You do not believe that there may have been some deity that intervened on his behalf?' Dumuzi asked.

'Superstitious nonsense!' Ishtar laughed. 'You and I both know better than to believe in gods, don't we, Dumuzi?'

Knowing little now that she did not allow him to think, Dumuzi did not reply. He forbore to give the obvious reply — that she herself was proof of divine intervention. But Ishtar caught the scent of this thought, anyway, and whirled about to face him down.

'You think that another like myself might be here, Dumuzi?' she said. 'Ah — I see in the dim, dark closets of your mind that you pray that someone might come to free you from me! How delightful! Despite my restraints, there is still a portion of your tiny brain where you possess a touch of individuality. No matter. When it suits me, I shall seek it out and devour it. Until then, let it hide and fear.' She wrapped an arm about Dumuzi's shoulder. 'It pleases me to enlighten you, my priest. I am not a goddess, such as you think of the term. I was once as human as you are, and as frail.' She tapped her beautiful features and enjoyed the strange bell-like sound that rang out. 'Behind this mask lies a mind that once knew the pleasures and follies and pains of flesh. But then I discovered the potential of cybernetics, Dumuzi, and now I am no longer prey to the ills and sorrows of the flesh. Nor am I limited by the shackles of one form or one mind.

'I was born centuries ago on a world that lies half a universe from this tiny planet. And I became its queen — its goddess. But there were some that refused my Touch, and who fought against me. In the end, I had to flee.' She glanced sharply up at him. 'Fool! I could see that thought as clearly as if you had shouted it from the roof tops. If they could make me flee, you dare to hope that they could come here, seeking me out?' She laughed, scornfully. 'I am not one to leave enemies in my wake, Dumuzi. When I fled that wretched planet, they discovered what it is to scorn my power.' With a cruel curl to her lips, she bent to stare into his eyes. 'I left behind only the smoking embers of a planet, priest. A burnt-out, lifeless hunk of a world. Do not even dream of freedom from me. If such a thing is even possible, then when I leave this world of yours, it will be as a void and a devastation behind me. I would wipe out every last insect from the surface of this planet sooner than allow anyone — *anyone* — to think that they could best me!'

Turning slowly away again, she began to glide back into the darkness. Over her shoulder, she called: 'If you wish to pray, Dumuzi, then pray that nothing angers me. Because if it does, then I shall destroy the human race utterly from the face of the Earth.'


There came a quiet rapping at the door to Ninani's room. The princess glanced up, and called: 'Come!'

The door opened, and Puabi ushered in a young girl, barely as old as the princess herself. 'My niece,' she explained.

It was more than apparent that En-Gula was one of the votaries of Ishtar. She was well-formed and pretty, with dark eyes and short-cropped dark hair that fell only to the base of her neck. Her bronzed skin shone from the oils that were used to keep her body pure. Apart from her sandals, and the band about her forehead that bore the insignia of Ishtar, she wore only a simple skirt. Her bare breasts marked her clearly as one of the priestesses of the goddess of love. As she entered the room, she slid quietly and simply into a kneeling position before Ninani, and bowed to the floor.

'Rise,' the princess commanded, studying the other girl as she obeyed. Though she was clearly aware of her inferior rank, the girl seemed at ease and confident. 'Are you not curious as to why I wanted to speak with you, child?'

En-Gula stared back, clearly studying the princess in her turn. Then she glanced back at her aunt, and moved one eyebrow slightly. 'Your maidservant seemed to think that you were interested in my knowledge, highness.'

'My maidservant had better mind her own business, then,' Ninani answered. 'And while she is about it, she can fetch us a little wine.' Puabi took the hint and vanished. Rising to her feet, Ninani circled the acolyte, examining her carefully for the Mark of Ishtar. Her father always did this, she knew, and he had explained that all who were Touched by Ishtar bore her Mark on their bodies somewhere — generally on their brow or temples. En-Gula seemed free from all bodily blemishes, which was, after all, one of the requirements of any who wished to serve Ishtar in a physical role. Her body must be free from any imperfection, as such blemishes would nullify the offering of herself.

Having circled the girl, Ninani sat down again. 'How old are you, child?' she asked.

'Thirteen,' En-Gula replied, carefully.

'And how long have you been in the service of Ishtar?'

'Since I was seven.' Seeing the surprise in Ninani's eyes, she added: 'My mother died at that time, and I was taken as a child into the temple. I became one of the priestesses only a year ago. Until then, I helped to clean, and to look after the other priestesses.'

Wistfully, Ninani murmured: 'You must have seen a lot of life, child.'

Shrugging, En-Gula sniffed. 'I should think that you see as much as I, princess. You are captive within the palace, I within the temple.'

An unexpected answer, and Ninani realized that this girl was no fool. 'You do not like your life?'

'Who am I to complain?' Despite her words, it was quite clear that En-Gula was complaining. 'I am an orphan, and have been given a steady job, and a good home.'

'But?' the princess prompted.

Abruptly, En-Gula laughed. 'My lady, you didn't bring me here to hear the temple gossip.'

The door opened, and Puabi backed in, carrying a tray. On it were a silver pitcher and two goblets — one silver, one bronze. Ninani held her tongue as Puabi filled the silver goblet with the dark wine and passed it to her. The maid then filled the bronze cup, and gave it to En-Gula. When she looked up again, Ninani gestured at the door.

'What!' Puabi snorted. 'Am I to fetch my niece and not learn why?'

'Yes,' Ninani replied. 'You are. Now, go.' Meekly, Puabi left. Glancing back at the other girl. Ninani saw a flash of a smile in her eyes. 'If you know your aunt at all,' she explained, 'then you know of her astounding capacity for carrying gossip. I would like as little as possible of that to be about me.'

'Wise, princess,' En-Gula agreed. 'But may I learn why you sent for me?'

Ninani sipped her wine, and gazed evenly at the other girl. Now that the princess had drunk, the priestess was free to do likewise, and did. Etiquette and social order was rigid, and always obeyed.

'En-Gula,' Ninani said, slowly, 'you were wrong when you said that I did not want to hear the temple gossip. That is exactly what I wish to hear.'

The priestess shrugged. 'Lady, if you really want to hear about who drinks too much, and who is sleeping with which nobleman, then I could tell you. Forgive me, though — but it seems beneath your dignity.'

Sniffing, Ninani nodded. 'And so it is. The antics of your brood of harlots do not interest me at all. It is Ishtar I wish to know about.'

The girl stiffened at this. 'You require religious instruction?' she asked, carefully. 'My lady, I do not think that it would be fitting for you to serve in the beds of the temple — unless you wished it, of course!' Then another thought occurred to her. 'Or...' She glanced at the door leading to the bedroom at the far end of the room. 'Am I here to serve in your bed?'

Ninani sighed. 'Does everyone in your family think of nothing but sex?' she chided. 'I am not interested in becoming one of Ishtar's whores, En-Gula. Nor did I call you here to seduce you. I want to know about the goddess Ishtar herself!'

Getting to her feet again, she started to pace the room. 'I know what has been told me by my father,' she explained. 'That the goddess has condescended to visit with us a while. What I do not understand is why the thought should terrify him so. Nor do I understand what is happening in the temple. I've known Dumuzi for years, but of late he's not been the man I grew up with. I want to know why,' She stared at En-Gula. 'Can you help me?'

The priestess warily put down her cup. It was obvious that she was fighting back some urge to speak, one that eventually got the better of her. 'My lady,' she said, carefully. 'This may cause some offence, but may I first ask a favour of you?'

Ninani shrugged. 'Speak.'

'May I touch your skin for a moment?'

Puzzled, Ninani nodded. En-Gula came in close, and then brushed the long hair from the princess's brow. Sighing with relief, she allowed the hair to fall back. 'I am sorry, lady,' she replied, 'but I had to be certain that you had not been Touched. To speak freely with one who had the Touch of Ishtar would have meant my death — or worse.'

This was beginning to sound like the start of a productive conversation. Curious, Ninani listened as the priestess talked.

'When the goddess came among us,' En-Gula explained, 'she was not strong. Dumuzi told us all that she had been on a long journey, down to the world below the stars and heavens above. He said that she needed to rest, and to regain her energy. Then she would be herself. Well, it made sense, of sorts — about as much sense as anything that the gods ever do. So we carried on, honoured by her visit and waited.

'Then several of the older priestesses vanished. There was no explanation for this given us. And a few of the others changed. They had all received the Touch of Ishtar. Now they served as her eyes and ears, and she learned all that they knew. If anyone spoke in their presence against the goddess . . . Well, they tended to vanish, or else they, too, bore the Touch, and changed.

'Finally, my curiosity got the better of me.' She shrugged. 'It's a curse I suffer from, lady. A family trait, I suspect. I wish to know too much.'

'The both of us,' Ninani replied, liking this girl. 'Speak on.'

'The goddess had taken over several of the larger rooms. I

had been a cleaner, as I mentioned, and I know a few less obvious ways into these rooms.' She didn't clarify. The princess would have no interest in the times she had been hungry, and sought food wherever she could steal it within the temple.

'I had seen the goddess, of course — she would come out into the aisles of the temple from time to time, to be seen by her worshippers. But I had never been summoned into her private rooms.

'One evening I heard strange noises coming from behind the main altar, where Ishtar's sanctum lies. I used my knowledge of the secret ways of the temple. The innermost of Ishtar's rooms has a balcony around it, and I crept into it. The noise was coming from below me: a humming noise, but rising and falling, like bees buzzing in a rhythm. And there was a strange silver glow that flared and faded with the humming. It was dark in the shadows on the balcony, and I was scared. But I had to look over the edge, I had to see.' She shuddered, and lifted her wide, dark eyes to stare at Ninani. 'I wish I hadn't looked, lady.

'The goddess was there. She was as beautiful as ever, tall and pale and glorious. But she seemed to be dead. She was completely still. She was standing against the wall, in the one place where the wall was not covered by the tall metal cabinets that the goddess had had brought down from her buried ziggurat in the wilderness. The space she was standing in looked like a sarcophagus, lady — my heart went out to Ishtar then. Her head was covered by a metal hood, and the hood was the source of the humming. She was naked, and I saw that although she has a woman's shape, she is not made as a woman is made. All these things I saw in just a few moments, and then the goddess moved. She stepped from beneath the hood like a body stepping out of its grave. Her eyes opened, and I ducked into the shadows.'

'It sounds terrifying,' Ninani said, imagining the punishments for spying on a goddess.

En-Gula shook her head. Her eyes were bright with tears. 'It was only just beginning,' she said. 'Ishtar was with me on the balcony. I couldn't see her, but I could feel her there in the darkness with me — hunting me. I have never been so afraid.

I did not dare to make a sound, but I could sense her here, in my head, seeking me out, and I had to move. I crawled on my hands and knees round and round the balcony, as fast as I could, like an animal in a trap. I could feel her eyes below me, as if her sight could pierce the floorboards of the balcony. She was playing with me, as a cat plays with a mouse. She could have pounced on me at any time, but I could feel her amusement as I crawled hither and thither above her...'

The girl started to sob quietly. 'What happened?' Ninani said, too excited to let En-Gula stop at this critical moment.

En-Gula sniffed twice, and wiped her eyes. 'The goddess was distracted, lady. She forgot about me. Dumuzi and one of the palace guards had entered the room below me. They had brought two priestesses to receive the Touch of Ishtar. I felt her eyes leave me, and after a while I found the courage to drag myself to the edge of the balcony and look down.

'I knew the priestesses, my lady. One of them, Belkeli, had been kind to me ever since I entered the temple. She was struggling in the arms of the guard. The other priestess was on the floor, asleep or unconscious or drugged.

'Ishtar did not cover her nakedness. She stood in the centre of the room, drinking in the sight of Belkeli's fear. And then she began to change.'

'Change? How?' Ninani breathed.

En-Gula gave a long sigh. 'I think the gods look like us only because we would shun them if we were to see their true forms,' she said carefully. 'Ishtar is not like us. She made of metal, my lady. She is a living statue. And although her arms and shoulders are like those of a woman, she had the body of a serpent. No legs, my lady. She writhes across the floor like a snake. A gigantic metal snake.

'And her face is worse, because it is so nearly like a woman's face. But hard, and cold, and sharp, with movements that are not supple, like the expressions on your face or mine, but that are like the twitching of an insect's legs. And instead of eyes, she has burning coals set in her head.

'I think I screamed, but any noise I made was drowned by Belkeli's yells as the goddess slithered towards her. Ishtar spoke quietly and cruelly, and stretched out her right hand. I could see Belkeli shaking as the goddess stroked her hair. Ishtar's hand reached Belkeli's forehead, and I heard the sound like the hiss of a snake. Belkeli stopped moving, and when Ishtar removed her hand I could see the mark on Belkeli's forehead. I could not stay to watch any more. I felt ill. I crawled away.

'When I met Belkeli the next day, she was different. She had no kind words for me, no gossip. I asked her if she was well, and she replied as if I were a stranger. The worst of it was that even as she spoke in a dull voice, and would not meet my gaze, I saw a tear gather in the corner of her eye.'

Ninani tried to keep her voice calm. 'And the other priestess?'

'I never saw her again,' En-Gula said. 'But I spoke to one of the guards, one who at that time had not received the Touch, who told me that he had helped to dispose of her body. Her veins were drained of their blood, my lady — and her brains were missing from her skull!'

Ninani was as appalled as En-Gula. Seeing the girl fighting back the wave of horror, Ninani threw aside her dignity and rank. She grabbed the girl, pulling her close. Like a baby En-Gula clutched at her, sinking her head onto Ninani's shoulder. Great sobs of pain shook her. Finally, she shook herself free of Ninani's compassionate embrace, and stood up. She wiped at her nose and eyes.

'I am sorry, my lady,' she whispered. 'It was so terrible to see.'

'It is almost as terrible to hear about it, En-Gula,' Ninani assured her. 'But now you do not have to keep it all to yourself. Let us be friends.'

Surprised, En-Gula nodded. 'As you wish, princess.'

'Good.' Ninani led the girl to her couch, and gestured for her to sit beside her there. Somewhat hesitantly, En-Gula did so. 'Now then, my friend — there is one thing I must know from you. This goddess you serve — how do you feel about your oaths now?'

En-Gula considered her reply very carefully. 'Lady, I am sorry for the first time in my life that I ever came to serve Ishtar.'

'That's what I hoped to hear.' Ninani smiled, but without

warmth. 'Because I want your help, En-Gula. I wish to destroy this goddess before she destroys us all.'

Shocked, En-Gula jumped to her feet. 'Lady!' she cried. 'It is not possible, surely!'

'It must be possible,' the princess insisted. 'You and I must find some weakness in her, or some magic that can overcome her. There must be something that we can do! There must be!'

'I am not as certain as you are, lady,' replied the priestess. 'But — well, the alternative is to keep on living as I do, while Ishtar Touches or eats my friends.' Resolutely, she shook aside her forebodings. 'I will do all that I can,' she agreed.

Ninani laughed, this time with real pleasure. 'Excellently spoken! En-Gula, whatever a princess and priestess can accomplish, we shall do. Let us only pray it will suffice.'

Ace found the city of Kish quite amazing. Despite her worries, Gilamesh had kept his mouth shut at the gate, and the four of them had been hurried through without exciting any interest in the guards. Once inside, they began to wend their way through the narrow, crowded streets.

Close to the gate was the merchants' section. Shops that looked very similar to pictures Ace had seen of the Middle East in her times lined the streets. Canopies kept the sun off both products and people. The wares were laid out on tables or mats for inspection. Fruits, vegetables, tools, cloth, clothing and pots were plentiful. Though most traders were now packing up for the day, there were enough wares still on display for her to realize that Kish was a prosperous city. She mentioned this to Enkidu who nodded in agreement.

'Kish and Uruk — the city we come from — have been the biggest two powers in the whole of Mesopotamia for as long as can be recalled,' he explained. 'Gilgamesh and his advisers think that Kish's day is done, but the king of Kish, Agga, is no fool, and his policies have built up both the army and the wealth of this town.'

Ace glanced back at Gilgamesh. 'I gather you don't agree?'

'Who am I to agree or not? I have no real voice in council, and I'm only allowed to hang around because Gilgamesh likes me. None of the nobles will listen to my ideas.'

'I would,' Ace assured him.

'You're an unusual person, then,' he smiled. 'My ideas are strange, I warn you. I think that Uruk and Kish would get along better if they were allies, rather than enemies. When I was a child, my mother told me that the reason my people died out is that we could not co-operate. These hairless humans took advantage of that folly, and managed to destoy my race. I've always been afraid that the same thing might happen to all humans one day.'

'Trust me,' Ace told him, 'the human race will be around for a good long time yet.'

'Of course I trust you,' Enkidu replied simply. 'You are the goddess Aya.'

'Right,' she sighed. 'I keep forgetting that bit.'

The Doctor stopped a few of the passers-by, and asked directions to a good inn. After the men finally agreed on one, the Doctor led the other three there. It stood just off the main street, and was a small building. Ace judged that it couldn't have more than five or six rooms, and was hardly surprised when she had heard the innkeeper telling the Doctor that he had exactly one room left, take it or leave it.

'We'll take it,' the Doctor told him. Nodding to Enkidu, he said: 'Pay the man, will you?'

Enkidu did so, counting over the copper discs with care. Ace tugged on the Doctor's sleeve. 'Oi,' she complained. 'Professor, I don't mind sharing a room with you, but I'm not so sure about his high-and-mightiness there.'

'Gilgamesh?' The Doctor seemed uninterested. 'Oh, he'll probably get roaring drunk and pass out. I know his sort.'

'So do I,' Ace snapped. 'I met plenty on Iceworld. Some of them just get drunk and make passes.'

'If you're worried about your virtue,' the Doctor replied, 'you could always go back to the TARDIS.'

She sighed. 'According to Enkidu, there are lions on the prowl at night.'

'Well, make up your mind — the lions out there or the wolves in here?'

'Thanks a lot,' she grumbled, and sat at the closest table. 'You're all hearts.'

'One of my failings,' he replied, dropping onto one of the stools himself. 'Innkeeper — beers over here, if you would, and have one yourself on us.'

Enkidu joined them. 'Let me guess,' he said, in resignation. 'I pay for the drinks, too?'

'You don't expect a couple of deities to carry money, do you?' the Doctor asked rhetorically. 'We've better things to do with our time.' The innkeeper put down four pots of barley beer, and accepted Enkidu's coins with alacrity. Gilgamesh grabbed his beer and downed it in two gulps.

'Have mine,' the Doctor offered, pushing it across. 'And Ace'll probably give you hers, too,'

'I'm old enough to drink my own,' she retorted, unwilling to give Gilgamesh anything at all of her own.

'Yes, but I doubt it'll be to your liking,' he told her, watching Gilgamesh making massive inroads on the second beer. 'It's hardly likely to win CAMRA approval.'

Sullenly Ace took a sip, and almost spat it out. 'What's this made out of? Pig vomit?'

'Close,' the Doctor smiled. 'Barley. They've not yet invented the sort of beer you'd like. To the natives of this time, that's ambrosia.'

'Don't you mean ammonia?'

'Right,' the Doctor said, getting to his feet. 'I'm not going to be long. Enjoy yourself.'

'What?' Ace couldn't believe her ears. 'I'm coming, too.'

'Not this time,' he said, pushing her back onto the stool. 'I'm just popping out to take a peek in the the local temple. You stay here and look after Gilgamesh. Try and talk to some locals, get the gossip, that sort of thing. I'll be back as soon as I can.'

'Don't do this to me, Professor,' she begged. 'Not with *him*.'

'Suffering builds the character,' he replied. In a conspiratorial whisper, he added: 'Ace, I could be wrong about this temple being so important. But Gilgamesh is vital — I really need you to stick with him and make certain nothing happens to him. He's destined to do a great deal in his lifetime, and I'd feel happier if I knew he had a rest of his lifetime.'

'And what about me?'

'You can rest later.' He winked. 'Just keep the drinks flowing. And keep your ears open.' Saluting her briefly with his umbrella, the Doctor slipped out of the door.

Ace stared unhappily across the table at Gilgamesh. He had just stolen her beer, and was making inroads on that, too.

It was going to be a very long evening.

# 8: Band On The Run

En-Gula glanced fearfully from side to side as she slipped through the shadows into the temple of Ishtar. Plotting against a goddess was a new venture for her, and she was half-expecting a very unpleasant reception when she returned to the temple that had been her home for half her life. Ishtar had eyes and ears throughout Kish, and despite her precautions En-Gula was by no means certain she had kept her scheming from the attention of the goddess.

However, everything seemed to be normal. The evening watch had sounded the trumpets, and the city gates had been locked while she was returning to the temple. Now the sacrificial fires were being banked for the night, and the priests getting ready for their evening meal before retiring. The few votaries left in the temple were finishing their prayers and departing with the setting sun. The cleaners were sweeping the flagstones, and it would soon be time for all the priestesses to gather for their final meal of the day. En-Gula was none too soon in getting back: her absence would certainly have been noted had she missed the meal. While it was unlikely that Ishtar would read anything suspicious into one such minor aberration, En-Gula was wise enough to know that while she was plotting the downfall of the goddess it was best not to draw any attention to herself.

Despite her brave front with the princess, En-Gula did not really think that they could succeed. Ishtar's powers were too immense, and the feeble strengths of even a priestess and princess could not match them. She and Ninani had agreed that what they needed more than anything was some hint of a weakness in Ishtar's armour, or some suggestion of magic that she might be vulnerable to. Until then they could only exchange information and plans.

It was hard to believe that she, a low-born orphan girl, should be granted the ear of the princess. To her astonishment she had discovered that Ninani was a likeable young woman, and quite human. Despite the social chasm between them, they had become cautious friends in the course of their conversation. En-Gula could never have imagined such a possibility even a few hours ago. The royal family of Kish was the subject of much speculation in the temple, but none of the priestesses had ever before been in contact with royalty, save for the times when King Agga had briefly visited the temple for the rituals.

Lost in her thoughts, En-Gula almost screamed when a strange figure stepped out of the shadows and politely raised his hat.

'Good evening,' the Doctor said, blessing her with his best smile. 'I do hope I've not called at an inconvenient hour?'

Realizing that this strangely-attired little man could not be one of Ishtar's messengers sent to call her to retribution, En-Gula managed to catch her breath. Her heartbeat gradually slowed. 'I — I'm sorry,' she stammered. 'You startled me.'

'I'm so sorry,' the Doctor murmured. He had thought about many things on his way to the temple, weighing up the pros and cons of his various choices. Should he keep his disguise and try to slip inside the sacred portals? Or should he cast aside the cloak and brazen his way through? He wasn't too surprised when he found himself deciding that the latter course might suit him best. Catch people off-guard, give them something out of the ordinary to consider, and then be terribly polite — it usually worked wonders. This time, he'd almost given some poor girl a heart attack. 'Take a deep breath, and let it out slowly.' he advised. 'It will help.'

En-Gula took his advice, and managed to calm her frayed nerves. 'Please,' she finally said, 'tell me what I may do to help you.'

'Actually, I just popped in on the off chance that the goddess might be in. Or, if she's busy, I'd be happy to talk to the high priestess. Or priest.' He studied her costume. 'Isn't it draughty for you, undressed like that?'

En-Gula blinked, trying to follow his speech. She glanced down at her bare breasts and looked puzzled. 'All of the priestesses of Ishtar dress like this, stranger. Did you not know that?'

'Having a little touble with the memory,' the Doctor confided. 'It's not as sharp as it used to be.'

'Oh.' En-Gula was totally lost by this remark. However, his request had been plain enough. 'You wish to see the goddess?'

'If I've come at an inconvenient time,' he smiled, 'I could call back. Or should I make an appointment?' His gaze wandered from the girl and took in the interior of the building. There was something at the back of his mind trying to catch his attention, but he couldn't quite tempt it into the open where he could see it.

'I do not really know.' The girl studied him. He seemed quite a nice man, despite his outlandish clothing and his strange manner. 'It's not always safe to speak with her,' she finally ventured.

The Doctor raised an eyebrow. 'You mean that I might be able to talk with her?'

'If you are sure that this is what you really want.'

'I'm not sure of anything,' he admitted. 'Usually when I call on deities they aren't at home, and I'm fobbed off with a high priest or some other butcher.'

Struggling to keep up with his strange words, En-Gula shook her head. 'You may be able to speak with Ishtar, stranger.'

'The goddess is in, eh? Splendid.' Despite his apparent enthusiasm, the Doctor was disturbed. In almost every case, in his experience the priesthood of any religion insisted on passing on messages for the gods. This girl seemed to be completely convinced that in this temple there was no need for an intermediary. He didn't know whether this was a good or bad sign.

At that moment Dumuzi moved from the shadows to join them. His grey, haunted eyes rested on En-Gula, who cowered slightly. If the Doctor saw her reaction, he didn't say anything. 'Is there a problem?' Dumuzi asked. 'The priestesses are not usually required to perform their functions this late in the day.'

Extrapolating from the girl's lack of clothing, the Doctor could easily imagine the kind of service she was expected to perform. He shook his head. 'I just dropped in for a chat with the goddess, actually.'

'Indeed?' As he stared at Dumuzi, the Doctor saw the man start slightly, and then the expression on the priest's face shifted. The tired look vanished, to be replaced by one that was eager and almost predatory. 'And why do you wish to see Ishtar?'

'Because there's something very wrong in this city.'

'Can you be more specific?' purred Dumuzi.

Tapping his nose with the ferrule of his umbrella, the Doctor confessed: 'It's mostly a whiff I get. Evil, pure evil. When you've been after it as long as I have, it starts to feel like a bad stench in the air. And this city is filled with it.'

'I see,' the priest murmured. 'And what, exactly, do you propose to do?'

'Isolate it and destroy it,' the Doctor said, frankly. 'I'm a sort of cosmic environmentalist. I like things to be tidied up and smelling pretty.' He smiled at the young priestess. 'Like this young lady.'

Dumuzi turned cold eyes on the girl. 'You may go now,' he informed her. 'I will conduct this stranger to the goddess myself.'

'As you command, lord,' she agreed, bowing low. Facing the Doctor, she couldn't stop herself from adding: 'I hope that you find what you seek, stranger.'

'So do I,' he replied, flashing her another smile. There was something about the girl that he couldn't place. Ah well, it wasn't important, probably.

En-Gula watched as Dumuzi lead the stranger away through the temple. An odd man. Yet, somehow, she had sensed great strength in him. He didn't look strong; quite the contrary. Yet there was strength there. It was as if the ridiculous little man was merely a cloak, covering what might lie in his depths. She began to feel a stirring within herself. Though she tried to chase the thought away, it came to her that this odd person might actually be the magical link she and the princess were after.

Ridiculous — wasn't it?

Still debating within herself, En-Gula crept through the darkened halls after Dumuzi. If she were to be caught... She fought down that fear. She couldn't afford discovery — but neither could she overlook this strange feeling of hope that the stranger had somehow kindled in her. She had to see what would happen when he met the goddess...

It was worse than Ace had feared. Gilgamesh had finished his sixth or seventh beer, and had called for more. He was not improving with the effects of the drink, and Enkidu was looking almost as worried as she was. The inn was starting to fill up as the locals arrived. Their tasks finished for the day, townspeople on their way home were drifting in for a drink and a chat. The other tables in the room were occupied now, and the background chatter was growing louder.

It reminded Ace of the atmosphere in a British pub. Some of her Mum's boyfriends had tried to curry favour by taking care of Ace from time to time. That had usually meant a quick helping of fish and chips, then a glass of fizzy at the local while the current boyfriend sank a few beers with his mates. Ace had never much cared for the smoky, smelly atmosphere of the public bar, and had spent her time playing darts, and stealing the odd mouthful of beer whenever she could get away with it. Those experiences had left her with a mean aim and a distaste for beer-drinking drunks.

The inn had the same sort of feel to it. No smoking, of course — tobacco was still a few thousand years in the future, as was the smell of fish and chips with plenty of salt and vinegar. But the wafting stench of beer was the same, and the rattle of inane conversations and crude jokes would probably never change no matter how many thousands of years might pass. The more things change, she reflected, the more some things stay the same. Like pubs.

Gilgamesh started on his next beer, then belched loudly. This seemed to wake him up somewhat, and he glanced fuzzily towards Ace. 'What? No drink?' he asked.

'I'm not interested,' she told him.

He leered at her, heavily. 'Then shall we retire for the night?'

She could kill the Doctor for this. 'I'm even less interested in that,' she snapped. 'At least with you.' She was definitely going to bring on another regeneration crisis for the Doctor in exchange for this.

'Nonsense!' Gilgamesh insisted, belching loudly again. 'I've bedded better-looking wenches than you.'

'Yeah?' One thing she'd learned from her mum's fancy men — never argue with a drunk. You couldn't win, and you might provoke them. She remembered a black eye she'd sported for a week after one of them had lost his temper with her quick tongue.

'Gods, yes,' he told her, warming to the subject. 'Why, the goddess Ishtar herself tried to entice me into her bed just a few weeks ago.'

What an ego he had! 'Can you blame her?' Ace smiled, leading him on. While he was drinking and talking he at least kept his hands away from her.

'Of course not,' Gilgamesh replied. 'But, despite her pleas, I turned her down.'

'Not good enough for you, eh?'

Gilgamesh tapped the side of his nose. It took him two attempts to find it. 'Not that,' he said. 'But you know what happens to mortals who sleep with the gods.'

'No, I don't,' Ace said, suddenly tired of the man and his boasting. 'And neither do you, if you're truthful.'

'Truthful?' he echoed. 'I'm always truthful! Don't you believe that Ishtar tried to seduce me?'

At this moment there was a snicker from the next table, saving Ace the trouble of either lying to him or picking a fight. Gilgamesh turned round to glare at the man who had laughed. 'Do you have a problem?' he asked. 'Or were you dropped on that face at birth?

The man, eyeing the empty beer pots lined up in front of Gilgamesh, obviously decided to humour the drunk. 'Friend,' he laughed, 'I've heard that when Ishtar wants a man, she takes him. She takes enough these days at the temple.'

'It won't be Ishtar who takes you,' Gilgamesh swore, starting to his feet. 'It'll be Belit-Sheri, recorder of the tablets of the dead!'

Enkidu grabbed his king's arm. 'Please,' he hissed. 'Don't start anything.'

Gilgamesh glared at his friend, but he was not so drunk that he couldn't see the worry in Enkidu's eyes. Reluctantly he nodded, and sat down again. He started to nurse his drink, turning his back on the other man.

Ace was doubly thankful — first, that Gilgamesh had calmed down, and second, that he had forgotten about trying to get her to bed. She glanced up as the man at the other table reached over and tapped her arm.

'Listen,' the Kishite told her. 'Keep an eye on your friend there. Not everyone in this town is as tolerant as me.'

'I appreciate it,' replied Ace. 'Thanks for the advice.'

The man hadn't finished. 'Where are you from, anyway?' He glanced over her. 'I've never seen skin that fair before. You're not from around here. What are you doing in Kish?'

That tore it! All they needed was some nosey native, prying into their business. 'I'm a traveller,' Ace said, hoping to stave him off before he started on Gilgamesh. The drunken king would give everything away as soon as he lost his temper.

'You're not a merchant,' the man said. 'You've no wares to display. So what *are* you doing here?'

Casting about for ideas, Ace could think of only one answer that might convince him. 'We're entertainers.'

'Oh?' It was the wrong answer, because the man's companions now turned to look at the trio. 'What does he do?' He gestured towards Gilgamesh.

'I'll bet he's a fire-eater!' one of the other men said, and laughed.

Gilgamesh caught this. 'I do magic,' he growled. 'I cut men in half.'

'And then put them back together in one piece?' howled another of the drinkers.

'Only if I like them.'

Before the situation could get completely out of hand, Ace broke in: 'I'm a singer.'

'Really?' The men stared at her, interested. 'How about a song, then?'

Now she'd done it. There wasn't a piano in the room, and there wouldn't be unless they all hung around for four thousand years or so. Well, there was only one thing she could do...

'Okay,' she agreed, getting slowly to her feet. What could she sing that wouldn't go completely over their heads? No jazz! Nothing too modern... She realized that everyone in the room — including Gilgamesh — was looking at her with interest.

Clearing her throat, she began to sing.

It was one of her real talents, her voice. She had perfect pitch, and only had to hear a song through a few times to get it down right. After the first line or so, she had them enraptured. She sang:

*I've been a wild rover for many a year*
*And spent all my money on whiskey and beer*
*But now I'm returning with gold in great store*
*And I swear I will play the wild rover no more.*

One of Mum's fancy men had been an Irishman. He was almost as full of folk songs from the old country as he was full of Guinness from the local, and he'd spent many evenings teaching Ace as many songs as he could recall. *The Wild Rover*, he had told her, was his theme song.

Ace had cried when she learned he'd been killed. He'd fallen, blind drunk, under the wheels of a bus. Fighting back the memories, she started on the chorus:

*And it's no, nay, never* — clap, clap, clap, clap, clap
*No, nay, never no more*
*Will I play the wild rover*
*No never, no more.*

The room had gone very quiet. Everybody was listening to her singing. She launched into the second verse, hoping that they could follow the meaning of the words.

*I went into an alehouse I used to frequent*
*And told the landlady my money was spent*
*I asked her for credit, but she answered me Nay!*
*Such custom as yours I can get any day.*

This brought a round of laughter. It had obviously struck close to home for many of the men present. She finished the final two verses, and had the audience clapping and joining in the chorus. For good measure, she repeated the last verse:

*I'll go home to my parents, confess what I've done*
*And ask them to pardon their prodigal son*
*And if they caress me as ofttimes before*
*I swear I will play the wild rover no more.*

At the end of the chorus, the men all applauded, slapping hard on the tables. The animosity towards her, Gilgamesh and Enkidu had dissipated. The man who had been questioning her smiled.

'Girl, that was uncommonly well done. Let me and the boys know when you'll be performing, and we'll be along to see you again.' The others chipped in with their agreement, and Ace grinned at them all.

A man materialized from between the tables, and bowed low. He was dressed well, in a rich cloak and trappings, but they all showed signs of wear. Unlike the townspeople he was clean-shaven, and his shoulder-length hair was not oiled or matted. He looked thin, and his grey-green eyes seemed to suggest he'd seen much.

'Lady,' he said, courteously, 'might I speak with you?'

Glad of any distraction, Ace nodded. The man pulled up a stool, and almost fell on to it.

'Allow me to introduce myself,' he said. 'I am Avram, the songsmith.'

'Songsmith?' Ace echoed.

He opened his cloak, to show her a small harp slung over one shoulder. 'Like you, a travelling singer, my lady...?'

'Ace.' She stuck out a hand, and he shook it, gingerly. 'Nice to see you.'

'Likewise.' He hesitated, then plunged on. 'I was wondering if you might be willing to take me on with your party, lady. Truth to tell, Kish is not a very good place for a musician at this time.'

To avoid replying to his question, Ace shot back: 'What's wrong with this place?'

Avram's eyes darted about, then he leaned forward, conspiratorially. 'People are not happy here. This does not give them a good spirit to listen to music.'

Wicked! Ace thought to herself. I'm a real spy. Getting the gossip for the Doctor. She asked: 'Why's everyone so hacked off then?'

Carefully, he whispered back: 'Because the goddess Ishtar dwells among them.'

Puzzled, Ace thought it over. 'I would have thought that was a bonus.' Striving to recall all she she could about primitive religions, she added: 'Doesn't she make the crops grow, and that sort of thing?'

'Hardly that,' confided Avram. 'She sits within her temple, preying on her worshippers. Devouring them, it is said.'

Ace suddenly felt a deep, gnawing wave of fear. 'In her temple?' she asked, weakly. 'In the city? Here?'

Gilgamesh leaned forward. 'Did I not tell you she was here, and trying to bed me?'

Ace pushed him away from her, fighting back nausea at the stench of his breath. 'If I listened to you, I'd be in dead trouble.' Ignoring the pained look on Gilgamesh's face, she turned back to Avram. 'Is this on the level?'

'Certainly, lady.' He seemed amazed. 'You must be a newcomer here. The city is filled with the news. Ishtar has come to dwell in her temple.'

'And the bit about her devouring people?' Ace prompted.

Avram shrugged. 'Many bodies have been found. No one speaks openly, but a songsmith keeps his eyes and ears open. I hate to speak of such an indelicate subject to a lady such as you...'

'You'd better talk' she said, finding it hard to restrain her impatience, 'or I'll rip your tongue out and feed it to my pet donkey here.' She indicated Gilgamesh.

'Well, they have been found with their heads broken open, and their brains missing.'

Anything that Ace might have said next was lost as Gilgamesh surged to his feet, glaring furiously at her. 'Your pet donkey?' he yelled. 'Girl, I will take no more of your impertinence!'

Not to be outdone, Ace jumped to her feet. 'Listen, you daft piss-artist!' she screamed back. 'I've had it up to here with your high-and-mightiness and that wandering hand syndrome of yours!' She turned to Avram. 'Let's get out of here. I want to talk.'

He nodded, happy to get away from the muscular giant. Gilgamesh was too stunned that Ace had answered back to react. As a king he was not used to being spoken to in such tones — nor to being turned down for a session of lovemaking. By the time he'd gathered whatever wits the drink had left him, Ace and Avram were gone.

Out in the cold, crisp night air, Ace felt she could breath again. Avram stood next to her, waiting. Finally, she asked him, in a quiet voice: 'Do you know where this temple of Ishtar is?'

'Of course. But it will not be possible for you to visit it.'

More certain than ever that this temple of Ishtar must have drawn the Doctor to it like honey draws flies, she looked grimly at Avram. 'Why not?' she demanded.

'Because no women are allowed within, save for the sacred priestesses.'

'Typical,' she said. 'Well, I'll deal with that problem when we get there. Now show me the way.'

Avram gave in to her strong will. Shrugging, he led the way through the streets.

Ace was absolutely sure that the Doctor must have gone to this temple. Gilgamesh's claims of meeting Ishtar she had taken with more than a pinch of salt, but Avram's quiet honesty had convinced her. If there was anything funny going on in Kish, it had to be in that temple. And the Doctor was bound to get himself into trouble there and need her help.

# 9: Nitro Nine, Goddess Nil

The shadows seemed to gather about Dumuzi as he led the Doctor through the temple precincts. There was something very unwholesome about the man, but the Doctor couldn't quite put his finger on it. These annoying little hints of danger and wrongness were beginning to annoy him. While things were rarely entirely clear in his adventures and crusades, he hated nothing quite so much as working in the dark. In this case, he reflected, looking about the stone walls, quite literally in the dark.

'Business not good?' he asked, sympathetically. 'Can't afford to burn the midnight oil?'

Dumuzi regarded him with detachment. 'The temple is visited by the goddess and good fortune,' he replied. 'We lack for nothing that we wish.'

'Well, that's handy,' the Doctor replied breezily. 'Most of us aren't that lucky. For myself, I'm beginning to wish I'd brought a large torch. Bit dark in here, isn't it?'

'That is how the goddess prefers it.'

'Oh, well, that ends the problem,' the Doctor observed. 'No arguing with a goddess, is there? Do you ever argue with her?'

'Never.'

'Didn't think so.' The Doctor stopped dead, looking with interest at the altar of sacrifice. It bore the marks of much use. 'Yes, I can see this is a busy place. I'm surprised that the goddess has the time to see me. She will be seeing me personally, I take it?'

Dumuzi gave him another of the curiously blank stares. 'Yes. She will have union with you.'

'Oh, well, I'm all in favour of unions,' the Doctor smiled. 'Trade unions, postal unions —'

'This way.' Dumuzi gestured for the Doctor to begin walking again. The Doctor, however, had no intention of plunging further into the gloom until he was completely ready. His instincts were definitely warning him of danger in these darkened halls. He had discovered over the centuries that evil preferred lurking in darkness to sunbathing. If this priest were kept off-guard, it might provoke some interesting responses. So far, his answers were far from satisfactory. The Doctor had let slip any number of anachronisms, and the man had questioned none of them. Highly unusual.

'It's not every temple that's visited by the goddess it serves, is it?' he asked, leaning against one of the pillars and giving the impression that he had all night to spare for chatting. 'How come you're so blessed? Win a competition for best-kept temple or most respectful sacrifice or something?'

'The goddess has her own reasons for whatever she deems best.' Dumuzi gestured again. 'She awaits you.'

'Does she really?' Peering into the face of of the priest, the Doctor smiled. 'How does she even know I'm here? I've not sent in my card yet, and I didn't see you use the telephone.'

'Your words are devoid of meaning,' Dumuzi replied.

'You're not the first to tell me that,' said the Doctor. A sudden impluse struck him, and he decided to act upon it. His impulses were rarely wrong. When they were, of course, they tended to get him into serious trouble. He hoped that this wasn't one of those times. 'I've been insulted by better men than you!' he yelled. 'You take that back, or put up your fists!' He struck a pose that Jack Dempsey had once shown him, fists clenched and raised, ready to strike.

Dumuzi seemed to be completely unmoved. 'This way,' he repeated.

'Certainly,' the Doctor agreed, cheerfully. So he couldn't annoy the priest. Interesting. The man was under some form of mind control. No matter how good his self-control, he should have reacted at least slightly to the Doctor's threat, but there had been no flicker of puzzlement or alarm in his face. Of course, in this light, it was impossible to be certain... But the Doctor didn't need to be certain of anything yet — just very, very wary. He followed his host through a doorway, then stopped dead.

'Now I know what that smell is!' he exclaimed. 'It's anesthetic! I always disliked hospitals, and that's what this place reminds me of!' He tapped Dumuzi with the handle of his umbrella. 'Now where did a primitive civilization like yours get its hands on anesthesia?'

Dumuzi made no attempt to answer him. Instead, two of the priestesses darted out of the darkness by the doorway and gripped the Doctor's arms tightly. Unable to break free, the Doctor yelped: 'Be careful of the jacket! I had it dry-cleaned and pressed last century!'

The priest bent to an alcove, and then moved forward, a pad in his hand. The Doctor caught a momentary stench of ether, and then the pad was pressed into his face. He kicked, and struggled, then gave one long, sharp intake of breath before going completely limp.

Dumuzi regarded him with the same lack of interest he had shown all along. 'The goddess will be pleased to devour the mind of this one,' he murmured. Then he gestured for the two women to bring the body through into the Holy of Holies, to await the pleasure of Ishtar.

Her heart beating furiously, En-Gula hid behind a pillar, wildly trying to think what she should do next. The stranger had been tricked and rendered unconscious by the minions of Ishtar. She had caught some of his words as she had followed the two men through the temple, and though she understood few of them, the certainty had grown that here was a man who might be able to help. If he was Touched by Ishtar, there would be no hope of any aid from him. His mind would be hers to mould or devour as she pleased. But what could one young priestess do, alone, to save this strange stranger?

Should she try and get word to Ninani? But what good would that do? By the time the princess could receive the message, make a decision and act, the stranger's brain would be long gone. No, if there was to be anything done, she would have to do it now, alone.

But what?

Ace found her fears growing as they approached the gray bulk of the temple. Maybe she was just imagining things, but her travels with the Doctor had honed her senses. She couldn't write off her mood as being simply the product of worry. There was something seriously wrong in Kish, all right, and this temple was the place where it dwelt. She had absolutely no doubt that the Doctor had blithely waltzed in here, trusting to his luck and improvisation to deal with whatever problems he encountered.

She felt he placed too much trust in his abilities. Without her to help him, he'd undoubtedly get into some real trouble. As she was about to move forward, Avram placed a hand on her arm.

'Stay, lady,' he advised, 'You will not be welcome within.'

'Dead right I won't be,' she agreed. 'But I'm going in. I'm certain that's where the Doctor must have gone.'

Avram sighed. He liked this young woman. She was pretty, talented, and bright, but she was too headstrong for her own good. 'Ace,' he explained, not for the first time, 'only the sacred priestesses are allowed in there. You would never be able to pass as one.'

'I wouldn't want to.' Avram had explained to her that the priestesses had one main duty — they had sex with any man who came into the temple with a sufficiently generous offering for the goddess. 'You can call them priestesses, but where I come from they're called something else.'

'It is an honest and honourable trade,' he replied, shocked at her attitude.

'Yeah, well, you would think that. You're a man, and you get the best of the deal.'

He snorted. 'I am unlikely ever to get the price needed to buy time here,' he told her. 'Not by playing my musical wares in this city.'

'You should go to Uruk,' she told him. 'Especially if you know any good songs about Gilgamesh. He's a heavy tipper.' She was only half paying attention to him or to what she said. She was studying the building ahead of them. 'Now let's have a go at getting in, and no arguments.'

Realizing that he would not be able to dissuade her, Avram nodded. 'At least let me go first,' he argued. 'I will make certain that there are no people about to see you when you slip in.' If they saw him, of course, he would play drunk, and pretend he was here for a session with one of the priestesses. He'd be thrown out, but nothing worse. If they found Ace within...

She reluctantly agreed to this, and he gently opened the main door, then slipped inside. The entrance hall was still. From a distance, he could hear the clatter of food being served. Shulpae, god of feasting, was the only deity being honoured at the moment. Good fortune smiled on them — at least temporarily. He turned back to the door and almost ran head-on into Ace.

'It's the time of the evening meal,' he whispered. 'We should be able to get within.'

'Great.' Ace followed him inside, then waited until her eyes adjusted to the gloom. 'Aren't they afraid of thieves?'

Avram stared at her in blank amazement. 'Thieves?' he echoed. 'Who would dare rob the house of the goddess?'

'Yeah, I forgot about that. Okay, lead on, pilgrim.'

Shaking his head, Avram moved quietly through the entrance hall, and into the main temple. Once again, he was relieved not to see anyone within. The sacrificial fires were barely more than embers now, left to burn gently overnight. Despite the gloom, it was clear that they were alone in this part of the building. he breathed a silent prayer of thanks.

Explaining Ace to anyone they might encounter would not be easy. He wasn't even certain he could explain to himself why he was doing this, risking his liberty if not his life. Surely not just because she had a pretty face and a fine singing voice?

They moved onwards, looking for any sign that Ace's friend might have passed this way. Neither saw anything out of the ordinary — though in Ace's case, she wasn't certain what might pass for ordinary inside the temple. Avram was congratulating himself on their good fortune when, naturally, it ran out.

Approaching the area near the altars Ace rounded a pillar and walked straight into one of the priestesses. Before the girl could open her mouth Ace had her in a hammerlock, and pressed a hand over the astounded harlot's face.

'Keep your voice down,' Ace warned the priestess. 'Or I'll break your neck.' She could see terror in the girl's eyes, and loosened her hold slightly. 'Understand?'

The girl nodded. Ace couldn't work out what to do next. Nor did she know why the girl had looked so scared when she had seen Ace. Okay, so Ace looked a bit outlandish, dressed in her leather jacket and jeans, but surely she wasn't terrifying? Or maybe the girl had just been listening to ghost stories, and had been spooked when Ace suddenly appeared? She didn't look much out of childhood, despite the unmissable development of her bare breasts.

'Hang about,' Ace muttered. 'How come you're not at dinner with the other girls? Been sent to bed without your supper?'

En-Gula shook her head as much as she could, trapped by the grip about her neck. When she had first seen Ace she had been scared witless, certain that Ishtar had discovered her treachery. But she wasn't so sure of that now. Ace cautiously loosened her hold a little more.

Avram cared for none of this. 'We'd best get out of here,' he urged Ace. 'Where there's one priestess, there's a hundred.'

'Like cockroaches, eh?' Ace asked, furiously trying to work out what she had better do next.

'No,' En-Gula volunteered, surprising even herself. 'There's just me here. Dumuzi has two more priestesses within, watching the stranger, but — ' She gagged on her words as Ace accidentally tightened her grip in excitement.

'Stranger?' she hissed. 'A funny-looking bloke with a hat and umbrella?'

'Bloke? Umbrella?' asked En-Gula, when she could speak again. 'I do not know these words. But he wears strange clothes and speaks just as oddly as you do.'

'I knew it,' Ace grinned. 'The Doctor's in there.'

'Is he a friend of yours?' asked En-Gula, hardly daring to hope that this unusual person might be of help.

'Sometimes he is', said Ace. 'Right now, I'm here to warn him about this place.'

'Then you are too late.'

Ace dropped her arm lock, and smacked the girl back into the pillar, shoving her elbow against the priestess's throat. 'What do you mean?' she growled, trying to suppress her fears.

'Dumuzi, the high priest, has drugged your friend to prepare him for union with Ishtar,' explained En-Gula, struggling to catch her breath.

'Drugged?' Ace shook her head. 'He always walks right into it.' Then, glaring at the girl, she said: 'Right, are you going to blow the whistle on us?' Seeing the lack of comprehension in her eyes, Ace added: 'You going to tell anyone about us?'

'I could not, even if I wished to,' En-Gula replied. 'I have no explanation for being here either. To turn you in would be to betray myself.'

Avram was having a hard time following all of this. 'Then what are you doing here?' he asked. The longer he spent in Ace's company, the less sense anything that he or other people did or said seemed to make.

'It's a long story,' En-Gula assured him.

'There's no time for stories, short or long,' Ace said, firmly. Pulling a can of nitro-nine from her pocket, she primed it, then met their blank stares. 'I'm going in there to get the Doctor out. Are you two going to help me, or what?'

'I'm a musician, not a soldier,' Avram said, hastily. 'I'd be of little use in the event of trouble.'

'Great,' Ace muttered. She glared at En-Gula. 'How about you? I could do with someone who knows her way about in there.'

Swallowing, the girl nodded, slowly. 'I will help you.'

Hoping she was doing the right thing in trusting this priestess, Ace nodded, then walked through the doorway. As he saw the two girls pass out of sight, Avram took hold of all his courage and followed behind them, into the portals of death.

The room was quite small, about twenty feet long and ten feet wide. In the centre was a stone altar, and stretched out on it lay the Doctor. His arms were folded on his chest, clutching his umbrella, and his hat lay atop them. He was snoring loudly. There was no sign of anyone else.

Clutching the can of explosive, Ace edged her way to the dais, watching all round. There was nothing to be seen, and no sound.

'Right,' she hissed at the others. 'You grab him and head for the front door. I'll cover the retreat.'

One of the Doctor's eyes flew open, and he groaned. Thinking he was coming round, Ace grinned sympathetically down at him. 'You'll be all right, Professor,' she told him. 'We'll get you out of here.'

'I don't *want* to be out of here,' he snapped as quietly as he could. She realized that he was completely conscious, and had been faking his snores. 'I've worked hard to get where I am today. Now, clear out of here before someone comes!'

En-Gula stared at him in shock. 'But... I saw you drugged, with my own eyes!'

'Ace,' the Doctor hissed, 'take your friends and get lost. You can explain to them about my respiratory bypass on the way out.'

It was too late. Dumuzi walked through the doorway from the inner rooms, and stared. His eyes swept over the three intruders, resting a second longer on En-Gula, and then looked down at the Doctor. Realizing he had been discovered, and that there was no longer any point in pretending, the Doctor sat up quickly, donning his hat.

'Thanks for the loan of the bed,' he said. 'I'm much better after my little nap. Ace, time to say your goodbyes.'

Misunderstanding him, Ace laughed and lobbed the canister of nitro-nine over the priest's head. She barely heard the Doctor's scream of outrage as she pushed En-Gula and Avram back the way they had come.

The blast behind them helped them on their way rather forcibly. Both the musician and the priestess were too startled to object to Ace's less than gentle prodding to keep them moving. Ace herself didn't pause to see if the Doctor was still with them. Her ears ringing from the sound of the blast she grabbed another canister of nitro-nine from her pocket, priming it as she ran. Ahead of them, blocking the exit, a squad of temple guards had started to form, many of them hastily swallowing mouthfuls of food.

No time to worry; Ace tossed the explosives as far as she could. The soldiers, assuming that she'd missed her aim with the missile, simply stood their ground and drew their swords for the fight. The nitro-nine detonated behind them, shattering one of the pillars and flattening the men in the blast. Chips of stone lacerated their bodies. Ace jumped over the prostrate forms, having no time to see if they were still alive or dead. She and Avram hit the doors together, and piled into the deserted streets. En-Gula hesitated for a second before following them. Dumuzi had seen her, and to stay now would be more than her life was worth.

Clouds of dust and smoke poured out of the doors behind them, and then the Doctor leapt out, one hand on his hat, the other clutching his precious brolly. Flames licked at the edges of his coat and trousers.

'Now you've done it!' he yelled at Ace, but didn't stop to hear her answer.

'You're welcome!' she howled, running after him. Avram and En-Gula fell in behind them, following without understanding what was happening, but knowing it would be certain death to stay to think things out.

The temple of Ishtar was a shambles. The surviving soldiers at the door battled the fires that had started on the wall-hangings and the rush mats. Further inside, the outer chambers of Ishtar's sanctum were destroyed. Dumuzi, ignoring the cuts and bruises from the blast that had felled him, directed the priestesses who had rushed in to start clearing a way to the inner rooms.

Finally, enough of the shattered stones had been cleared to allow Ishtar to emerge from the wreckage. The can of nitro-nine hadn't exploded close to her, but her dignity and pride were severely bruised. The debris and rubble interfered with the traction of her metal coils on the floor, and she shook with rage and impatience. The eyes that glared at Dumuzi were pits of crimson fire.

'Fool,' she hissed. 'The stranger was not felled by the drug. He must have called for help in some way. And look at what has happened to my temple!'

Calmly, Dumuzi stared back at her. 'You were in my mind, goddess, when the stranger was drugged. You believed that he was unconscious as much as I did.'

Ignoring this inconvenient fact Ishtar spun furiously to glare at the closest of the priestesses. The girl, one of her mind-slaves, simply stood passively. 'And one of you — you, my servants — helped the intruder to escape. Who is she?'

The girl saw the mental image that Ishtar projected. 'She is called En-Gula, goddess.'

'Is she gone from the temple?' Ishtar asked, swivelling to face Dumuzi.

'She was seen leaving with the others.'

'She cannot flee beyond my vengeance,' Ishtar vowed. She slithered furiously back and forth across the floor, grinding rubble to dust beneath her scales. 'Neither her, nor that stranger, nor the other two. They are all to be killed. Is that clear?'

'When they are found, they will die,' Dumuzi agreed placidly. 'I shall send out the guards to look for them.'

'Good,' Ishtar said. Calming a little, she added: 'Has any trace of Gilgamesh been found in the city?'

Dumuzi shrugged. 'I have heard nothing, lady. As you know, there are patrols out looking for him also.'

'I am surrounded by incompetents,' she spat. 'Can none of these idiots find me anyone?' Sweeping from the room, she retreated into her chamber to brood. Once again the problems with her conditioned slaves were resurfacing. Without her guidance they proved to be of little use. The only answer now was to take full control of their minds, no matter how much it drained her powers. Settling into position against the wall, she began to tap into the neural networks, scanning the minds of the various soldiers that she had Touched. She began the work of directing them, oblivious to everything but her desire for revenge on all those who had opposed and humiliated her...

Enkidu was on the verge of wringing his hairy hands in despair. Following the departure of Ace, Gilgamesh had retreated once again to the beer flasks. He hated to be crossed or turned down, and Ace seemed to delight in goading him. It didn't make Enkidu's task any easier. Knowing Gilgamesh, he realized that the king's pride had been hurt. The problem was that the king tended to take out his frustrations on those about him.

He was like a child, really. As long as he got his own way the king was a charming and cheerful soul. In Uruk, of course, he always got his own way. There were plenty of grumbles about his behaviour of course. But such grumbles came mainly from the men whose women were either seduced or raped and were spoken, naturally, outside the king's hearing. The women, of course, had no say in the matter. But here, supposedly on a spying mission, Gilgamesh couldn't claim his divine rank — and especially not with Ace, since she was possibly a goddess. As a result, he sat and pouted, and — of course — drank to drown his frustrations.

Now Gilgamesh was at the stage in his drinking that Enkidu feared most: he was ready to start picking a fight with anyone. The problem was that Gilgamesh could kill people with his bare hands without being aware that he was doing so. All it took was a small spark to set him going.

One of the drinkers at the next table unwittingly supplied that spark. As he shifted on his stool to get at his drink, his elbow caught Gilgamesh in the ribs. It was a minor blow that the king hardly felt, but it was enough to make him growl.

'Sorry, friend,' the drinker said. 'But I should think with your huge frame, you get bumped a lot.'

That was enough cause for Gilgamesh. 'What?' he roared, leaping to his feet. 'You think you can punch a king and then joke about it?'

'Hey,' the man muttered. 'It was an accident, and I apologized.'

'That's not good enough,' Gilgamesh growled, grabbing the man by the throat and swinging his hand for one good, clean punch. To his annoyance, Enkidu grabbed his arm and held it firm. Enkidu was the only person Gilgamesh had ever met that could match him for strength. 'Let me be,' the king said in a low voice.

Fearing that their cover was blown and their mission finished, Enkidu nevertheless tried to salvage what he could from the wreckage. 'Lord, let him go, He's not worth the effort. I think it's time we left, and —'

'Wait a minute!' one of the other drinkers yelled, pointing at Enkidu. The cloak the Neanderthal wore to cover his hairy body had fallen open as he struggled with Gilgamesh. 'Look at that fur!' the man continued. 'Only one person looks like that — the monkey-man that Gilgamesh of Uruk keeps as his pet!'

There was a chorus of agreement that petered out as the crowd gradually realized who the giant trying to throttle one of their friends had to be. The men fell back, and Enkidu knew that they were on the verge of sending someone for the guard. Subtlety was not called for at this point, so he let go of Gilgamesh's arm.

'I believe we've outstayed our welcome,' he said, sighing. As the king punched the man he held and tossed the body aside, Enkidu grabbed the edge of the table they had been seated at, and heaved it towards the crowd. It took down several of their number with a splintering of timber and bones.

Gilgamesh's hands flew to the battle-axe hidden under his cloak, and he swung it out and free.

'Right!' he grinned. 'Who wants to die?'

That cleared the room. Those that could shot out through the door. A couple managed to wriggle out of the windows. The innkeeper ran out the back way. Laughing, Gilgamesh walked to the inkeeper's desk and scooped up all the loose money he could find. 'It was lousy beer,' he explained. 'It would be an insult to allow that crook to keep our money.'

Enkidu hardly cared about that. It was time to leave Kish before the patrol arrived. Kicking open the door, he led the way into the street. Getting his bearings, he started for the gate through which they had entered the city. It was bound to be barred and guarded, but against problems from without, not within.

A group of soldiers appeared ahead of them. Even in the low light he could make out at least a dozen. Enkidu cursed but reckoned that if he and Gilgamesh were quick, these men would never be able to send for reinforcements.

Gilgamesh reacted in a more visceral fashion. With a scream of joy, he ran at the men. His axe scythed the air, leaving blood, entrails and limbs in its wake. Enkidu followed, his sword slashing at the remaining troops as he guarded his king's back.

All twelve of the patrol died within moments. Enkidu felt vaguely disappointed that they had not put up a better fight.

Gilgamesh had had most of the fun. Another patrol came into sight from the opposite direction. Enkidu frowned. How could they possibly have known where to come to?

The leader of this new group smiled — a hollow, haunted grimace. 'Gilgamesh,' he said in dangerous tones. 'Did I not promise you that I should have my revenge?'

The king snorted. 'I've never seen you before, lad — or you'd be dead.'

'O king,' the man's voice mocked grimly, 'do you forget me so soon? Ah, but when last you saw me, I was a bewitching woman, and my ziggurat in ruins.'

Shocked, Gilgamesh blurted: 'Ishtar!'

'So you can remember that far back!' The man laughed with his voice, but his eyes remained dead. 'Now, O king of foolish words, it is time to die.'

Enkidu could have told the man he was making a mistake in talking to Gilgamesh instead of fighting. The axe whistled, and the man's head left his body. The corpse stood a second, belching blood, then fell into the dirt of the street.

'Some revenge!' Gilgamesh shouted as he launched himself at the others in the squad. Enkidu was about to follow him when a third body of men arrived, marching from the same direction as the first, dead, party had come.

The leader of this group signalled the attack, and Enkidu leaped to stand them off. The leader's voice called out: 'Gilgamesh, you cannot destroy a goddess as easily as that!'

Without even turning his head, Gilgamesh let forth a loud laugh. 'Ishtar, I am glad to hear it. I had been afraid that you'd be no fun at all!'

Together, king and companion battled on, hacking, slashing, and parrying the blows of their attackers. Screams from the fallen died away as the wounded were swept up by merciful death, taken by the servants of Erishkigal, the queen of the underworld. Strong as Enkidu and Gilgamesh were, the constant fighting was taking its toll of their stamina. Besides, the blood in the street made for difficult footing.

'I think it's time we left,' Enkidu panted over his shoulder, as he stove in the skull of another soldier.

'What?' Gilgamesh asked, all trace of his inebriation gone. 'Bored already?' He slashed out, severing the arm of an attacker. The mutilated man screamed, so Gilgamesh clove his head to quieten him.

'There's something very strange about these soldiers,' Enkidu managed to explain. He blocked a blow that might have gutted him, then backhanded his attacker. 'They've not bothered to send for reinforcements.'

'Maybe they want to die,' Gilgamesh suggested. He rammed the butt of his axe into an advancing stomach, then hacked upwards with the blade, severing another head.

'But I hear more soldiers approaching,' protested Enkidu. 'This squad must have made signals of some sort for aid.'

'They are beyond aid in this world,' Gilgamesh chuckled, impaling the last of his foes and watching the man drop. 'Still, perhaps we'd better leave some men alive so that the next time we stop for a visit, there'll be something to do.'

Enkidu agreed quickly and finished off the final man he had been fighting. Together, he and Gilgamesh turned and ran for the city gates. Enkidu wondered how they would get out of the city if the rest of the guards acted as if guided by the same preternatural communications as the three parties they had encountered so far.

The problem of getting through the gates was resolved fairly simply. As they neared the wooden barriers, ready to kill the guards and hack down the gates, there was a sudden light in the sky, followed by a deafening noise.

'Well,' Gilgamesh managed to comment, when his ears had ceased ringing and the smoke was clearing from the ruins of the gate, 'I think we now know where Aya went.'

'Let's follow her,' Enkidu suggested.

'I'm with you there!' Together, they sprinted through the shattered timbers and injured guards, and out into the darkness beyond.

# 10: Ace In The Hole

The roar of a lion broke the stillness of the night air. Ace huddled closer to the dark mass of the TARDIS and glared at the Doctor in disgust.

'You're just being difficult,' she snapped. 'Why won't you let us into the TARDIS? Just because you're choked about being rescued, you're going to let the lions eat us?'

'If the lion is roaring, it's because one of the lionesses has just made a kill,' the Doctor said crossly. 'It would hardly howl like that if it was stalking anyone, would it? And I don't want Gilgamesh inside the TARDIS. It might affect the course of human history.'

'Him? He's too thick to understand what the TARDIS is — and too drunk.'

'Will you stop arguing with me?' The Doctor had had quite enough of Ace for one evening. If she had any sense, she'd just shut up and let him think, but she ploughed on instead, making her mistakes worse by the minute.

'Look, how was I to know you'd used your respiratory bypass to avoid being drugged?' she asked, annoyed. 'I thought I was helping you out of another one of those stupid mistakes you make.'

'I never make stupid mistakes,' he retorted, trying to muster all his dignity. 'Only very, very clever ones. And then only when I think you might actually do as you're told for once. Leaving Gilgamesh alone like that could have been a disaster. He might have been killed by those guards. And if you hadn't interfered, I might now know what's happening in Kish.'

'If I'd stayed with Gilgamesh I'd have topped him myself,' Ace snapped back. 'And if I hadn't rescued you, you could have been killed. Then where would we be?'

Avram had endured all the bickering he could take. He had given his cloak to En-Gula — her skimpy garments might be suitable inside a heated temple, but not in the cold night air — and the chill was making him irritable too. 'Please,' he begged, 'can you two refrain from arguing? It is quite clear that neither of you is listening to the other.'

'That's fine by me,' Ace said, turning her back on the Doctor. 'I've had all I can take from him, anyway.'

'Good,' the Doctor said peevishly. 'Now we'll get some peace. And perhaps I'll be able to think.'

The strained silence was better than constant arguments. Avram nodded, and went back to where En-Gula was huddled by the small fire they had decided to risk lighting. Both Gilgamesh and Enkidu were sleeping silently, worn out after their battle. Avram was glad, because the nobility always made him uncomfortable. At least he could talk to the girl.

She glanced up, a worried look on her face, as he smiled down at her. She tried a thin smile of her own, but it didn't work well.

'Troubled?' he asked sympathetically.

'I dare not return to Kish,' she said, sighing. 'Ishtar would kill me if I tried. What is to become of me now?'

Ace had wandered over, and she sat down beside the girl. 'Why not go to Uruk with us?' she suggested. 'You could probably find a job there.'

'Job?' En-Gula asked blankly.

'You know, work. Employment. What can you do?'

En-Gula shrugged. 'What I have been trained to do. I am a priestess of Ishtar. I serve in her temple by lying with her votaries.'

'Great,' Ace muttered. 'A professional ceiling inspector.' She glanced at Gilgamesh's sleeping shape. 'Well, he'd probably appreciate you. Can't you do anything else? Something useful?'

'What I do is useful,' the girl retorted, hotly. 'Without my sacrifice of love, how will Ishtar bless the wombs of our people? How will Enki give us his sweet waters of life? How will Nisaba give us her divine gift of the corn? How will Ennugi keep watch over —'

'I get the picture!' Ace broke in, dreading a complete list of the gods and goddesses in the Mesopotamian pantheon. 'If you stop giving out, they stop giving out.'

'Your words are strange,' En-Gula said, 'but they do seem to be correct.'

'Did you ever stop to think that maybe the corn would grow without you having to go to bed with anyone who'll pay you?' asked Ace. She hated to see people being used like this in the service of dull superstition.

En-Gula laughed. 'Surely, you joke! If the gods were to leave the corn unattended, then it would not grow at all! We should all starve! What I do is vitally important to the welfare of our people.' She thought for a moment, and then added: 'Besides which, it is not difficult work, and I am not required to perform it too frequently. And I am told that I am very good at it.'

Ace laughed bitterly. 'The hours are short and the pay's good,' she commented. 'Gorden Bennett, I feel sorry for you.'

The Doctor tapped her on the shoulder. 'It's a few thousand years too early to start feminism here, Ace,' he told her. 'They don't understand your philosophy.'

'And you're in favour of tarts in the temple?' she snapped.

'My own feelings have little to do with this civilization,' he told her piously. 'I'm not supposed to interfere with its natural development. Unnatural development, on the other hand, is a different bucket of fish.' He smiled down at En-Gula. 'Young lady, from your speech I gather that you are employed in the temple of Ishtar?'

The girl shrugged. 'I suspect that I am no longer welcome there.'

'Well, we'll settle that later.' The Doctor sat cross-legged in front of her. 'Meanwhile, perhaps you could tell me something of what is happening in Kish? Especially anything to do with Ishtar.'

En-Gula found herself, for the second time in one day, telling a new friend about the terrible deeds she had witnessed. Ace, spellbound, actually stopped complaining to the Doctor. Avram was taking mental notes, clearly for his own future use. At the end of her tale, En-Gula told the Doctor: 'The Princess Ninani fears that Ishtar will destroy the whole of Kish. She seeks a way to defeat the goddess first.'

'Perceptive of her,' the Doctor commented. 'But it's not simply Kish that this goddess of yours might destroy. She may be endangering the whole planet.'

Ace was getting an attack of the creeps. 'Do you really think she's some kind of goddess?' she asked, quietly.

'No,' replied the Doctor, thoughtfully. 'From the sound of things, I'd say that Ishtar was some form of robotic or cybernetic organism. Clearly, she can mentally communicate with her servants, and somehow has an electronic bond with them...'

'Electronic?' Ace asked, slowly, an idea forming in her mind. 'You use copper in electronics, don't you?'

'Among other...' The Doctor stopped as he caught Ace's drift. 'The walls! Of course! Ishtar is lining the walls with copper in patterns...' He leaned forward, and started scribbling in the dirt with the tip of his umbrella. 'Avram, En-Gula, help me. I want to sketch a plan of the walls of Kish. Those that Ishtar has put her so-called artwork on.'

Puzzled, since they had no idea what the Doctor and Ace were talking about, the two did as they were asked, using sticks to try to fill in portions of the walls that they knew. After a short while, and much arguing, there was a crude diagram in the dirt. The Doctor rocked back on his heels and stabbed at it with the point of his umbrella.

'A radio generator of a very sophisticated kind,' he announced in awe. 'Linked to the right power source, it could transmit a signal that could blanket the entire Earth.'

Ace said, thoughtfully: 'I remember reading at school that they dug up a crude battery somewhere around here, Professor.'

'Probably one of Ishtar's prototypes,' he said. 'There would have to be a lot of work done. There's virtually no native technology to speak of, and she'll need some serious power if she's going to do what appears to be on her mind.'

When he didn't say anything more, Ace knew he was waiting for the inevitable question. For a moment she considered annoying him further and not asking it. But then she'd never get to know what was going on. 'What do you think she's up to?'

'From what I've been able to piece together,' he lectured her happily, 'I'd say that Ishtar has some sort of link into the brains of selected people. Like that high priest —' He glanced at En-Gula.

'Dumuzi,' she supplied.

'Dumuzi,' the Doctor continued. 'It explains his blank look, and lack of surprise. She can't have those devices in too many people, because the power requirements would be staggering. And even with computer enhancement, she'd have trouble organizing the thoughts from more than a dozen brains at one time. This kind of transmitter —' he jabbed at the map on the ground again '— would enable her to expand her links to anywhere on Earth. Given key individuals, she could rule the entire planet in a matter of decades. Quite ingenious, really. All she needs is a good power source.'

Ace snorted. 'They're still using wood for fuel, Professor. Where could she get any power from?'

'The place is littered with it,' the Doctor retorted. 'Why, there are vast oil fields under this land. And hydro-electric possibilities in the rivers. Power's the least of her problems, I'd say.'

Ace had a sudden vision of Kish, with oil wells, generators and even automobiles ... four and a half thousand years too soon. 'That could muck up history a bit,' she commented.

'Just a trifle,' the Doctor agreed, absently. 'Avram, how long has this building project been going on?'

Unable to follow the Doctor's conversation with Ace, Avram had almost dozed off. He jerked back upright. 'What? Oh, a few weeks at most. Forty days, I'd say.'

'Hmm...' The Doctor studied the plan again. 'Then I'd say we've got probably the same amount of time left to defeat her. Once that radio transmitter is built and powered up, she'll be too strong to be stopped.'

En-Gula seized upon his words. 'You believe that it is possible to stop the goddess?' she asked, eagerly.

'Oh, yes. With a little luck, and a lot of brilliance. Both my specialities, I might add.'

103

'Good job it's not modesty that's called for, then,' Ace said. 'Or we'd really be up the creek.'

The Doctor glared at her again, but only said: 'I wonder how Ishtar got here?'

En-Gula shrugged. 'She came down from the heavens.'

Ace snapped her fingers. 'Old gonads-for-brains over there —' she pointed at Gilgamesh, '— said he met this Ishtar character in the hills, halfway towards Uruk.'

'Did he indeed?'

'Yeah,' Shrugging, she added: 'But I wouldn't believe too much of what he says.'

'Nor would I, without proof,' the Doctor agreed. Crossing to the sleeping king, he prodded the man gently with his umbrella. Gilgamesh leapt to his feet, one hand going for his axe before he saw the startled Doctor, and let out a huge sigh.

'It is dangerous to wake me like that, Ea. What do you want?'

Gesturing at Ace, the Doctor said politely: 'My companion tells me that you met the goddess Ishtar in the hills.'

'That I did,' Gilgamesh growled. 'A fast-talking, sly-thinking harpy. She tried to trick me.'

'Fancy that.' Putting one arm as far as he could about Gilgamesh's muscular neck, the Doctor added: 'Do you think you could show us where it all happend, on our way back to Uruk?'

Gilgamesh shrugged. 'If you feel it's important.'

'It is, Gilgamesh.'

'On the morrow, then.' The king yawned. 'Right now, I need my sleep.'

'Good idea. Let's all get some shut-eye.' The Doctor fussed over the others until they all settled down for the night. He didn't sleep. Leaning casually on the TARDIS, he watched the rest of them like a hawk. When he was certain that they were all in the arms of Morphius, he quietly unlocked the doors and went into his craft.

The Doctor stood on the lip of the impact crater and stared into the dark depths. 'I don't know how I do it,' he muttered, mostly to himself, but Ace caught it.

'Do what?' she asked.

'Start off with just one person and end up with a circus troupe.' The Doctor stared over his shoulder at their four travelling companions. Avram and En-Gula had been talking in low tones all morning, in distinct contrast to Gilgamesh and Enkidu. To Ace's astonishment, the king had woken with no trace of a hangover and ready for a good, long walk at a steady pace. Though she considered herself fairly fit, she was secretly glad of the chance to rest for a while.

The Doctor, curious as ever, seemed inexhaustible. He started down the slope, and looked back at her, raising an eyebrow. With a sigh, she followed him. It never seemed to occur to him that she might appreciate a bit of a rest. The others fell into a silent line behind her.

'Oi,' Ace called out ahead of her. 'How come this Ishtar thing didn't send some troops after us last night?'

'Her radio link is probably limited to the vicinity of the city,' the Doctor replied, absently. 'And she can't trust uncontrolled guards to get Gilgamesh. Look what happened when she tried that yesterday morning.'

'So we're probably safe here?'

'Whatever gave you that idea?'

Glaring at the Doctor's back, Ace muttered: 'Thanks a lot. That really encourages me.'

'Don't be so — aha!' He stopped suddenly, and Ace ran into his back. He was staring into the bottom of the pit. From one of his pockets he drew a large electric torch. It was was one of the items he'd picked up in the TARDIS the previous night. He switched it on and handed it to Ace. In the strong, white beam he scuttled across to what he had spotted. It was the glint of metal.

Avram was staring at the torch in wonder. 'Now I begin to believe that you are truly Aya!' be breathed. 'Light from your hand!'

'Leave it out,' she growed. 'It's just a trick, not a badge of divinity.' After a while, being taken for a goddess was getting on her nerves. 'Oi, Professor, what is that?'

The Doctor was examining the metal fragment he had found. Then, tossing it blithely away, he said: 'Bit of a heat shield. There's more over here. Come on.'

Gilgamesh peered into the darkness, feeling uneasy. 'This is where that tricky Ishtar sat,' he said. 'Is it wise to proceed?'

'Probably not,' replied the Doctor, heading off anyway. 'Stay behind me, all of you.'

He led the way down, while Ace did her best to keep the patch illuminated. After a few more minutes, during which they passed further scraps of metal, they arrived in the bottom of the pit. Ahead of them was a cone of sorts, very battered and scarred from a fiery descent. It was about twenty feet high at its tallest point, and shaped like an old — or, in this time, future — Apollo space craft.

'Escape capsule,' the Doctor mused. 'Ishtar must have been in serious trouble, then. Main ship broke up about her, I should think. There's scarring from various chunks of metal, as well as the burning of re-entry at the wrong angle.'

'That is her ziggurat,' Gilgamesh growled. 'You are certain she is not in it?'

'She's in Kish,' the Doctor explained. 'But I'd be very surprised if she hadn't left us a little present.' Bending down by the main hatch, he grinned. 'Christmas is early this year!'

'What is it, Professor?' Ace moved to join him. He gestured into the doorway, and she saw a faint gleam of a wire strung across the threshold.

'Primitive,' he said, scornfully. 'But she probably couldn't spare any power for anything more sophisticated. Mind you, this would be enough.' He stepped gingerly over the trip-wire, and followed it a short way. It terminated in a small bundle. 'You'd like this, Ace. Thermite bomb. A bit rudimentary, but effective. If we had tripped that trap, we'd be out of this mortal vale of tears.' Disconnecting the detonator, he tossed the bomb to his companion. Ace caught it with ease and immediately started to examine it.

Taking the torch from her, the Doctor played it around the interior of the craft. Bare stanchions and bits of wire hung down. There was none of the equipment left. Sand, dust and bits of plant-life had drifted inside. 'She's taken most of the trimmings to Kish, by the look of things.' The beam caught something, and he stopped.

It was a bas-relief moulding, with some alien script under it. The raised shape was of three triangles, points down, two atop the third, and making up a larger triangular form.

'Any idea what that is?' Ace asked.

'None at all,' the Doctor replied, examining it with interest. 'It's some language I've never seen, and the picture's no help.'

'I've seen it before,' Avram offered, from the doorway. The Doctor spun on his heels to face the singer.

'Really? Travelled a lot, have you?'

'A musician always travels, Doctor,' Avram replied. Reaching into the pouch at his belt, he withdrew a small metallic disc. On the front was the same symbol as on the wall of the ship. On the reverse, the Doctor noted with satisfaction, was a small printed circuit design.

'Where did you get this?' he asked. 'On the plain?'

'Nowhere in these parts,' Avram replied. 'It was when I was in the mountains of Mashu. I took it from the Zuqaquip.'

'The who?' asked Ace, blankly.

'The scorpion men,' explained Avram. 'There were two of them, in the form of men, but with bodies and stings like those of scorpions.'

Ace stared at him. 'You're pulling my leg, aren't you?' she asked, hopefully.

He glanced down at her feet. 'No one is touching your legs.'

'I mean, you're not serious about scorpion men, are you?'

'Of course,' He seemed puzzled that she doubted him. 'Have you not heard the story of Utnapishtim?'

'There's time for that later,' the Doctor decided, abruptly. 'Come on.' He shot outside once again, and wandered over to Gilgamesh. 'I think it's time we returned to Uruk,' he decided. 'We've got to start making a few plans, I think.'

Grinning hugely, Gilgamesh clapped the Doctor on the back, almost felling him. 'Capital! War plans, eh? Time to attack that harpy Ishtar and destroy the benighted city of Kish?'

En-Gula gave a short gasp of horror, and the king looked at

her. 'No offence,' he said good-naturedly, 'but Kish is a cesspit under the gaze of the gods. Fit only to be pissed on or burned down.'

'I was thinking more of liberating Kish than destroying it,' the Doctor replied.

'Oh.' The answer seemed to disappoint Gilgamesh. Then he brightened, and winked. 'I get it — liberate the city! Ha! Capital idea! Let's liberate it right into my control.'

'Gordon Bennett,' Ace muttered. 'He's completely hopeless.' While the Doctor wasn't looking, she slipped the thermite bomb into her jacket pocket. You never knew when such a thing might come in handy, especially when you were following the Doctor around. She didn't bother mentioning that she'd appropriated it. Despite his affinity for dangerous situations, he didn't seem to possess any understanding of the usefulness of weaponry.

'We'll discuss that back in Uruk,' the Doctor suggested to Gilgamesh. 'Over a good meal and a jar of beer, eh?'

'Doctor Ea,' the king grinned, 'I like the way you think!' He slapped the Doctor's back again, then set off once again out of the pit.

Swaying, the Doctor managed to catch his balance and follow. The rest fell in line behind, and the strange procession set off once again.

King Agga was not in a good mood at all. He had returned from yet another conference with Ishtar, and this had left him in a black temper. The goddess was furious about the violation of her temple and the possible damage that might have befallen her precious secrets. She had vented her anger on the king, and he, in turn, was brooding blackly in his palace.

Ninani, her fears for her father etched into her face, prostrated herself before him. She was determined to try to speak to him again. After a moment, he glanced up, and scowled.

'Daughter,' he said, in a low growl, 'this is a bad time to talk. The temple of Ishtar has been attacked, and the goddess is furious. She has voiced all kinds of threats against the city. I must think. Leave me alone.'

Obeying his commands despite her fears and worries, Ninani

retreated from the throne room. As the guards closed the doors, shutting her off from her father, she turned to see her maid Puabi, almost hopping from foot to foot.

'What is it, old woman?' the princess asked rudely.

'My lady, terrible news.' She fell into step beside her mistress as they returned to the princess's rooms. 'Strangers have attacked the goddess Ishtar in her —'

'I have heard that news,' Ninani said coldly. 'It's a shame that they didn't drive her out.'

'Have a care, saying such things!' Puabi whispered in horror. She glanced about them, in case anyone had heard this remark. 'We are blessed by her presence. But ...'

'But what?'

'Lady, according to one of the acolytes that I spoke with, one of the temple girls was helping the strangers that attacked Ishtar. My niece, En-Gula!'

Stunned, Ninani whirled about. 'What happend to her?' she asked urgently. 'Does she live? Has she been captured by the goddess?' She could imagine what might happen if Ishtar made the girl speak.

'The attackers fled,' Puabu replied. 'En-Gula went with them. Lady, I'm so sorry! I didn't know that she was such a wicked child! Attacking the goddess in her temple! What is the world coming to? Young people in my day —'

Ninani let the nurse prattle on, and thought hard. Whatever En-Gula was doing, she alone knew that the princess was plotting against Ishtar. A few words from the girl, and Ninani might well be doqmed, for all her royal blood. What was happening? Ninani shivered, imagining all of the possibilities. If Ishtar were to find out ... Or her father, even ... Who had the girl plotted with, and what was she doing now?

Her stomach churning with uncertainty and fear, the princess of Kish felt the corridor spinning about her. With a cry, she collapsed to the hard, stone floor.

# 11: Party Piece

To Ace's surprise Gilgamesh's palace was nowhere near as grungy as she had feared. Uruk looked similar to Kish — a city with walls, next to a stream — and about the same size. A bridge led across the river to the main gateway, where winged lions carved from imported stones stared down at her. The roads were wide, and astonishingly clean. Trees were planted in the streets and squares, and the buildings were in good repair. To her eyes, the oddest thing was that there were no windows in the buildings. She mentioned this to Avram, who smiled.

'It is for privacy, lady,' he explained. 'Each house is built about a central open courtyard, and the windows let onto this. It would be unseemly for a family to allow themselves to be overlooked by the most casual of passers by, would it not?'

Ace remembered the rows of windows in Perivale, all looking out onto the road and all protected by frilly nylon curtains. 'You may have a point,' she agreed.

In the centre of the town a huge ziggurat stood. This was a stepped pyramid rising over two hundred feet into the air, with a temple atop it. It had seven levels, each with a walkway leading around the entire structure, and with altars on every level. People swarmed all over it. The edifice dwarfed all of the other buildings including the royal palace, which was a mere two-storey building, albeit built on a grand scale.

The guards at the city gates had alerted the council of nobles to the return of Gilgamesh as soon as the party had been sighted approaching the city. Several of the nobles appeared as Gilgamesh led the way to the palace, and they fell on their faces in the street. It didn't do anything for their clothing, since the roads were not particularly dry.

Obviously pleased with his reception, Gilgamesh reached down to touch one of the prostrate nobles. 'Get up, Ennatum,' he said, with mock severity. 'I trust all has been well since I left?'

Ace didn't like the shifty look on Ennatum's bearded features. Despite his oily words, he didn't seem overjoyed to see his king return. 'Lord,' the adviser said, rubbing his hands together, 'the city prospers, and all rejoice that you have returned safely. A feast is being prepared —'

'Good,' Gilgamesh said dismissively, striding on towards the palace. The guards fell in about him, and the growing procession continued.

Glancing about Ace saw another of the nobles, a short, fat man who struggled hard to keep up. He seemed as white as a sheet, and she wondered why. Didn't he like Gilgamesh? Well, she couldn't blame him — the king was certainly a royal pain in the backside — it seemed odd. Then it clicked. Gilgamesh had been ambushed as he had tried to enter Kish — and someone must have told the Kishites to expect him. With a wicked grin, she made her way to the tubby traitor, and nudged him in the ribs.

'Oi,' she said, softly. 'Who rattled your cage? Surprised to see the king back, are you? Didn't think he'd make it?'

The man stared at her and almost fainted from terror. Bingo! Hit it in one! she grinned at his terror. 'Chill out,' she said. 'If he's too thick to notice what's going on, I won't tell him.' She sauntered on, leaving the stunned traitor to his own terrified thoughts.

Ennatum had seen Ace approach Gudea, and the fool's ashen face had spoken volumes. Why couldn't he mask his emotions? The girl, whoever she was, didn't glance at him, so he was safe — for now. It was obvious, though, that it was time to dispose of Gudea before he blabbed.

Avram stared around curiously. He'd never been in Uruk before, but it looked like a wealthy city. A musician might make a good living here, he mused. Especially if an idea he'd been mulling over bore fruit. He smiled encouragingly at En-Gula. She looked pale: she'd been brought up in Kish to look upon the inhabitants of Uruk as murderers and rapists at best. This trip was merely the lesser of two terrifying evils for her, despite Gilgamesh's assurances of royal protection. Both Avram and En-Gula knew that kings have notoriously short and fickle memories.

As for the Doctor: his thoughts were his own. He fingered the devices he'd slipped into his pockets after the midnight trip into the TARDIS, and hoped that his conclusions were correct. So far, all the evidence pointed the same way.

They arrived at the palace. Guards threw wide the main doors, and Gilgamesh strode in, regally ignoring everyone who threw themselves down in his path. He made his way directly to the throne room, and collapsed into his throne.

'Right,' he said, when everyone was gathered around. 'First, I'm taking a bath and oils. Then I want a feast. After that, Doctor, you and I will talk with my council and lay our plans. Ennatum, see to it that the Doctor and his friends have one of the royal suites. They'll need to refresh themselves before the feast, too. And get them some clean clothes. Well — what's everyone waiting for? Get to it!' He clapped his hands, and a whirlwind of activity began.

Ace was escorted away by a couple of servants who were measuring her up even as they walked alongside her. She saw the Doctor and Avram taken through one set of doors, and she and En-Gula were politely but firmly ushered through another set.

She looked about the room torn between mortification and amusement. It was a bit different from her old bedroom in Perivale. The stone walls were broken only by small, high windows. Light was provided by reed torches, soaked in foul-smelling bitumen, set in holders at intervals on the walls. There were two low beds, covered in furs and a coarse kind of cloth. Instead of pillows there were wooden blocks. A few chairs and small tables were scattered about the room, most carved into uncomfortable-looking animal designs. Panthers and antelopes seemed to be the favourite themes.

En-Gula seemed equally to be stunned by all of this. 'Such luxury,' she whispered, staring about her.

Ace snorted. 'If you like this lot, you'd love Perivale,' she grinned.

The girl stared at her. 'Is Perivale the home of the gods?' she asked.

Ace was momentarily lost for words. She replied carefully. 'Not exactly. More like the back end of nowhere. But compared to this pad, even a council flat is luxury.'

En-Gula shook her head. 'I do not understand you.'

'Don't worry,' Ace told her. 'Sometimes I don't understand myself. Oi! What are you doing?' she demanded, as one of the servants started to tug at her jacket.

'Preparing you for your bath,' the young girl replied, bowing low.

'Well, keep your hands to yourself,' Ace snapped. 'I don't need any help to take a bath.' She had to admit, though, that after the events of the previous night she felt that it would be lovely to lie back and soak in a tub.

En-Gula shook her head slightly. 'Lady,' she said, 'I do not know how it is where you come from, but here you must allow them to help. It is their duty.'

Glancing around at the four young girls, Ace shook her head firmly. 'Push off,' she told them, as kindly as she could. 'Just point me to the bath, and I'll handle it myself.'

She obviously wasn't getting through to them. Trying again, En-Gula explained: 'Aya, these girls have been ordered by the king to help you. If they do not, he might have them executed.'

'What?' Staring at the servants, Ace realized that the priestess was telling the truth. And she wouldn't put it past that regal loonie to kill the girls, either. Sighing, she held out her arms. 'Okay. But be careful with the jacket, or I might save Gilgamesh the trouble of killing you.'

Though En-Gula was more used to serving than being waited on, as the king's favoured guest she too submitted to the ministrations of the serving maids. She and they were equally amazed at both the quantity and kind of clothing that Ace wore. After they had fussed over her underwear and sneakers long enough, Ace yelled at them to get on with the bath.

Ace had expected a good soak in a tub. She was disappointed. Two of the girls brought in what looked like the type of old tin baths she'd heard pensioners talk about using in front of their fires half a century before she was born. Standing in one as she was directed, Ace gave a shriek as a bucket of cold water was tipped over her head.

'Grief!' she finally managed, teeth chattering, 'don't you heat the water here?'

The chief serving girl looked puzzled. 'Whatever for, lady?'

'Well, I think you'd live longer with less shocks like that,' Ace managed to say before a second pail was tipped over her. Spitting out cold water, she flinched as two of the girls began to scrape at her with what looked like butter knives. 'Oi, what are you doing?'

'Cleansing you, lady,' the maid explained.

'Just pass me the soap,' Ace complained.

'Soap?'

The rest of the bath was no less like a nightmare. After the maids had scraped her skin almost raw, they tipped two more buckets of ice-cold water over her. While she was still shivering, they attacked her with rough towels that virtually finished the job of removing all her skin. Then they brought in two vases filled with some oozy liquid that smelled like a department store perfume counter after an elephant had trampled on all of the bottles.

'Don't tell me that's the shampoo,' she protested. 'I'm not having that stuff in my hair.'

'What?'

'Women must have a pleasing aroma, lady,' the servant explained. 'It charms their men.'

'Well, it doesn't charm me,' Ace protested. 'I'll smell like a walking anti-perspirant spray if you throw that stuff on me.'

Puzzled, En-Gula asked: 'Does the Doctor not like you to be scented?'

'I don't care what he likes,' Ace said, firmly. 'I do as I please.'

This confused the maids and the priestess. The king, the

Doctor and a seemingly endless queue of suitors featured in the babble of protestations. 'Oh, get on with it,' she finally sighed to shut them up. Looking relieved, the girls began to massage the oil into Ace's skin. Once the shock of the powerful aroma wore off Ace had to admit that it felt rather nice. Sort of like a good massage, she supposed. Her raw skin was cooled by the oils, and she decided she could get used to the smell eventually.

She drew a line at the clothing, however. They brought her only two pieces of cloth, and a pair of sandals. 'What's this?' she demanded.

'Your robe, lady,' the maid told her.

Ace regarded the scraps of purple cloth. 'I've got bikinis more respectable than that,' she told them, regardless of the fact that they couldn't possibly understand her. She marched back to the other room, trailed by the wailing servants. 'I'll wear my old gear again.'

'It would be a great insult to the king,' the chief maid cried, with tears streaming down her cheeks. 'He selected your clothing himself.'

'That explains it,' Ace said. 'He's a sex maniac.' The maids seemed distraught at the idea of her ignoring a command from the king. Unwilling to cause the girls more worry than she had to, she agreed to try the outfit on.

It was as skimpy as she had feared. The smaller cloth was wound about her hips, roughly in the place of her knickers. The main cloth was draped about her shoulders like the saris her friend Manisha used to wear, and pinned in place by a very ornate gold brooch.

'No way,' she decided firmly. Too much leg showing, and definitely not enough protection against Gilgamesh and his wandering hands. She stripped down again, and in spite of the protests of the maids she pulled on her old underwear and her jeans. Then she had them redrape the sari over that. She eyed her jacket, but reluctantly decided to leave it. To the wailing maids, she said: 'It's this or I don't go to the feast.'

'The king will not be pleased,' En-Gula commented. She herself wore a white version of the sari, and although her legs were bare her breasts were covered for the first time since Ace had met her.

'Stuff the king,' Ace commented. For a moment she thought the servants were going to faint, but they managed to pull themselves together. Ignoring them, Ace grinned at her companion. 'You're looking more dressed now.'

En-Gula glanced down. 'It would be unseemly to pose as a priestess of Ishtar in the palace of the king of Uruk,' she explained.

'Come off it,' laughed Ace. 'He'd love it. And he might leave me alone if you were flaunting your boobs in his face.'

'You do not like his attentions?' asked En-Gula, puzzled.

'Right on,' Ace agreed.

'But it is an honour,' the girl tried to explain. 'To be the paramour of a king is to be especially blessed.'

Ace snorted. 'Then I'll bet Gilgamesh has blessed every woman in the city at least once. He's just not my type.' This concept was obviously beyond the grasp of the young priestess. Ace decided to give up. 'I'll just skip this honour,' she said. 'Now, how about looking for that feast? I'm famished. I could eat a horse.' Something dawned on her. 'Hey, what *do* they serve for food here? Not really a horse, I hope.'

En-Gula shrugged. 'Probably roast birds, corn bread and the like. The king eats very well. There may even be meats and real bread.'

Ace raised her eyes to heaven. 'I'll never complain about Perivale again,' she muttered. 'I'm dying for a bacon butty.'

Ishtar regarded the fragments on the table in front of her with interest and wary curiosity. They were all the scraps that the guards had been able to find from the wreckage of the device that had caused the damage to the temple rooms.

'An explosive of some kind,' she mused, her tail swishing back and forth on the hard stone floor. 'Bits of aluminium, and a nitrogen-based compound.' She switched off her analyzing scanners, and swept the pieces to the floor with her hand. 'Quite obviously beyond the abilities or imaginations of you primitive humans,' she told Dumuzi. He was waiting, servile as ever, just inside the doorway. She spun about to glare in his direction again. 'Yet, I do not think either the man or the woman you saw were from Utnapishtim's coven of cowards.' She forced his mind to return to the images of the pair.

'The girl...' said Ishtar, thoughtfully. 'Now, she could be from my world. She looks considerably more lively and interesting than your pallid race, Dumuzi. She would make me a fine servant — or a tasty feast.' She brought the image of the man to the front of the high priest's mind next. 'Strange clothing, strange manners,' she said, softly. 'And he somehow managed to resist the effects of the drug he was given. He cannot be one of Utnapishtim's lackeys — they would not have the ability he displayed.'

'Lady?' asked Dumuzi, grimacing in pain as the memories were ripped from his mind. 'I do not understand. Did you not say that no one from your home was left alive after you poured out your wrath upon them?'

She released the link almost contemptuously. 'I do not expect you to understand. I expect you only to obey.' She glared at him. 'And there may have been a few who survived my wrath — it is nothing to you.'

Recovering from the attack, he managed a short bow. 'This — Utnapishtim that you speak of. He is your foe?'

Laughing in derision, Ishtar stared down at her priest. 'Dumuzi, never forget that I can read your every little thought. Oh, don't be afraid — I shan't punish you for daring to hope that Utnapishtim might come to destroy me and free you. Leaving you the dream and desires for freedom amuses me.' She glanced inwards. 'But even if Utnapishtim lives, he believes me dead, little man. And by the time he discovers otherwise, I shall be far too strong for him to defeat. No, place no hopes in him.' She smiled again, and raised his chin with her metal hand. Her red eyes burning directly into his. 'I'll tell you what — if you want to maintain those foolish fantasies about getting free of me, try placing them in the hands of that stranger who was here, I tell you this, Dumuzi — he has a better chance of defeating me than Utnapishtim. That worm is dead, or if he lives I will crush him when it suits me. This other, though —

he is an unknown force. He clearly has unusual powers. Dream on, with him as your hero, foolish priest!'

Laughing to herself she moved back into her sanctum, and left Dumuzi to wonder.

To Ace's surprise the feast was not the torture session she had expected. The hall had been prepared with a dozen long tables arranged in a square about the walls, leaving the centre of the room empty. The tables were all ornamental, their legs carved in the forms of humans and animals which were holding up the table tops on their arms or shoulders. They were inlaid with the bright blue of lapis lazuli, and even jade or some other green stone that she didn't know. The plates and cups were mostly of silver, except the set for Gilgamesh which was of pure gold. Finger bowls abounded, Ace noticed, but the only utensils were knives.

Behind each of the tables were cushions, soft and comfortable. The tables were low, and En-Gula explained that the guests would lie on their sides on the cushions to eat. Though she would have preferred a chair, Ace decided she could play along with this style of eating for a change. She was glad that she'd insisted on wearing her jeans, though — lying down in a short skirt would definitely have been asking for trouble. Didn't the local women have any notion of modesty? Or, with Gilgamesh about, of safety?

The maids showed both girls and the other arriving guests to their places. Ace was placed at the end of the largest table, next to the Doctor, who didn't look as if his skin had been scraped and who had obviously insisted on wearing his old clothes. He'd even brought his umbrella along with him. He'd clearly won all the arguments with the servants about changing. He had a way of doing things like that which she envied. To Ace's disappointment, both En-Gula and Avram were placed at a table at the far end of the room. Seeing her wave forlornly to them, the Doctor smiled.

'It's a matter of status, Ace,' he explained quietly. 'You and I are honoured guests, and thus allowed to eat at Gilgamesh's table. Avram's just a musician, and En-Gula is just a defrocked priestess. The local hierarchy probably didn't even want her here. So they have to be seated as far away from the nobles as possible.'

'I'm surprised they were allowed in at all, if it's just a matter of having the right name and enough gold thread in your robes.' Ace hated the attitudes that dictated the seating arrangements. She wanted to be with people she liked, regardless of their status.

'I think it's because Gilgamesh doesn't want to offend us,' the Doctor told her. 'Otherwise I'm sure they'd have to forage for food in the kitchen.'

'It pays to have connections, eh, Professor?'

He winked at her.

The entertainment began. There were court musicians playing crude wind instruments, drums and harps. There were dancers, conjurers and acrobats. There were trained monkeys juggling nuts and bright baubles. All of this went on, almost unnoticed, as the food was served and eaten.

To Ace's relief, Gilgamesh had taken his place at the centre of the table, with Enkidu on his right. The oily adviser, Ennatum, lounged next to Enkidu. On Gilgamesh's left was a pretty woman with an extremely well-developed chest. The king didn't bother Ace all evening, but he laughed a lot and pawed the woman frequently. She, in her turn, was clearly enjoying the attention, and with obvious delight fed Gilgamesh little delicacies as his hands roamed inside her robes.

'Thank God for small mercies,' Ace muttered to the Doctor. 'Who's she, the queen?'

'No.' The Doctor's face was perfectly blank. 'She's the wife of Gudea.' He nodded in the direction of the fat man that Ace had enjoyed scaring earlier.

'What?' Ace spluttered. 'And his randy majesty is feeling her up in public? Don't they have any laws in this town?'

'Of course they do,' the Doctor chided her. 'This is a civilization, after all. But don't forget that it's Gilgamesh who makes the laws here.'

'Oh.' She watched the king as he bobbed for grapes down the woman's dress. Both of them were quite obviously enjoying themselves. Gudea, equally obviously, was not. Ace began to appreciate the hidden emotions that could drive a man to betray even a successful king. 'Doesn't seem right to me.'

'I didn't say it was right, Ace,' the Doctor sighed. 'But in this culture it's considered acceptable. Gilgamesh is a warrior king, and a hero by anyone's count. Because of his strength, Uruk is one of the greatest powers in the known world. If he feels like fooling about with the wives and daughters of the nobles — well, they may not like it, but to them it's a small price to pay. To them, the king is almost divine. She probably feels it's an honour to gain Gilgamesh's attentions.'

'Sounds pretty sick to me,' Ace replied. 'If he wants to keep his fingers intact, he'd better keep them well away from me.'

The Doctor regarded her sadly. 'Ace, these trips of ours are supposed to broaden your mind. Stop thinking in twentieth century terms for a while and try to see these people through their own eyes. I know you don't like Gilgamesh, but by the standards of this time he's actually quite a decent chap.'

'That's because they have low standards.'

'At least they have standards.' He shook his head. 'I've been to times and places in which Gilgamesh would look like a veritable angel.' He winced as the king let loose a loud belch. 'And others where he would be flayed alive for behaviour like that. It's not just the TARDIS that has relative dimensions, Ace, but the societies that we visit, too.'

Ace shrugged. She didn't agree, but there was no point in arguing with the Doctor. She tried the food, which proved to be filling but fairly bland. There were few herbs or spices used in the cooking. The meat dishes — mostly birds, with some pork and scrawny beef — were all roasted. Flat slabs of warm bread were served, and there were several sorts of vegetable soup. This was clearly considered to be five-star catering. Ace tried to decide whether she had ever eaten better food in school. Some of the canteen meals had been only one step up from pig swill.

It took her a while to get the hang of eating these dishes, since there were no spoons. Bowls of the steaming soups or stews would be placed in front of every three or four guests, who would break off pieces of bread and use them to dunk for vegetables or chunks of meat. Ace wasn't too keen on sharing her dishes with other guests, given the standards of hygiene practised here, but there wasn't any choice. After a few tries she managed quite well. The finger bowls, she noticed, got quite a lot of use. With no towels to hand, the diners simply wiped their wet fingers on their clothing. It wasn't surprising that Gilgamesh's robe was getting quite stained.

There were plenty of fruits around, and she stuck mostly to those. The grapes, apples and pears were all tasty, but the oranges were bitter. On the other hand, she realized that bananas and pineapples, her own favourites, had not yet been discovered in Mesoptamia.

For drink there was either the foul barley beer, quaffed in large quantities by the men, or a sort of watery red wine. Ace stuck to the latter, though she was by no means fond of it. The lesser of two evils, really. She wished that tea or coffee had been discovered — or even a bit of carbonated water.

Finally when the feasting was done, Gilgamesh straightened, removed his hands from wherever they had been on Gudea's wife's anatomy, and clapped loudly. The chatter that had permeated the room ceased, and everyone looked at the king.

'Friends,' he said loudly, 'Enkidu and I have returned from a rare adventure. Chancing our lives, we went on a spying expedition into Kish.' There was quite a tumult of applause at this, people banging their fists enthusiastically on the table. Whether they liked Gilgamesh or not, they knew how to stay on his good side.

'Toadies,' Ace shouted. The Doctor glared at her.

'We learned much there,' the king continued, beaming happily at the applause. 'And we were joined on that adventure by two of the gods themselves — Ea and Aya.' He gestured at the Doctor and Ace. Again there was applause.'

'He makes us sound like a double act on the telly,' Ace complained under her breath. Still, she'd been half-terrified that the crowd would bow down and start worshipping them or something. She'd never have managed to keep a straight face if they had.

'And we also met with a new songsmith,' Gilgamesh said. 'Since he's accepted our hospitality tonight, I think it's about time he paid for his food, eh?'

There was a general roar of approval at this, and Avram rose to his feet, clutching his harp. Moving to the centre of the room he struck a chord, and quiet fell. 'My lord king,' he said, formally. 'Lords, ladies ...' I am indeed honoured to be allowed in such distinguished and noble company. I am eager to perform for your entertainment. Is there any song that you might like to hear?

'Yes,' the Doctor called out, before anyone else could speak. 'I'd like to hear the one about Utnapishtim, if you don't mind.'

'A new song?' Gilgamesh asked, surprised. 'Well, Ea, if you like. Then he can sing about Ishtar and the seven drunken nights, eh?' The woman next to him sniggered, and whispered something in his ear that made him roar with laughter. 'Later, you bawdy thing! Music first!'

Avram bowed to the king, and again to the Doctor. Striking another chord, he began. His song consisted mostly of chanted lyrics, with the harp being used for emphasis rather than accompaniment. Silence fell over the hall as Avram spun his song for them.

# 12: Avram's Tale

Praise to Shulpae, god of feasting! He has given us food to delight us.
Praise to Ashnan, god of the barley! With his aid, we quench our thirsts.
Praise to Gilgamesh, king of men! By his protection, we are safe, and warm, and fed.

Listen!
In the east, by the waters of Ocean, there stand great mountains
Jagged, and strong, they challenge the realm of Anu, father of gods.
Men call them the mountains of Mashu, gateway to the day.

In the rocks, the ibis frolics. In the peaks, the itubi-birds sing.
In the pathways, the zuqaqip stand. They are tall, like men,
Tall as the sons of men! And strong they are.
In one hand, they can crush a boulder; yes, even a stone the size of a man.
Their skins are not as the skins of men, nor like the fur of the beasts.
In the place of hair, they are clothed in metal. In the light of Shamash, they glow.
When the sun falls upon them, bright is their appearance!

They stand at the gateway to the gods, and they neither slumber nor sleep.
Ever-watchful, they wait, and waiting, they serve.

Strong is the arm of the zuqaqip, but stronger yet his sting!
Like the arrows of Adad, whose storms sweep the land
The arrows that fly and bring fire to the land
So are the stings of the zuqaqip, the watchers by the way.
Like the arrows of Adad, they fly and burn. Like the arrows of Adad, they cut and kill.

Who can withstand these stings? Can mortal man?
Can a man crush a rock, till like sand it falls?
Can a man call out, and cause Adad to rise?
Can a man stay without sleeping seven times seven days?
Who can withstand the strength of these watchers?

And what do they guard, these zuqaqip?
What secret so great could they keep from our eyes?
Listen!
Beyond those mountains lies the garden of the gods.
In those fields, the first-born sons of the immortals dwell.
Even the kin of Utnapishtim!

Who is this Utnapishtim? Who but the saviour of his people.
In a far land they dwelled, in peace and comfort. None there worked, save so they wished. None there toiled, nor dug, nor spun.
In their place, their servants worked. For their praise, their maids toiled.
All of the sons of Mashu were blessed. All of their lives were gentle and long.

Then came among them Ishtar the great. Ishtar the beautiful, Ishtar the proud.
'Shall men forever sit idle?' she asked. 'Shall their lot be ease? No!'
Instead, she enchained them, and made them toil. They who had known rest
Now knew only work. They who had led their gentle lives now sweated
To give Ishtar praise, they laboured.

Then Utnapishtim, strong and wise, saw what had befallen.
He wept, and cried, and tore at his hair in despair.
'How far are you fallen, children of dawn! How hard it is for you.'
And, kind father, he made vow: 'Soon shall you be free!'
Setting his powers to work, Utnapishtim, wise and cunning,
Loosened bolts of thunder, and arrows of Adad.
Storms raged! Wind rose! Waters grew! The very earth shook!

Then Ishtar, seeing this, grew angry and afraid.
'If you do this,' she cried, 'then men will die. Man will perish
Never to live again. Be still!'
But Utnapishtim would not. Again, he loosed his bolts; again
the arrows flew.

And again the earth shook, and the waters grew stronger.
And, seeing this, the wise Utnapishtim took him men.
Craftsmen, and artisans, and dreamers and planners — all he took
And came to them, and said:

'The waters rise, and we shall perish. The earth shakes, and we shall be devoured.
Make for me a boat, a hundred cubits long, a hundred cubits high, a hundred cubits round.
And in it place there floors, and rooms, and doors, and torches.
And in the roof, a single door, that I alone will close.'
And the craftsmen and artisans and dreamers and planners came to him and said:
'All you have asked of us is done, lord. Speak on!'

And Utnapishtim, lord of men, spoke:
'Of all the animals, take you two of each kind, and place them in my ark.
Of all the birds, likewise two. And place those within also.
And of the sons of men, gather up all who live, and place them with the birds and beasts.
And when all of this is done, there will be peace.'
So the artisans and craftsmen, dreamers and planners, all did

as he directed.
And when the ark was full, they came to Utnapishtim and told him.
So Utnapishtim rose, and sealed his ark.

Then the waters rose, and covered the lands. The earth shook, and swallowed the waters.
The day was gone, and night dwelled on the face of all that existed.
For six long months, there was no day. Within the ark was peace
But outside dwelled only chaos on all the face of creation.
And when the months were passed, then came the ark to rest.
In the mountains of Mashu it found the ground again.

And Utnapishtim rose, and opened up the boat. And there was Shamash!
Shamash the golden, Shamash the glorious! Shamash, shining from on high.
And so were all the kin of Utnapishtim the wise
Saved from death, and the fury of Ishtar.
And to this day, within the mountains there they live!

Avram finished singing and stood still, waiting. For a moment, while the feasters gathered their wits, there was silence. Then a wave of applause broke, and Avram smiled. The nobles pounded on the tables, until finally Gilgamesh clapped for silence.

'Right,' he said, grinning. 'A fine tale, well sung. But let's have a real song, eh? Sing of the drunken nights, and the lovers of Ishtar, songsmith!'

As Avram bent to obey, the Doctor nudged Ace, none too gently, with his bony elbow. 'How'd you like the song?'

'Well, it's no match for U2,' she grinned, 'but I think he's pretty good. All he needs is a decent backing band, and he could get on *Top Of The Pops* easy.'

The Doctor sighed. 'I didn't ask you to sign on as his manager. What do you think of the story itself?'

'Bit silly, isn't it?' she asked. 'Sounds like something from the Bible to me.'

'The flood legend?' The Doctor shrugged. 'A common theme, really, at this time. Given the nature of the land — as flat as a pancake, and about as interesting — any sort of flood would be a catastrophe. On the other hand, what about the rest of it?'

'What? The scorpion men? And the six months of darkness?' She frowned. 'You don't take it seriously, do you?'

'I take everything seriously,' the Doctor replied. 'Except myself.'

'Come off it, Professor. It's just a song. Nothing more.'

'Never jump to hasty puddings,' he told her. 'They're usually the wrong ones, and sticky to boot. Remember what I told you about not judging cultures by their own standards.'

This was too much for Ace. 'That's exactly the opposite of what you told me last time.'

'Of course it is,' the Doctor agreed, blithely. 'Haven't you ever read Hegel?'

'I don't know. Did he write *Watership Down*?'

'No he didn't.' The Time Lord frowned. 'Take this seriously, for a change. You can't hide yourself away from the world behind a barrage of explosions forever, you know. Hegel suggested that you take an idea — a thesis — and its opposite — the antithesis — and put them together to get an end result, the synthesis. So, apply yourself. Avram's song is quite correct, and tells a true story. But it's culturally biased, based on his own experiences. Use your imagination, and what you know of the Universe through my tuition, and take a guess what it's really talking about.'

Ace hadn't listened to most of the lecture; she's already been thinking. 'Professor! That ark — was it really a spaceship?'

He beamed. 'I knew you'd get there, sooner or later, with my help.'

'The six months darkness — the trip! No sun, of course. And the scorpion-men — people in space suits? With lasers?'

'I do believe you've got it,' the Doctor approved. 'And the story had other interesting aspects, didn't it? Utnapishtim and Ishtar were foes. According to En-Gula, Ishtar is now living in Kish. According to Avram, Utnapishtim and his band of merry men landed in these mountains of Mashu. That talisman Avram has is some sort of electronic key, lending credence to his story.

Fascinating, isn't it?' Then his face fell. 'The only thing is, what do we do about it all, eh?'

Ace had no idea, but that was generally the Doctor's department, anyway. He was the planner. She preferred to act. 'Why don't we sleep on it?' she suggested.

'Why not?' The Doctor turned his attention back to Avram's latest song. Somehow, he wasn't at all surprised to discover that Gilgamesh's choice of entertainment was about the sexual exploits of the gods. The king was probably hoping to emulate them later, he mused.

In Kish, things were less festive. Ishtar, too anxious to wait, had summoned King Agga. She slithered about the main altar, lashing her tail back and forth. The human was infuriatingly slow! Granted, it was night, and he was probably resting, but that was a pathetically poor excuse for keeping her waiting.

Finally the King arrived, looking haggard. 'What is it?' he growled, not in a good mood.

'I think, in light of recent events, Agga,' Ishtar ordered, 'that we will step up the rate of work. I want more men assigned to laying the copper pathways to the walls. And I need a second team of slaves. They are to begin work on my power supplies. I am impatient to reach the culmination of my plans.'

'What are these power supplies that you speak of?' he asked, curiously. 'The words are meaningless to me.'

'Of course they are!' she sneered. 'To you and this pathetic little town of yours, power is measured in terms of slaves and the work they can do. I speak of real power, Agga, king of dust and sand! Power to move mountains, to level the hills! Power to fly, or build up. Power, should I so choose, to destroy. Ah,' she said, disgusted at his lack of understanding, 'I don't know why I bother talking to you insects. You are too feeble to comprehend.' Then she smiled, coldly and evilly. 'But one thing you will understand. I know that you have been curious about what lies within my inner sanctum. Come, and see — and fear!'

She didn't bother to check whether he was following her. She knew that he would not dare to decline her offer. Moving through the inner rooms, she reached her own private chambers. Quickly, unobserved, she disconnected the defences she always placed, and led the way within.

All of the equipment from her damaged shuttle was here. The electronic devices that sustained her, the controls that linked her mind to those of her slaves. They were all beyond the limited mental prowess of King Agga, of course. He stared in wonder at the blinking lights and the snake-like traces across the VDUs. The computing potential of the equipment was meaningless to him. However Ishtar knew that there was one device that even he, stupid and dull as he was, might understand.

It was a smallish box, about a foot in each direction. She stroked it tenderly, and smiled down at him. 'One of the reasons I came here, Agga,' she purred, 'is that I could detect a source of radioactivity in the area. So far your men have mined a small amount for me, and it powers all that you see. In the past few days, I have garnered enough spare material to fill this box.'

Agga shrugged. 'It means nothing to me,' he confessed. 'What difference does it make what is in that box of yours, Ishtar?'

She laughed long and hard, enjoying his foolishness. She stopped. 'O king,' she smiled, 'you saw the damage done to my temple by the intruders, did you not? Well, it was accomplished using some simple explosives. They made quite a mess. This,' she stroked the case again, 'is what is known as a thermo-nuclear bomb. It is linked to me electronically. Just a grain or two of the minerals in here could create the same effect as the bomb that harmed my temple. And in this box is several pounds of the destructive ore. If anything happens to me, Agga — anything at all — then this will explode.'

Trying to understand this, Agga ventured: 'You mean that if you should somehow be destroyed, then your box will demolish my city?'

'Your city?' Ishtar laughed again. 'Agga, this box will destroy everything that you've ever seen, or even heard of! It will despatch this portion of your miserable little planet into complete oblivion!'

Agga stared at the box with increased respect. And he could see in her eyes that Ishtar would be more than happy for such a catastrophe to happen.

# 13: Split Infinities

Despite all the carousing Gilgamesh was up bright and early the next day, having called a council meeting. The Doctor brought Ace, Avram and En-Gula to it, despite the frowns aimed in his direction by Ennatum and the other nobles. They were not keen on either women or commoners attending the sacred sessions. The Doctor didn't particularly care what they liked.

Gilgamesh was the only one allowed to be seated. Even the powerful lords had to stand while tactics and plans were discussed. As soon as everyone he had sent for had arrived, Gilgamesh rapped on the stone floor with his sceptre, and silence fell.

'As you all know,' the king explained, 'Enkidu and I visited the city of Kish on a spying mission. We discovered some very disturbing things. First of all,' he stared around the room, at each of the dozen or so nobles present, 'the people of Kish knew that we were coming. My initial thought was that someone had made my plans known to them.' He looked directly at Ennatum, who withstood the stare without a flicker of doubt appearing on his face. 'Where is Gudea?' Gilgamesh asked, deceptively mildly. 'He seems to be missing.'

Ennatum spread his hands. 'I have sent messengers to try to locate him, O king. So far, though, I have heard nothing from them or him.'

Gilgamesh nodded, and then continued with his lecture. 'But there is another possibility. It seems that the goddess Ishtar has blessed Kish with a personal appearance.' The noblemen murmured sceptically until the king stared them down and appealed to the Doctor, who nodded unsmilingly. Gilgamesh continued. 'She now resides in her temple in Kish, and she controls the warriors of that city. Enkidu and I had to fight our way out by night, and she knew where and when to send troops to attack us both. Clearly, then, she was responsible for discovering our approach earlier, and not some traitor on this council. For which, you may all be thankful.' He stared directly at Ennatum. 'Nevertheless, I would like a few words with Gudea when you locate him.'

'As you wish, lord,' Ennatum replied, smoothly. Nothing in either his eyes or his bearing indicated the panic churning his insides.

'Now, the king said, gesturing again towards the Doctor, 'we ourselves are blessed with divine visitors. It would appear that this season a number of the gods walk among us. This is Ea, god of wisdom, and he has brought Aya, goddess of the dawn.' Ace wondered if she was expected to curtsy at this. Instead, she elected to smile sweetly. 'They wish to help us in our struggles against Kish.'

The Doctor stepped forward, and leaned on his umbrella to face the council. 'As your king has said, nobles of Uruk,' he began, 'the city of Kish is host to someone calling herself Ishtar. However she is no goddess, but a demon from the pits of hell. She can cloak herself in the likeness of a goddess to deceive men. Lying, she tries to claim the glories due to the gods alone. She infects the minds of those she touches, and she is preparing to lead Kish in a war against Uruk.'

'If she is a demon, O Ea,' Ennatum asked, 'then why does the real Ishtar not blast her to pieces with divine wrath?' There was a murmur of agreement from the other nobles at this display of logic.

'Because, O man,' the Doctor answered, 'there is a deep balance to the eternal battle between good and evil. True, the gods could simple destroy this false Ishtar — but what would mortals learn from that? No, this must be a battle fought by men.'

Another of the advisers, an older man named Lagash, stepped forward. 'While you sit and watch?' he asked, cynically.

'No. Aya and I will aid you in the ways that are permitted to us. We can offer you guidance, and also a little physical help. But this must be your fight, and not ours alone.' He smiled disarmingly at them. 'And there is one other who will aid you — Utnapishtim.'

Even Avram looked amazed at this piece of news. The Doctor paused for a moment to revel in the surprise he had caused, and then explained: 'He and the demoness are foes from ages past. When he knows she is in Kish, he will help to destroy her.'

'Are you sure about that?' Ace whispered to him, while the nobles considered the news.

'It can't be a coincidence that there are two different starships from two unrelated races here in one small part of the Earth at the same time,' he answered. 'Ishtar's ship is an escape capsule, and shows signs of scorching from radiation weapons. I'd hazard a guess that Utnapishtim's forces destroyed her main craft, and thought she perished in the fight.'

'Could be,' Ace agreed, sounding less than completely convinced.

'Trust me,' the Doctor grinned.

'Do I ever have any choice?' she sighed.

The Doctor rapped on the floor with his brolly, silencing the chatter. 'Now, what I would suggest is this: we send a party to speak to Utnapishtim and to seek his aid. Meanwhile, the rest of us will stay here plan how to get back into Kish to probe Ishtar's temples and defences. Since Utnapishtim is such a great man, only the greatest man in Uruk would be fitted for the task of meeting him.' He looked at Gilgamesh.

The king laughed aloud with pleasure. 'Ea, your words have a strong ring of truth to them. I would like to meet this man who survived the great flood that destroyed the lands. Enkidu and I will prepare to leave immediately.'

'I would suggest not,' the Doctor said, carefully choosing his words. 'If anything should happen while you are gone, such as Ishtar making a move, then Enkidu would be an invaluable helper for me here. He alone could act with your authority.'

Gilgamesh frowned. 'Ea, you are not suggesting that I travel alone to meet with this Utnapishtim? It would not be fitting, either to myself or to him.'

'Of course not, O king,' the Doctor replied. 'You must take with you Avram, who knows the way to the mountains of Mashu. He will be your guide. And also the lady Aya, who will advise and aid you.'

'What?' Ace screeched in disbelief. 'Doctor! Don't do this to me!'

'Do as I ask,' he pleaded quietly. 'I need you to keep an eye on Gilgamesh.'

'You can't keep pulling that excuse on me,' she said. 'He'll be safe without me around — I'm more liable to kill him than anyone.'

The Doctor smiled reassuringly. 'Excuse us, just a moment,' he begged, and then dragged Ace outside. 'Ace, just this once, please — do as I ask.'

Furious, Ace refused to listen. 'This so-called monarch really gets up my nose,' she stormed. 'And there's no way I'm putting up with going on a cross-country trek with him. Absolutely not. If you want him to go and see this Utna-whoozit bloke, you take him.'

The Doctor sighed. 'Ace, don't be difficult. It has to be this way. I've got to stay here in Uruk in case Ishtar makes any changes to her plans. But I need someone to go with Gilgamesh who's used to dealing with aliens, who won't be overawed, and who won't overreact. It *must* be you. You're the only person I can trust.' He smiled at her in what he hoped was a winning way.

Unwilling to be swayed by his logic, Ace retorted: 'Why are we doing this the hard way? Can't we just let them all sort it out? Zip over to find Utna-whoozit in the TARDIS, bring him back and let him do the job?'

The Doctor shook his head. 'It's not that simple. I've no idea where Utnapishtim's base is. I could never get the TARDIS there. And remember, we've supposed to be here for an appointment with a Timewyrm, whatever it is. I don't want to chance using the TARDIS. After all, if this creature is somehow connected to time, then it will zero in on something. I don't want to move the TARDIS.'

'But the TARDIS is outside Kish,' Ace pointed out. 'How will you know what's going on?'

He pulled a small device from his inside pocket. It looked like a pocket calculator. 'I removed the time path indicator from the TARDIS,' he explained, 'while you lot were asleep. It will register any activity in the Vortex heading for the Earth and the TARDIS.'

'I've not seen that before.'

The Doctor shrugged. 'I don't have a lot of use for it. It's not often that there's another time machine on my trail. Haven't used this since...' He broke off, remembering the last time he had called on the device. It had been the time the Daleks were chasing him, seeking to regain the Tarranium Core he had stolen from them. A long time ago, before his first regeneration. That had been the time that Sara Kingdom and Katarina had died. He firmly shut his memory on those events. 'Anyway, if a Timewyrm is heading for the Earth, I'll detect it. Which is another reason I have to stay here and you'd be better off with Gilgamesh.'

'I don't like your reasoning,' scowled Ace. 'But I don't think arguing will get me anywhere. But if I've got to go with randy rex in there, you tell him to keep his hands well away from me — or he'll be sorry.'

'I'll make it very clear,' he promised her in a voice that did nothing to reassure her.

'You'd better.'

The Doctor put an arm about her shoulder. 'I know how you feel about the king,' he said, sympathetically. 'He's not someone I'd choose to go on a hiking holiday with, either. But at the moment, he's our best chance to defeat Ishtar. Believe me, if I could think of any other way to do it, I wouldn't put you through this.'

'Yeah,' Ace agreed, knowing he meant it. 'But that doesn't make it any easier to take, Professor.'

Gilgamesh stared thoughtfully at Ennatum. He had never liked or trusted the man, but so far the adviser had been far too cunning to be caught out, either in deceit or in a lie. It was only a matter of time, Gilgamesh knew. Ennatum twisted and squirmed so much behind the cold mask of his face that one day he would betray himself. Gilgamesh could wait.

'You say you found Gudea?' Gilgamesh asked. 'Then why is he not here?'

'Alas,' Ennatum replied, looking anything but sad, 'I am afraid that it is beyond his powers to come to you now, O king. It seems he had a troubled mind, and to settle it he drank some poisoned beer.'

'Indeed?' Gilgamesh raised an eyebrow. 'Curious. I wonder whether he knew that he was doing so?'

Ennatum feigned a look of surprise. 'Do you mean that he may not have killed himself?'

'I hardly care,' replied the king. 'It saved me the bother of having to kill him myself. On the other hand, I shouldn't like to think that there might be further examples of people drinking the wrong thing.'

Bowing, Ennatum murmured: 'I am sure that he will be the only one, lord.'

'I am sure that he had better be.' The king dismissed his adviser from his presence, but not from his mind. As soon as Ennatum had left the room, Gilgamesh beckoned Enkidu to him.

'Enkidu, my friend, I shall be leaving in the morning on this quest for Utnapishtim. Whether we shall find him, I cannot say. My heart is heavy that you will not be with me on this venture.'

The hairy man nodded. 'Mine too, Gilgamesh. Ah, you'll have many an opportunity to add to your story! What an adventure this will be.'

'Aye, perhaps.' The king took the cylindrical seal from about his neck, and placed it over Enkidu's ugly head. 'Here is my seal, Enkidu. It confers on you my full authority. Use it wisely, my friend. And be very wary about Ennatum. While I am certain that Gudea plotted to have me killed because of his wife, I suspect the same of Ennatum, but cannot prove it. The man is an insect, but one with a sting. Take care about him.'

Nodding, Enkidu asked: 'And what of the Doctor, and his young companion? Do you believe that they are truly Ea and Aya?'

Gilgamesh laughed. 'Ah, you hairy monster, you too have your doubts as to their divinity? Well, I'm with you there. As to whether they are gods, who can say? But I feel that we can trust them. There is much mystery in them both, but little guile, I feel. They have their own reasons for what they do, but they work with us — at least for now.'

'Travel well, my king and my friend.' Enkidu reached out and clasped Gilgamesh's arm in a strong grip. 'Return as quickly as you are able. I feel that we are living in dangerous times.'

'True,' Gilgamesh agreed. 'But those are the best of times. With danger comes the chance to grasp glory — aye, and perhaps even immortality. And it staves off the boredom of life, eh?'

'There are worse things in life than boredom.'

'Ha! Name one.'

With a sober glance at his king, Enkidu replied: 'Death.'

Gilgamesh shrugged. 'Death is not to be feared, my friend. When my time comes, I shall die willingly enough, with my battle axe dripping the blood of many enemies. The people shall sing of me forever!'

'A week?' Ace howled, furiously. 'A week with that... that...'

'King?' suggested the Doctor, quickly. He turned to Avram, and clapped the musician's shoulders. 'Take care of yourself, songsmith. And keep an eye or two on Gilgamesh.' He looked at Ace. 'I've a feeling he may need all of the help he can get.'

# 14: The Mountains of Mashu

It was the longest week of Ace's life. In the Doctor's company she had faced both danger and boredom often enough in the past, but this trip took every ounce of patience she could muster.

Gilgamesh was actually quite well behaved, at least for him. He didn't attempt to either seduce or rape her — the Doctor must have somehow made it clear to the king that Ace was out of bounds — and he seemed to be trying to be charming and thoughtful. Unfortunately he fell far short of both virtues.

His biggest problem, Ace decided, was that he had been brought up to think that he could do no wrong. She had mentioned this to Avram one evening, while the king was hunting for supper. The singer seemed surprised at her comment.

'Lady, he is the king of Uruk. His mother Ninsun is rumoured to be divine. The people of Uruk believe he is two thirds god and one third man. How then can he do wrong?'

'Give me a break!' said Ace, disgustedly. 'He's got the manners of a pig, an ego the size of a mountain and a libido that just won't stop.'

Avram shrugged. 'For the last, there are many women who are honoured to have him in bed. I see that you are not one of them, but he is not troubling you now, is he? He is not foolish enough to press his attentions where they are not wanted. There are plenty of arms open to him, should he choose them. As to his manners, he is no worse than the others of his court. Perhaps where you are from, Aya, his manners seem strange. But to him they are normal.

'As to his ego... He paused. 'Lady, what do you know about the king?'

'More that I care to.'

He laughed easily. 'Gilgamesh is a hero, lady. His leadership has kept Uruk safe from attack, and he has strengthened it through the years. The merchants prosper, the people are content, and his nobles find their wealth increasing. He is stronger than four normal men, and he is unsurpassed when hunting either man or beast. His arrows never miss their mark, nor his axe its target. If he is proud of these deeds — well, ask yourself: does he not have reason to be?'

'Well — OK. But can't he keep his ego to himself? He could pretend to be humble occasionally, couldn't he?'

Avram laughed. 'Would you have Gilgamesh add dishonestly and dissembling to the list of defects you see in him? He is a plain man, and it is a great strength in him.'

Ace grunted noncommitally. 'What are you, his agent?'

'I do not understand you,' the musician said.

'Sometimes I don't understand myself, Avram,' Ace admitted. 'Gilgamesh rubs me up the wrong way, but it's just not that. There's so much, and so much you wouldn't understand.'

Avram shrugged. 'At least I have a patient ear,' he told her. 'If you will feel better, speak on. I cannot promise advice, but at least I could sing a song to lift your spirits later.'

Unsure herself what she would say, Ace kicked moodily at a stone. 'It's not easy for me,' she confessed. 'I just sometimes wonder what I'm doing with my life. Here I am, like some galactic tourist, following the Doctor all over the place — getting beaten up, shot at, attacked, betrayed, and worse. And having to put up with loonies like Gilgamesh. And none of it makes sense to me.'

'Then it can hardly be clear to me,' smiled Avram. 'But — well, you have a choice, don't you? You could take your leave of the Doctor. Follow some other path.'

'Yeah, I could.' She tried to convince herself of that, and finally she shook her head. 'No, I couldn't. I'm stuck with him for now.'

He regarded her curiously. 'And why is that? Does he have

some magical hold over you?'

Laughing, Ace said: 'You could call it that. You know what he did to me the other day? He robbed me of all my memories. Every one them. I didn't know who I was, or where, or why. Nothing.'

'Was he trying to punish you?' Avram struggled to understand this strange event.

'Nah. he just made a mistake. Luckily he put me back together again. Otherwise I'd be in a right state. But he does things like that — you know, really stupid things — and doesn't even seem to know he's doing it.'

The musician frowned. 'It seems to me that you live a very uncertain life.'

'You can say that again.'

'So then why do you stay with him?' he persisted.

Ace dug down into her self, and was afraid she had come up with no answers. 'Well, it's better than things used to be. I come from this place that was — naff and boring. Life might be dangerous now, but it's never dull with the Doctor around. Not like Perivale. You can't imagine how I hated that place. I felt like a prisoner there. As if I was an alien. Didn't belong. And you know what I hated the most?' Memories flooded back to her. 'People hated each other. People with white skin hated people with dark skin. Poor people hated the rich. Men wouldn't trust women. Women were afraid of men. And there I was — a girl, poor, and thick, too, they said. Mixing with the wrong sort. I couldn't bring myself to hate anyone, really. Except the people who hated other people. And that was just about everybody. What kind of life could I have? But the Doctor — well, he's got his faults, but there's not an ounce of prejudice in him. In fact, it's the other way round. He's ready to take up the flag and fight for anyone's rights.' She grinned. 'He even gave some of his own people bloody noses when they tried to stop him. He cares about people, but in a funny sort of way. He might seem callous, but it's a sort of skin, I think. To stop getting hurt. I think he really does care for me, but he knows that I'll leave him in the end, so he won't let himself get too attached to me.' She sighed. 'It must be very hard for him. He's

139

over a thousand years old, you know.'

'He doesn't look it,' Avram said, politely.

'Well, when he gets a bit worn out, he sort of... Well, he changes. He told me he's done it six times so far.'

Considering the matter, Avram nodded. 'Like the snake sheds its skin,' he suggested. 'To allow for new growth.'

Ace stared at him with respect for this insight. 'Yeah, I bet that's one reason he regenerates. It must be hard being fresh and decisive for a thousand years without getting tired.'

At that moment Gilgamesh arrived back in the camp, the carcass of an antelope slung across his shoulders. He roared. 'Who wants the liver? A delicacy for our footsore goddess?'

*Yuk*! was what Ace thought. But she found herself saying: 'Not for me, thanks.'

'More for me,' he grinned, and Ace smiled back.


'Think, Doctor, think!'

Fingers pressed to his temples, the Doctor tried to apply all of the techniques that his old mentor K'Anpo had taught him. Lose the self, free the mind to its potentials. But it was no good. He was too tense, too worried. He uncurled from the lotus position, and instead stretched out flat on the stone floor.

The trouble with his mind, he decided, was that it was too cluttered. Despite the cleaning out of his memories the other day, there was still too much general nonsense left. And much that was important was either buried too deeply or else had been lost over the years — including the reasons he had recorded the warning to himself.

He knew the background to the warning. It had been at the time the Sontarans and their gullible henchmen the Vardans had managed to invade Gallifrey. He had been in his fourth body at the time. He had been forced to enter the Matrix to find out what was going on.

But he'd managed to find out a bit too much, and the Matrix had unravelled his memories. In fact, he remembered none of this directly — the Matrix had very effectively wiped clean those portions of his mind. No, it was all pieced together from other places — K9's memory banks, that last tea he had taken on

Gallifrey with his old companion Leela and that silly husband of hers back — how long? Well, no matter.

Maybe the Timewyrm warning was a mistake. The product of his addled brain, freshly scoured by the Matrix. Ishtar was the problem now, and more than enough to be going on with. He'd managed to stave off Ace's doubts and get her out of the firing line for now. She was obstinately loyal, and this plan of his could turn out to be very dangerous. Maybe he was overreacting, but his recent memory scans had brought back to him many painful events: Katarina, killing herself to save a Universe she didn't even comprehend; Sara Kingdom, dying to defeat the Daleks; Adric, perishing in a fireball over prehistoric Earth to stop the Cybermen from destroying the human race.

And on top of that, a chilling image of Ace — her brain being sucked dry by a snake-like creature.

A memory of the future? Or just his overactive imagination? He couldn't take any more chances with Ace. She was in danger from Ishtar; she had to be kept away while he tackled Ishtar himself.

He was abruptly aware that he was no longer alone. Opening his eyes, he stared up at the bemused face of En-Gula. 'Hello,' he smiled, sitting upright.

'I am not disturbing you?' she asked, worried.

'Mmmm? Oh, not at all,' he fibbed, getting to his feet. 'Just doing a little thinking. I like to keep my mind in shape. Did you want something?'

The young girl seemed very unsure of herself. The Doctor let her take her time, and finally she blurted out: 'What is to become of me?'

'I beg your pardon?'

'I do not know if you are truly Ea, god of wisdom,' the priestess sighed. 'But you do speak with understanding. Can you tell me what will happen to me?'

'What will be, will be,' he replied, then rubbed his chin. 'That reminds me of a song, but I can't quite place it. Oh well. Perhaps you could explain a little more clearly what it is you want to know?'

'Doctor, all I ever knew was my calling as a priestess of Ishtar,' En-Gula said. 'I was happy, and I like to think that I was a good priestess.'

'Despite lying down on the job, eh?' he joked. 'Do go on.'

'But when this false Ishtar came, everything changed for me. I began to hate the temple, and everything connected with it. Now I have cast my lot to fight this demon, but I have betrayed my calling, and I have destroyed my life. What is to become of me?'

The Doctor raised her chin, and stared into her dispirited eyes. 'Listen to me,' he said, quietly, but with authority. 'You have done what you knew was right. You have taken a stand against evil. Whatever you have done, it is with pure motives. I promise you that when Ishtar is defeated, you will be happy once again.'

En-Gula swallowed, and nodded. He could see the hope flooding back into her. 'Thank you,' she said simply, accepting his word implicitly.

*And if not happy*, he thought, *at least you will have been yourself.*

'Meanwhile,' he said hastily, not wanting to think about the promise he had given, 'you may be able to help us further. I need to have a quick peep in Kish to find out what's happening there. Do you know of anyone who might help us, or somewhere we could hide?'

She nodded, eager to be of assistance. 'The princess Ninani also hates and fights against the false goddess. She will shelter you, and will offer you aid in your fight.'

'Capital!' He rubbed his hands together. 'Well, let's find Enkidu, and be off, shall we?'

She stared at him, puzzled. 'But are you not going to await the return of Aya?'

'No, no, I don't think so,' he said. 'She's pretty busy, I imagine. Anyway, she'll find her way to me. She always does. I just want a little look into Ishtar's sanctuary without worrying about it getting blown up about my ears.' He put an arm about her shoulders, leading her from the room. 'Between you, me and the lamp post, Ace does have a tendency to blow things up first and ask questions later.'

'What's a lamp post?'
'Ask me later.'

Shading her eyes against the glare of the sun, Ace followed the line of Avram's arm.

'There,' he explained. 'That's the only pathway into the heart of the mountains of Mashu. It is where the zuqaqip stand their guard. We should be there in the morning.

After the vast expanse of the flat plain, Ace was glad to see something that stood taller than a molehill. But this was a real range of mountains, and they looked high. The dying embers of the sun gleamed off their pinnacles. Ace automatically felt for the coil of nylon rope in her rucksack. 'How far up do we have to climb?'

The singer shrugged. 'Who can say? I went only as far as the guardians. They should allow us to pass, since you are with us.'

'And if they don't,' Gilgamesh growled, 'then I shall kill them.'

'Knock it off,' Ace advised him. 'We'll get further if we asked questions first and fight later. Or not at all.'

The king didn't like this. 'Then what is the point of living if we do not fight?'

Ace shook her head in despair. 'Don't you think of anything but fighting?'

'Yes,' he grinned. 'But you won't do that, either.'

'Thanks a lot, Professor,' she muttered under her breath. 'I always wanted to go mountaineering with a psychotic sex maniac.' Aloud, she said: 'I think we'd better make camp for the night, and press on in the morning. Who's for left-over antelope leg?'

# 15: Guardians At The Gate Of Dawn

The Doctor patted the side of the TARDIS fondly and stared out across the irrigated fields towards Kish. 'They've been busy, haven't they?' he observed.

The copper patterning was all over the stone walls now. They had almost finished the work during the past week. He'd decided to come at precisely the right moment, as usual. Another example of prescience, he wondered, or just plain luck? Well, did it much matter, as long as they were here?

'What is it for?' Enkidu asked. 'To waste all of that metal simply to make patterns ... No. There must be a point to it.'

'Quite right,' the Doctor approved. For all of his apparent similarity to an ape, Enkidu had a keen brain. 'I've always been impressed by the reasoning powers of the Neanderthaler. Met one of your relatives a few thousand years from now who was pretty bright, too.' He smiled. 'Think of Ishtar as a spider. This metal is her web, within which she will entrap the minds and souls of everyone in Kish.'

Enkidu frowned as he considered the idea. 'She wants to take over the thoughts of all in the city?'

'Oh, I suspect she has grander aims than that,' the Doctor said, airily. 'The world, probably. Maybe even the cosmos. Depends on the blatant egocentricity of the creature. But Kish will serve her well for an appetizer, I should think.'

En-Gula struggled to take in this conversation. 'Can we do something to stop her?' she asked.

The Doctor smiled, and tapped the side of his nose with the handle of his ever-present umbrella. 'We can always do something,' he replied. 'The question is, will it be enough?' He pulled his cloak tighter about himself, and gestured for the others to do the same. 'Right, time to pay her a visit. Won't you come into my parlour...'

The final part of the climb was the hardest. Ace scrambled uphill, stubbornly refusing Gilgamesh's offers of assistance. Her only consolation was that Avram was having a rougher time of the climb than she was. As a musician he wasn't used to the rigours of mountaineering. Eventually they reached the small pathway that Avram had been guiding them to, and paused for a rest.

Gilgamesh didn't see the need for the break himself, but acquiesced to Ace's growls. 'I do not think,' he replied darkly, 'that you should be taking command of this party. I am, after all, king. And you are just a woman.'

'Goddess,' glared Ace back. 'Remember that big bang I saved your neck with? Well, I could repeat it right here, and take off all that ugly weight you're carrying on your shoulders. It would make the going quieter.'

He was clearly unwilling to push her that far. While she could see that he didn't really think she was divine, he obviously did recall her powers and was not going to challenge her authority directly. On the other hand he was not going to give in to her with good grace. 'I don't like this idea of talking to the guardians,' he objected. 'If they are soldiers, then force is the only logic that they will respect.'

'Look, *king*,' Ace snapped, 'if it was up to me, I'd love you to go in there and get yourself cut to pieces by them. But the Doctor wants you in one piece, and I'm going to try my best to see you stay that way. If those guardians have half the stuff I think they've got, they'd make a chicken à la king of you in seconds. So we do this my way, okay?'

Her anger did get through to him, and he subsided. 'Very well,' he said, reluctantly. 'For the moment, we will do this as you wish. But if it doesn't work, then it's my turn.' He fingered the edge of his axe. 'Agreed?'

'Whatever you say,' replied Ace. 'Okay, Avram, let's finish

this leg of the trip.' She pulled herself to her feet and she and Gilgamesh followed the songsmith down the narrow pathway between the rocks. Within a few moments the mountains had closed in on them, and they were winding their way down between two walls of sheer granite. In a way it was very beautiful, but she was in no mood to appreciate the fact. Her feet hurt, her temper was frayed, and she had a growing suspicion that the Doctor was up to something behind her back. The sooner this trip was over the better.

Avram halted abruptly, and gestured ahead of them. 'The guardians,' he breathed.

Ace shouldered him gently aside, and her gaze followed the curve of their trail.

It was worse than she had expected. The guardians of the dawn were not soldiers in space suits. They were robots.

There were two of them, each about eight feet tall. Humanoid in shape, they stood at attention. Long metal legs were hooked to a squat body. Two long, jointed arms ended in claws fitted with what looked like needle-pointed guns. Atop each body, with no intervening neck, sat a head of sorts. They had eyes like camera lenses, small gratings below the eyes, and then what seemed to be antennae or mandibles sticking out from the lower part of the faces. Ace didn't like to think what they were for. She stepped forward.

Two heads spun to face her, and the arms clicked up, weapons covering the small group. She braced herself for attack, but the robots intoned in unison:

'Approach and identify.'

The voices were metallic, but they were neither lifeless nor monotonous. They sounded almost like the buzzing of wasps. Ace moved forward hesistantly, followed by Avram and a very quiet Gilgamesh. Something had finally managed to make an impression on his ego, it seemed.

The two robots heads clickly slightly, and spun to face each other. Both guardians produced several of the buzzing noises before the heads rotated back to face the trio.

'Approach,' the first one repeated.

'Identify,' added the second. There was a slight difference

in pitch between the two voices. Ace mentally christened them One and Two.

'We are approaching,' she said. 'And I'm Ace. These are Avram and Gilgamesh.' She gestured towards her companions. The robot heads followed her movements, resting for a long moment on Avram's nervous features.

'Returned,' One said, then buzzed.

'Singer: Avram,' added Two.

'State —' One told Ace.

'— your purpose,' Two completed.

Not knowing which of them to look at, Ace shrugged. 'We're here to see Utnapishtim.'

'Not possible,' One clicked.

'Sees no one,' Two explained.

'Nergal's blood,' Gilgamesh growled, unsheathing his axe. 'I told you it was a mistake to try to talk to these creatures. Let me take them apart.'

'Attack?' hummed One.

'Illogical,' added Two. Before Gilgamesh could make a move, both robots spat laser beams from their mandibles. A rock beside the king glowed and melted into a small pool of slag. Gilgamesh did an almost comic double take, and realized that he was outmatched. Carefully, he replaced his axe over his shoulder.

'Wise —'

'— move.' The robots turned back to Ace. 'Utnapishtim —'

'— is to be protected.'

Mentally cursing Gilgamesh, Ace tried again. 'We're not here to harm him,' she said. 'We're here to ask his help.'

The robot heads regards Gilgamesh again. 'Some —' began One.

'— help,' finished Two.

'Don't blame him,' Ace sighed. 'He can't help being overaggressive. But Avram and I aren't like that.'

'Avram —'

'— isn't,' robots agreed. 'But —'

'— you?'

Carefully, slowly, Ace took her hands from her pockets. In her right hand, she held Ishtar's bomb. The guardians' arms swivelled up to train on her. 'Wait!' she called out. 'It's safe!'

The antennae twitched. 'So —'

'— it is.' The arms stayed in position, however. 'Explain —'

'— your actions.'

Moving slowly towards the two poised robots, Ace held out the bomb. 'Look at this. Could anyone from this culture or time period have constructed such a device?'

The antennae twitched again, a little longer this time. 'No,' One agreed. 'It was —'

'— built on Anu,' Two completed. 'Interesting. Where did —'

'— you get it?'

Ace was beginning to think she should have called them Tweedledee and Tweedledum. She explained: It comes from a wrecked escape capsule, near the cities of Kish and Uruk.'

The robots heads swivelled to regard each other. 'Wait —'

'— a moment.' There was a short pause, during which Ace could hear the sounds of machinery emanating from the robots. Then she felt a slight tug on her arm.

'What are they doing?' Avram asked, looking worried.

'Probably communicating with Utnapishtim or one of his people,' Ace told him. 'There's only one conclusion that they can come to — that Ishtar escaped their attack on her. They're bound to want to know more.'

The two heads swivelled back to cover them. 'Passage —'

'— agreed,' they said. 'Follow —'

'— this path.'

Ace replaced the bomb in her jacket pocket, and sauntered up to the robots. She patted them as she passed. 'Good boys,' she approved.

'Praise —'

'— non-essential.'

Gilgamesh favoured them both with a much darker stare, but kept his temper in check as he moved beyond them. Avram brought up the rear, smiling nervously at the unresponsive robots. Ace led the way down the narrow chasm. When she looked over her shoulder, both guardians were ignoring the human party and were watching the approach once again. 'Weird,' she muttered.

'Now what?' Gilgamesh asked her, crossly. 'Does this path lead to Utnapishtim?'

'Let's hope so. We'd better follow it to find out, hadn't we?'

'Well, I don't like it at all.' Gilgamesh pointed up the sheer cliffs of rock on both sides of them. 'All an enemy has to do is to drop stones on us from above, and we're doomed. We have no room to fight in here. It stinks of treachery.'

'Look, rocks-for-brains', Ace told him, 'if they'd wanted to kill us, those two guardians back there could have fried us where we stood and nothing you or I could have done would have stopped them. We're safe here just as long as we do exactly what we're told.'

'No man tells Gilgamesh what to do,' the king complained, scowling. 'And no woman, either, even if she claims to be a goddess.' He looked pointedly at Ace. 'I am willing to go along with your schemes only so far, Aya.'

This was all she needed: Gilgamesh in a grouchy mood and itching for a fight. It was like having to deal with a child, constantly keeping him in line. What had she ever done to deserve this? Hoping that the walk would tire him out, she marched on round the next bend in the canyon, and stopped dead.

The passageway opened out abruptly as the cliffs retreated on either side. They were on the rim of a vast hollow in the mountains, into which the pathway now led downwards. She looked about her and saw that the cliffs circled to meet on the far side of a huge lake. Abruptly she realized where they were.

'It's an extinct volcano,' she exclaimed. 'A lot of them have lakes in their centres, like this.'

Avram nodded. 'There are tales that this mountain once was host to the gods,' he told her. 'The smoke from their feasting fires rose for many years, then stopped. The gods moved on.'

'I hope this was a long time ago,' she muttered. She couldn't quite recall, but she vaguely remembered something about extinct volcanos having lakes in them. Or was that just wishful thinking on her part?

'Down there,' Gilgamesh growled, pointing. Following the line of his finger, Ace saw that there was a small shack of some sort by the water's edge. Next to it was an even smaller boat. 'Think you that is where Utnapishtim lives?'

'It seems a bit grubby,' Ace replied, uncertainly. 'I'd expected something much larger. And metallic.' The sun didn't penetrate into the crater. Peering, she asked: 'Is that some kind of island in the centre of the lake there?'

'Perhaps,' the king agreed. 'In this shadow, it's hard to tell. I never trust the dark; anything might lurk within its embrace. Still, things may be more visible when we reach the house.'

Ace agreed, and they started off down the slope towards the small building. It was easy going — perhaps a bit too easy. Stones rolled out from under their feet, gathering momentum as they skitterd down the slope.

The ground levelled as they approached the lip of stone that the shack stood on. To Ace's keen gaze it seemed a peculiar building. It looked as if it had been carved out of whitish plastic, instead of the wood or stone or brick of the buildings in Kish and Uruk. As she drew closer she realized that her guess had been correct: the hut was made from some sort of artificial material.

It wasn't large — about twenty feet long and wide, and about eight tall. There were no windows, and a single door. Feeling somewhat uncertain she approached and lifted her hand to knock.

'Not much point,' a voice said, lazily, from the direction of the boat. They spun around to see a gaunt figure unfolding from within it, yawning. 'There's nobody inside. Just me out here.'

Ninani sat before the polished metal of her mirror, carefully applying the kohl make-up to line her eyes. She would have to look her best, when she met her father later this afternoon. King Agga had been in a constant foul temper since his last conversation with Ishtar. Ninani was determined to break him out of it. Provided, of course, Ishtar had not yet discovered the plotting that she had tried to do against the goddess.

It gave her the chills just to think about that. It was more than a week since En-Gula had vanished, and nothing had been said about the young priestess having visited the princess. Was it possible that no one had known of it? Or did Ishtar know that the two girls had been conspirators and was simply biding her time?

Swallowing her doubts and fears, Ninani reflected that she was probably not cut out to be a conspirator. It was too hard on her stomach and nerves.

There was a quiet rapping on the door. Assuming it was Puabi with fresh clothing, Ninani called out imperiously for her to enter. Gazing into the mirror, she smeared the kohl across half of her face in panic at what she saw there.

En-Gula had returned.

With a cry Ninani spun about, torn between her terror that En-Gula was a ghost and her expectation that the girl would be followed through the door by the temple guards and an order for the arrest of the princess. Instead the priestess was followed by two improbable figures, both swathed in the robes of merchants.

Falling to her knees, En-Gula kissed the closest of the princess's feet. 'Lady,' she murmured.

Panic was followed in Ninani's mind by caution. One of the two odd figures closed the door silently, after glancing into the corridor to be certain that they were not observed. The Princess managed to shake off her fears, and could not restrain her curiosity. 'En-Gula,' she asked, 'where have you been? What has happened? And who are these people?'

The Doctor slipped out of his disguise with a thankful sigh. It had been hot wearing the heavy woollen cloak. Enkidu contented himself with just throwing the hood back from his hairy visage. Ninani choked back a scream when she saw him.

'You — you're that — that creature of Gilgamesh's!' She looked ready to scream for help. En-Gula leapt to her feet.

'Peace, lady!' she hissed. 'He means no harm! He is here to help us with Ishtar. As is this other, the god Ea.'

Uncertainly, Ninani subsided. Staring warily at the Doctor, who doffed his hat politely, she finally said: 'Forgive me, but I find it hard to trust any visiting divinities after witnessing what Ishtar has done.'

'And quite rightly, too,' the Doctor agreed. 'Terrible state of affairs here. But I'm here to do something about it. En-Gula has been telling us that you want her power broken.'

The princess nodded. 'She is evil, and disturbs both my father and my city.' She looked him over, curiously. 'Can someone such as you truly help us to defeat her?'

'I'm probably the only one who can,' he assured her. To En-Gula, he added: 'Perhaps you'd better tell the princess what happened to you.' He stood patiently by as the priestess told the tale of the finding of the Doctor, and Ace's raid on the temple. The Doctor tried to restrain his annoyance at this part. The girl then told of the planning session in Uruk, and finished her tale.

Ninani looked at each of them in turn. 'So,' she finally said. 'Gilgamesh, Aya and the singer have gone in search of Utnapishtim, while you three have come here. To what purpose?'

The Doctor took up the conversation. 'I really need to get a look into Ishtar's inner rooms,' he explained. 'All her equipment is there. I know she has implanted some kind of transponders in the minds of a number of people, by which she can control them. I'd like to sever that link, if possible, before we actually destroy her.'

'So,' said a low, hard voice from the doorway, 'you plot treason now, Ninani?'

They all spun around. Ninani paled with shock. In the open doorway stood her father, backed by several of his soldiers.

# 16: The Lake of Souls

As the man stepped out of the boat Ace sized him up. He was tall, well over six feet, and his face was weather-beaten and lined. His hair was pure white, and rather straggly. It had obviously been slept on. The stranger ran his bony fingers through it, trying to get it into shape.

He was dressed in what at one time had clearly been some sort of uniform. It was hard to tell exactly how it had looked, as it was torn, patched and dirty now, but the basic pale brown was still discernible in spots. His boots were in much better shape, and a pair of gloves lay within the boat. A belt finished off his clothing, and strapped to it was a small pistol of some kind that he made no move towards.

'Who are you?' Gilgamesh asked. 'And why don't you prostrate yourself before me?'

Regarding the king with some amusement, the scarecrow replied: 'The name's Urshanabi, strangers. And as for the prostrating part —' He shrugged. 'I've not had much call for that sort of skill. You're the first visitors we've had in all the weeks we've been here. Now, suppose you tell me who you are?'

Annoyed, Gilgamesh stepped forward. Ace could see he was ready to make a grab for his axe. 'I am Gilgamesh, king of men,' he informed Urshanabi, coldly. 'My companions are Aya and the musician Avram.'

'Really?' The man didn't seem impressed. 'Travelling far?'

'We're here,' Ace broke in quickly. 'to see Utnapishtim.' She glanced uneasily at Gilgamesh, whose face made it plain that he was running out of patience.

'Are you indeed?' Urshanabi scratched his chin, and thought for a moment. 'You must have been allowed through by the Guardians.'

'Of course we were,' Gilgamesh pointed out, barely restraining his temper. 'You yourself said you don't get many strangers. How else could we be here?'

'You have a point,' the man agreed, infuriatingly calm. 'But only so far. The Guardians are fine soldiers, but they're a bit limited in their logic functions. Suppose you tell me why you want to see Utnapishtim?'

'Suppose,' Gilgamesh thundered, dangerously, 'you just let us past, and mind your own business?'

'This is my business,' Urshanabi explained. 'I decide who gets to the island.' He pointed across the lake.

Ace saw that even from this close, the waters looked almost black. Too little light penetrated the cone to illuminate it. The effect was one of wild desolation. She shivered. Urshanabi saw it and laughed gently.

'Yes, it's a depressing place. We call it the lake of souls. Sort of chills them within you.'

'Speaking of souls,' Gilgamesh interrupted him, ominously, 'if you wish yours to stay within your body, then I suggest you take us to Utnapishtim right now.'

The man raised an eyebrow and regarded him with an amused expression. 'We do this at my pace,' he answered. 'I make the decisions here. Not some muscle-bound moron with an axe.'

This was too much for the king. 'By the backside of Lugulbanda,' he roared, 'I will take no more of these orders from others!' He grabbed for Urshanabi, who tried to back away, but not quickly enough. Gilgamesh's huge fist closed on his tunic front, and the king hauled him off his feet.

'Stop it!' Ace yelled, jumping to grasp the fist Gilgamesh had poised to strike with. She might as well have tried to stop a tree falling. Shrugging her off the king returned to his consideration of pounding some respect into his captive.

But Urshanabi had lost his veneer of calm; he drew his weapon and trained it on Gilgamesh. For a second Ace was tempted to let him use it but, mindful of the Doctor's instructions, she reluctantly realized that she couldn't take the chance that it was just intended to stun. She smacked the gun down, and Gilgamesh's fist collided with the unfortunate Urshanabi's face.

Ace was amazed that the poor man's head didn't simply cave in. The blow looked and sounded as if it had broken his nose, and blood flowed out and down his dirty uniform. Gilgamesh tossed him aside, his temper still flaming. Drawing his battle-axe he attacked the only other target within range — the boat.

With a cry of despair Ace tried to stop him. Again he brushed her aside, and hacked at the oars until they were match-wood. Still berserk, he launched himself at the little craft's single mast. The tall mast cracked like a tree in a storm and collapsed, half in and half out of the boat. Panting a little at his efforts, but still not satiated, Gilgamesh looked about for another target.

Ace had had quite enough of his petulant behaviour. She scooped up Urshanabi's fallen gun. It seemed pretty simple to operate, so she fired it at the king's feet. With a hiss, the sand fused into globs of writhing glass. Obviously it had not been set on stun. Had she not knocked it away, it might have killed Gilgamesh. Still, the king couldn't be certain she wouldn't use it on him. 'Enough!' she ordered. 'Calm down!'

Gilgamesh looked at her blackly, but he wasn't stupid enough to walk into the path of whatever it was that she now held. Muttering under his breath, he subsided somewhat. Ace ignored him, and turned her attention to the fallen Urshanabi.

Avram had wetted a piece of his own tunic and was using it to wash the fresh blood from the stunned man. Ace was amazed to see that Urshanabi was still conscious, despite the power behind the blow he had been given. Kneeling beside the musician she grimaced at the scarecrow, who was clearly tougher than he looked.

'You'll have to forgive Gilgamesh,' she apologized. 'He's a bit impulsive at the best of times. And these aren't the best of times.'

'I gathered as much,' Urshanabi agreed weakly. His voice sounded nasal, which was hardly surprising. He pushed aside

Avram's dabbing efforts and managed to struggle into a sitting position, from which he surveyed the damage.

'Sorry about that, too,' Ace added, glumly. 'He got a bit carried away.'

'Which is more than you will be,' Urshanabi managed, in a pained voice.

'What do you mean?'

He gestured at the boat. 'That boat is the only way out to Utnapishtim's island. So even if I wanted to take you, I simply can't now that idiot's destroyed the mast and oars. We're stuck on the shore here.'

With a sinking heart, Ace realized that he was telling the truth. 'Can't we replace them?' she asked.

Urshanabi almost managed a small laugh at that. He gestured all around. 'And do you see any trees?'

He was quite right: the volcanic landscape showed a few scrub-bushes, grasses and plants, but nothing of any size that would be workable as a mast or oars. The last tree she had seen that would suit such a purpose had been three days earlier... The thought of trekking back three days, and then trying to haul the wood here was too much even to consider.

So — now what? She stared over the black waters and wished heartily that she could sink Gilgamesh under the surface. Preferably with concrete blocks on both feet.

The Doctor realized that he was the only person standing, and that his companions were all prostrate on the floor in front of the King. Cheerfully, he struck out a hand. 'How do you do?' he asked politely. 'You must be King Agga. I've heard a lot about you. I understand you've got a problem that I can help you to sort out.'

Ignoring him completely, the king moved forward slowly. The tip of the mace of office he carried rested briefly on Ninani's shoulder. 'Rise,' he told her, in a weary voice. As she hastily complied, he shook his head. 'Daughter, what are you doing here?'

'Trying to help,' she said, miserably.

Agga snorted. 'And talking treason is supposed to help?'

'We were not talking treason!' she flared. 'We were talking about destroying the hold that Ishtar has over you.'

Agga gestured with his mace at Enkidu. 'And I suppose this isn't the ape-man that moves at Gilgamesh's behest?'

Ninani glanced uncertainly down at the Neanderthal. 'Well, yes — but he says he wants to help us.'

'I'm sure he does,' Agga agreed smoothly. 'He wants to help Gilgamesh to my throne. We all know that the king of Uruk views us as his rival. Or as a prize to be plucked.' He stared down at En-Gula. 'And who is that?'

'She is a priestess from the temple of Ishtar, lord,' Ninani replied meekly.

Nodding, the King spun about to face the Doctor, who politely raised his hat and smiled. 'I see. And you wouldn't happen to be the supposedly-unconscious man that Ishtar was interested in, shortly before her temple was damaged?'

'Ah, yes...' the Doctor answered. 'Well, I can explain that. You see —'

Agga gestured for silence with his mace. 'There's really no need to explain anything to me. I'm not interested. But I will explain something to you.' His eyes burned darkly into the Doctor's. 'For what you and your companions did to her temple, Ishtar almost destroyed my city. I will not risk that happening again. She tells me that she has a box that can lay waste to the all the lands of men. I believe her when she says this, and will not risk raising her fury by even listening to fools that plot against her.'

'If you do not fight her, she will consume you,' the Doctor assured him.

'No,' Agga replied. 'If we try to fight her, she will destroy us all. I cannot take that chance.'

'You're making a big mistake if you give in to her blackmail.'

Uninterested, Agga turned to his guards. 'Take the ape-man and his companions to the cells,' he ordered. 'I will stay and speak with the princess alone.' He watched impassively as they obeyed him. The Doctor gave him one final glance of pity and scorn before being led away. Then the door was closed. With a heavy heart, Agga turned back to his daughter.

'Ninani,' he sighed. 'I love you as I loved your mother. I realize that what you did, you did out of concern for me. But —' and steel crept into his voice, '— do not ever even think of helping me in such a way again. I make my own decisions, and you will obey them utterly. Otherwise, beloved daughter or not, you will be punished. Do I make myself quite clear?'

Her face burning with emarrassment and suppressed anger, Ninani nodded tightly. He was treating her like a stupid child!

'Good.' The fury in her eyes was not lost on him. 'I understand how you feel, daughter. You only did what you felt was right. But if you were the ruler of Kish and not I, you would soon discover that there are many, many things to consider when you make decisions. A wise king cloaks his thoughts and keeps his counsel close. Your idea of attacking Ishtar might have seemed clever, but it is insanely dangerous. She has powers that we do not understand, and her anger, if it is kindled against us, could destroy us all.'

Ninani could keep her own anger bottled no longer. 'So we sit here, doing nothing, and allowing her to act as she wills?' she cried. 'Why do you think that her plans will not kill us all anyway? Surely it is better to die fighting for our freedom than to die like slaves?'

'It is never better to die for any reason,' her father reprimanded her. 'While we are alive, we can hope.'

'Hope?' Emboldened by his soft words and inflamed on her own passion, Ninani charged on. 'How can we hope when out of fear for her you imprison those that might aid us?'

Agga glared at her, his emotions churning. Finally, tightly, he told her: 'Mind what you say, daughter. Any further outbursts from you and — princess though you may be — you will be placed in the stocks alongside your friends. And whipped till that tongue of yours stops its prattling. Now be silent, and do as I tell you!'

Turning, he stormed out of her room. The waiting guards closed the door behind him.

Ninani realized that her hands were so tightly clenched that her nails were drawing blood from her palms. Forcing her fury down, she slowly unclenched her fists. She stared at her bloody palms, not seeing them at all.

If her father thought he had beaten her spirit, he was wrong. And he was wrong to think that appeasing Ishtar was the best course to take. The goddess had to be fought, whatever the cost. Taking a deep breath, Ninani tried to calm down. She had to plan. Of all the conspirators, she was the only one left free. It was all up to her now. She knew that her father would truly punish her if he felt that he had to, but she had to take that chance. More and more certainly, she knew that Ishtar was evil and threatened to destroy everything. How could her father even think of trying to placate her?

Moving to the door, she listened carefully. As she had rather expected, she heard the sounds of someone fidgeting outside. Her father had made her a prisoner in her own room.

But that would not stop her. She had only to find a way out.

Urshanabi was getting over the punch that had floored him, and he started to toss the wooden fragments from Gilgamesh's destruction into a small pile. Ace watched his tidying up with no interest, frustrated at having come so far only to be stuck because of the temper tantrum Gilgamesh had thrown.

Avram was talking in a low voice with the ferryman, obviously gleaning background details for another of his songs from the man. Gilgamesh sat on a rock, lost in his own thoughts. Ace enjoyed the thought of pushing him into the water and dropping rocks onto his head.

She watched Urshanabi enlist Avram's help to get what was left of the shattered mast out of the boat. One long fragment almost brought something to her mind, but she couldn't think what. She concentrated furiously, and then it came.

Grinning, she dashed down to the two men. 'Oi,' she called, exitedly. 'How deep is this here lake?'

Urshanabi shrugged. 'Not deep. A little more than the height of a man, I'd say. It's not had time to get very deep. But don't think abut swimming out to the island.'

That wasn't what was in her mind, but she was puzzled and asked: 'Why not?'

As an answer, he tossed a stick into the waters. The blackness bubbled all about it for a moment, then subsided. He saw her look of shock, and smiled grimly. 'Utnapishtim stocked the waters with a species of killer fish,' he explained. 'To stop unwelcome visitors.'

Ace shivered. 'With those robots at the gate, and his pet barracudas here, he must really like his privacy.'

Urshanabi gave her an odd look. 'We're just defending ourselves,' he told her.

*Against what?* Ace wondered. Aloud, she said: 'Well, we needn't swim across. Why don't we make a punt?'

'A punt?'

'Yeah.' Grinning, Ace explained. 'They're dead popular a few thousand years in the future. You push the boat along with a long pole. About the length of what's left of the mast, in fact. And if the water's only eight feet deep, it should be a doddle.'

Rubbing his chin, Urshanabi considered the idea. 'It might work,' he finally agreed. 'But it'll take some heavy work to push us over to the island.'

Ace grinned maliciously at Gilgamesh. 'Well, I know someone who's very strong, and has lots of excess energy to work off...'

Though he did not feel at all confident about Ace's plan, Gilgamesh could raise no real objections when she explained it to him. For all of his faults, he was not a stupid man. He realized that he had, after all, almost wrecked the expedition, and he had been cursing himself silently for his impulsive actions. Here, now, was a chance to redeem himself. He had to agree to try it, at least. Carefully, with Urshanabi sitting in the prow, and with Ace and Avram behind him, Gilgamesh climbed into the stern, and used the mast fragment to push off from the shore.

There was a bubbling motion about the boat that had little to do with the water and considerably to do with the hungry fish investigating the intruder. But the pole was inedible and they eventually swam away out of boredom.

Though not used to punting, Gilgamesh caught on quickly. Muscles rippling, he raised the wood, then sank it until it touched bottom. Pushing hard, he raised and swung and lowered... The boat skimmed out across the black waters of the lake of souls, towards whatever might await them on the heart of the island.

Ace couldn't help wondering what sort of a reception might greet them. So far, all the signs that Utnapishtim had given seemed to be of the *survivors will be prosecuted* variety. Why was he so paranoid about visitors? And could they really expect him to aid them in their fight against Ishtar?

The Doctor waggled his feet experimentally, and then looked around. 'I've been in worse dungeons,' he told his companions cheerfully. 'And these stocks aren't really all that tight.'

In the gloom, he could just about make out Enkidu's grimace. 'Fine,' the warrior answered. 'That's the good news. The bad news is that they're probably going to leave us in here forever.'

'Defeatist,' the Doctor replied.

'Oh?' Enkidu laughed bitterly. 'And can your magic powers get us out of here?'

Regarding with an offended expression the crude wooden device that imprisoned his feet, the Doctor had to be honest. 'No. They're a bit too simple for me. Electronic locks, or even a good, old-fashioned padlock — those I could be out of in an instant. But they've not been invented yet.' Each set of stocks was simply two blocks of shaped wood that held their feet together. The pieces were joined by the simple but effective means of driving large wooden wedges through holes in both halves of the stocks. The only way out would be to hammer the wedges loose from below the stocks.

From a separate set of stocks facing the Doctor and Enkidu, En-Gula made a sobbing noise. The Doctor wished he had a hankie he could pass her. 'There, there,' he said, hoping he sounded comforting. 'It's probably not as bad as all that.' Privately, he was rather worried. For all her air of confidence in the past En-Gula was actually little more than a girl who had been forced into adulthood by her profession. Inside she was still a child and needed reassurance. He'd never been all that good in such situations. He wished that Agga had at least given her a cell of her own. Then he could have ignored her problems and concentrated on his own for a while. Rummaging about in his pocket, he found a tattered paper bag. Holding it out, he offered: 'Liquorice allsort?'

En-Gula ignored him and sobbed quietly. How far she had fallen! A few weeks ago, she had been a cheerful acolyte in the temple of Ishtar, enjoying her work, and desired by men. Now here she was, imprisoned in the cells under the palace, with a hairy half-human creature and a strange madman. The whims of the gods were too much for her. Her dreams had crashed about her and nightmares were gnawing at her spirit.

Meanwhile Enkidu was not idle. Carefully, he tested the strengths of the individual joints on the stocks. His hairy skin covered powerful muscles, but they would not be of much help here. He simply could not apply his strength usefully, trapped like this. Still, he considered, he had been in worse spots before. He was a warrior, and was quite prepared for whatever came to pass. If he had to endure hours, or even days, in these stocks, then he might as well put the time to good use. He was just about to try to settle down for a nap when he heard the Doctor muttering to himself.

'Come on, come on,' the Doctor snapped, annoyed. 'There must be a way out of this thing. There's too much to do to be idling my time away here.'

Enkidu laughed. 'You are talking to youself, my friend.'

'That's because I like intelligent conversations,' retorted the Doctor tartly. 'I can't waste all day like this.'

Shrugging, Enkidu observed: 'We have little choice in the matter. Do as I shall: get rest while you can. Who knows when we shall need our strength?'

'Oh, very philosophical,' the Time Lord muttered. 'Eat, drink and be merry, for tomorrow we shall die — is that it?'

'A good way to live,' Enkidu suggested. 'What will be, will be. Our portion is to endure what the gods send, and to do our best. Then we shall be remembered after our souls have passed into the keeping of Belit-Sheri, who records all in the book of the dead.'

'Well, I'd like to do something a little more constructive than that,' the Doctor told him.

'We all would, but some things are inevitable. Death cannot be denied.'

'Oh, I don't know,' the Doctor grinned. 'I've put it off once or twice myself — though it never left me the same man again.'

Enkidu couldn't follow this strange line of speech. He sighed. 'I do have one regret about dying, though.'

'Only one? If I was about to die, I'd produce a list the size of the Encyclopedia Brittanica. Well, what is your regret?'

'That I am the last of my kind. After me, my race is gone forever from the Earth.' Enkidu stared sadly at his feet. 'My people will never be remembered.'

The Doctor poked him in the ribs. 'Then I've got some good news for you.' As Enkidu looked up in disbelief, the Doctor went on: 'You're not the last of your kind. Right now, a character called Nimrod is sleeping. He'll be awakened five thousand years in the future. Ace and I have met him. He's quite a nice chap, though he's a dreadful butler. He'll carry on the legacy for you.'

Struggling with this, Enkidu finally smiled. 'Then I am not the last?'

'Not by a few thousand years.'

'Good.' With a contented sigh, Enkidu closed his eyes. 'Now I can die in peace.'

The Doctor glared disgustedly at him, but it was of no use. The Neanderthal had fallen asleep. Envying this ability, the Doctor continued to try and think of a way out of the cell. Perhaps Enkidu could take matters lightly, but he couldn't. He had a grim feeling that matters were coming to a head, and he had to be free when things began to happen.

# 17: Utnapishtim

Urshanabi moored the boat to a pylon on the island, and led the small party ashore. There was little to see but rocks, and no sign of anywhere that Utnapishtim could be living. The four of them moved through the volcanic debris across ground that was rising slightly. Finally they reached the lip of a large depression. Urshanabi merely gestured downwards. Reaching the crest Ace followed his gaze, and stifled an exclamation.

They were on the edge of a huge pit, almost a mile across. It was impossible to judge how deep it was because the entire depression was filled with what looked like a gossamer city. Minarets of light and air shimmered in front of them. Towers, pathways and ramps seemed to have been spun from magical materials. Long paths entwined among the jagged buildings, leading into the brighter depths. It was as if they were gazing into a fairy city, unreal and insubstantial.

Gilgamesh swore, and even Avram muttered a protecting prayer. Both men halted behind Ace, reluctant to move further.

'What — what is that place?' Ace managed to say.

Urshanabi smiled. 'That is no place. That is our ship.'

'Ship?' Gilgamesh echoed. 'But — where are the oars? The slaves? The sails? How can it move?'

'Through the air, my impetuous friend,' Urshanabi explained. 'Through the voids between the stars.' Then he grimaced. 'When it's in good shape, that is. Right now, there it is, and there it stays.' He moved into the lead again. 'Come, follow me.'

'Down there?' asked Gilgamesh, warily.

'Of course. How else will you meet Utnapishtim? He dwells within the ship.' The ferryman looked up in amusement. 'Don't tell me that Gilgamesh, king of men, is afraid?'

'Nobody calls Gilgamesh a coward,' the king growled, reaching for his axe. 'I am merely being cautious.'

Ace smacked his hand. 'Then be cautious after me,' she suggested, and began the descent behind Urshanabi. Scowling, Gilgamesh started after her, with Avram, still dazed, bringing up the rear. The going was slow, for all but Urshanabi were mesmerized by the flashing display of lights below. It was as if the city were a living creature, and the pastel colours some kind of blood flowing just below the skin. Ripples of lights played across the street, buildings and ground. It was weird, unearthly, and indescribably beautiful.

It occurred to Ace that she was probably suffering more from culture shock than even Gilgamesh and Avram were. Both men had simply accepted that the whole matter was completely beyond them, and now nothing that they saw suprised them. To them, the craft was simply magic. Ace, on the other hand, had seen much in her travels with the Doctor — the wonders of Iceworld, the terrors of Paradise Towers, the evil of the Psychic Circus. But this was of a completely different order from anything she had yet witnessed.

The sheer scale of the place was stunning. They entered through what was obviously an airlock, but instead of stepping into sterile metal corridors and the kind of spaceship that Ace had come to expect, they had walked into a wonderland. The outer skin of the ship was suffused with the glowing, writhing lights. Inside, the walls, floor and roof were all aglow with this dancing brightness, illuminating what lay within. Roads stretched through parks. Buildings punctured what was supposedly the interior sky. There was even the sound of running water, and she saw a stream flowing beside the road.

The plants and trees were subtly different from anything she had ever encountered. Vast orchid-like plants grew next to spiny bushes. Something that seemed like a cross between moss and grass grew underfoot. Weird, exotically-shaped trees wound about one another, reaching for the shifting artificial sky. She could see people moving in the buildings and on the walkways.

'Incredible,' she finally managed. 'Wicked!'

Urshanabi smiled off-handedly. 'We quite like it. Anu looked a lot like this once.'

'Looked?' Ace echoed.

'We'd best get along to Utnapishtim,' their guide said, evading the question. He gestured them to what seemed to be a large set of bathroom scales with the readout on a rod at one end. 'Climb aboard.'

Ace did as she was directed, stepping lightly onto the base. Both men, still silent, joined her, and Urshanabi took his place behind the stalk. His fingers flickered, and Ace felt a slight, not unpleasant feeling about her ankles, holding her in place as the small vehicle rose into the air.

'Magic indeed!' Avram breathed, staring at the fields flashing below them.

'Directed gravity fields,' Urshanabi murmured. 'Faster than walking. And far less tiring.'

'Yeah,' agreed Ace, enjoying the sensation. 'Better than a funfair.'

They headed directly towards one of the larger buildings, zipping over the lower edifices and whipping between the taller ones. Just as it looked as if they would collide with a wall in front of them it grew a hole which dilated, and they flashed inside, coming to an instant halt. There was no giddiness; the vehicle simply sank to the floor, and the tightness about their ankles ceased.

'This way,' their guide said, gesturing for them to follow as he left the room.

It was like almost any office building Ace had ever been in — not that she was a frequent visitor to such places. Soft carpeting covered floors, and the walls were of pastel hues, mostly blues and greens. There was no obvious source of lighting; it was as if the whole building gave off the soft glow that illuminated the place. Urshanabi stopped at a double door, and placed his hand against a small plate set in the wall. After a short hum the doors slid open, and he led them inside.

Not knowing what to expect, Ace was vaguely disappointed

to walk into an ordinary office. A large one, granted, but an office. It was some forty feet across, and the whole of the far wall was a window looking out over the cityscape. Directly in front of this was a massive desk some ten feet wide and four deep. The surface was pure white, with nothing at all visible on it. Several chairs faced the desk.

To one side was what looked like a white blackboard, and close by it was something that looked like the bar on Iceworld. Bottles of exotic designs and contents filled several shelves behind it. Several glasses lay ready on it, and Urshanabi moved over, indicating that the visitors approach the desk. He didn't have to suggest this; they were all drawn there by the man seated behind it.

He was tall, and would have been almost seven feet high if he had been standing. He wore a uniform similar to Urshanabi's, but crisp and clean. The whiteness of it was almost dazzling. His face was lined and etched with time and fatigue, but his golden eyes were bright and curious. His hair and beard were both short, and pure white also. He looked like a colourless Santa Claus.

'So,' he offered, in mild, conversational tones. 'You wished to see me? I am Utnapishtim.'

'Yeah,' Ace agreed, holding out her hand. 'I'm Ace. These are Avram, a singer, and Gilgamesh, the King of Uruk.'

Utnapishtim nodded politely to the men, and ignored Ace's hand. She was unsure if he didn't understand her gesture or simply chose to ignore it. Embarrassed, she let her hand drop. Despite herself she felt in awe of the man. He had an air of authority about him that even Gilgamesh seemed to sense.

'Are you a god?' the king asked, staring about the room in wonder. 'Is this heaven?'

Utnapishtim laughed good-naturedly. 'No, I am no god. And this is merely where I work. Far from heaven, and sometimes uncomfortably like hell, I fear.' He looked at Avram. 'I believe you were almost here once before. The Guardians reported a singer who talked with them a few weeks ago.'

Avram swallowed, and nodded, nervously. 'I told the lady Aya about you,' he stammered. 'She and the lord Ea were most interested, and she has come to seek your help.'

Urshanabi interrupted them, quietly handing out drinks from a silver tray. Ace took one, politely, and sipped it. It tasted like fruit juice of some sort, and was very welcome after the trek she'd endured. Utnapishtim accepted a drink also, and smiled when he saw that Gilgamesh eyed his suspiciously.

'A harmless blend of fruit extracts,' he assured the king, sipping at his own glass to reassure Gilgamesh. 'You looked in need of it. Now, why don't you take seats, and explain your purpose in visiting me here.' He eyed Ace, somewhat wryly. 'You don't seem to be from this land. And I did not think that this civilization recognized women as the equals of men.'

'It doesn't,' Ace answered. 'I'm not from this country — or time.'

'Temporal travel?' asked Utnapishtim, curiously. 'Could it be? I have heard mention that such things are possible, though only...' he broke off. 'Still, go on.'

'Well, the Doctor and I are sort of wanderers in space and time,' Ace explained. 'We landed here, and discovered that there's a serious problem that we think you could help us with.'

'I'm not sure that we can — or should — help you at all,' sighed Utnapishtim.

Ace suddenly sensed trouble. 'Do you mean that you're unwilling to help,' she asked, 'or unable?'

'Both.' He stood up, and hesitated a moment. 'Urshanabi, perhaps you would be kind enough to see to our two guests here?' He gestured towards Gilgamesh and Avram. 'I would speak with...Ace? Ace, privately.'

Urshanabi nodded. 'Of course.' To the men, he said: 'Perhaps a little food would make you more comfortable?'

'A feast?' Gilgamesh asked, an eager gleam in his eye. 'With beer? And — are there any women here?'

'Lots,' the ferryman answered, his eyes sparkling. Let the king try making passes at any of them, and he'd regret it.

'Then I may enjoy my stay.' Gilgamesh stood up, eager to begin his explorations. Avram looked less certain, but Ace nodded in what she hoped was an encouraging manner. Urshanabi led them out of the room, and the door hissed shut.

Utnapishtim gestured for Ace to join him at the window. For a moment, they both looked out of the buildings. 'My heritage, and my problem,' the old man explained. 'There are almost seventeen thousand of us in this city. The genetic banks hold the stored materials for almost a million more.' He looked at her directly, and she could see real pain in his eyes. 'And this marvellous city-ship of ours has power to sustain us for barely six more weeks.'

She looked at him, suddenly beginning to see what he meant. 'And then?'

'Then we must leave.' Suddenly tired, he turned his haunted eyes onto her face. 'We must all leave this ship, and look for a home, here on Earth.' He sighed, and sank into his chair. 'And I do not like that. We are an ancient people, and must adapt this planet to our needs. We will be forced to fight, I can see that. We are a technological race, and the native humans will never accept us as we are. There will be problems, and conflicts.'

A chill shook Ace. 'You're talking about war...'

'Yes, Ace. Now do you see why we cannot help these humans? Gods of Anu forgive us, we are going to have to steal their planet from them.'

Ace felt her confidence draining away, along with the blood from her face. 'War?' she repeated blankly.

'I don't like the idea any more than you do,' Utnapishtim answered. 'I am, after all, a civilized man. But I am no fool.' He gestured out of the window at the cityscape again. 'I know that any attempt to move all of this out into the primitive world beyond our island will cause terrible problems. Yet I have no options. My duty to my own people is paramount. The heritage of Anu must survive, and if it must be here...' He shrugged. 'Then so be it.' He turned again to face her, and she could see the horror in his own eyes. 'I do not like what I do, but as the leader here, I must make that decision. And then live with the consequences, for good or for ill.'

'You don't understand,' she finally managed to say. 'You can't do what you're talking about.'

'Ace,' he said, sadly, 'I know how repugnant the idea is to you, but I have no other — '

'It won't work,' she told him, desperately hoping that her uncertainty would not show. 'I'm a time traveller, remember? Well, I won't be born for another five thousand years or so. On this planet. To the human race. Not your descendants.'

Ace's interpretation of temporal causality, however shaky, impressed Utnapishtim. Realizing what she meant he turned once again to stare out of the window. 'The Earth stays human?' he said, softly. 'Then what becomes — became — of my people?'

'I don't know,' she replied. 'I've never even heard of Anu before. And though I've travelled about quite a bit, I don't recall ever having heard of your descendants.'

Sinking wearily into his chair, Utnapishtim propped his head on his right hand. 'Is this it?' he asked, not really talking to her. 'After everything, have we survived for nothing? Will we simply perish here?'

Feeling sorry for him, Ace tried to help. 'It's a big universe. You could be anywhere out there in my time, and I'd never know. What happened to bring you here? Tell me about it,' she suggested. He would never offer to help the Doctor while he was in this state. 'I know I don't look like much, but maybe I can help you.' She ignored the thought *fat chance* that her subconscious sent her. She was also pushing back another uncomfortable thought: maybe this was the crisis that would affect all future life on Earth! Maybe, in some split-off plane of reality, Utnapishtim and his people *did* take over the planet?

It was a harrowing idea, but the Doctor seemed to be certain that the danger they had to combat was Ishtar. Then again, the Doctor had been wrong in the past — what if he was wrong this time? And so far there hadn't been a sign of anything that might be considered a Timewyrm.

She fought this idea away and tried again with Utnapishtim. He looked about ready to break down, here and now. The strain on him must be terrific. 'Tell me,' she asked again. 'What do you mean about the heritage of Anu?'

'Why not?' he ran a distracted hand through his short, white hair, and tried to collect himself. 'It will at least pass some time.' He gestured for her to sit, and when she did so, he continued.

'This ship, this city we are in, represents all that is left of our home world, Anu. It lay many thousands of light years from here, Ace, and was once very beautiful indeed. This ark is all that we now have, and that for not much longer.'

'Anu was probably not the paradise that we all tend to think of it as. There were undoubtedly problems, many of them, but we were happy enough there. Out cities were much like this — pleasant, green places, where we could work and relax, and be happy. Our sciences had progressed to a satisfactory level, and life was simple but elegant for all.

'Then came Qataka.' He buried himself in his memories for a moment, lost in his own mind. Then, realizing this, he straightened up, and threw Ace a wan smile. 'Where she was from, no one is sure. She was probably just another person initially. But she had a terrible fear of dying, and would not accept that even with our life spans of almost a thousand years, death would come to us in the end. She had heard stories, probably, as we all have, of a race of beings calling themselves Time Lords, who live forever. They're just tales, told to amuse children, all over space.'

'No, they aren't,' Ace said, quietly. 'The bloke I travel with is one of them. His name's the Doctor.'

Utnapishtim raised an eyebrow. 'Forgive me. At any other time I would be excited by the thought of a mythical being turning out to be flesh and blood. But at this moment...' He sighed again. 'Worries drive pleasures out very effectively, I am afraid. Well, however, she got the idea, Qataka decided that she would not die. She experimented with cybernetics — replacing parts of living flesh with mechanical analogs.'

'Yeah, I know what cybernetics is.' Ace could still recall the cold grip of the Cybermen she had faced quite recently. The end result of tissue replacement, they were grim, implacable, logical hell on two legs, and numbered among the Doctor's greatest foes.

'Well, she made breakthroughs. Oh, our people had toyed with cybernetics in the past, but abandoned the field. With our medical knowledge, we were able to regrow lost limbs, and to keep the body functioning pretty well up to the ultimate point of death.'

Puzzled, Ace asked: 'If you could regrow things, then how come you have to die?'

Utnapishtim nodded. 'You make a good point. We could regrow most things, but the dividing line between *most* and *all* was in brain tissue. It inevitably degenerated beyond the stage where we could do anything. Our living minds simply wore out. You might say we die not of disease or accident, but simply through tiredness.'

'Qataka would never accept this, despite our knowledge. Instead, she managed to come up with a way to stay alive. Instead of attempting to regrow her mental tissues, she simply replaced it periodically.'

'How?'

'Putting it crudely, she steals it from other living beings.' Seeing Ace's look of revulsion, he nodded. 'Our thoughts exactly. When we discovered what she was doing, she was instantly condemned for her actions, and sentenced to the death she so feared. Would that it had been that simple to carry it out!' He was lost in his memories again for a short while. Finally, he looked up. 'She had known, of course, that one day the authorities would discover what was happening. And she had planned for it. While she had worked on keeping her brain alive with these periodic implants, she had made another discovery that was, if anything, more terrible than her first.'

'She had faced a problem with storage of her own memories — with the breakdown of the brain cells data would inevitably be lost. The fresh cells would be wiped clean of the owner's thoughts, and would be blank until she could imprint them. What she did, then, was to link her own living mind to a computer backup memory. It kept, if you like, a second set of everything she had on file. And she discovered that she could use this mind as if it were her own. She built little radio receivers that she could implant in the skulls of others, and then connect to this second mind of hers in the computer, which could then take over the infected person. She could see through their eyes, think through their brain, experience through their bodies...'

After a moment, Ace prompted him: 'And then what?'

'Oh, we were blind fools. We managed to isolate Qataka, and she was put to death, screaming and pleading for mercy. Mercy! She didn't ever understand the word.' Looking sick, he wiped his brow. 'But at the end she stopped her begging, and threatened us. While she was being put to death, she promised that she would have her revenge. I myself was the one appointed judicially to kill her, and as I did so I saw in her eyes that she was telling the truth. I knew that she really believed that she would have her revenge, even after death. But I could convince few people of this.

'I was scared, Ace, terribly afraid. I believed her when she promised destruction, though I had no idea what she meant. So I had this ark built, just in case. If she was somehow able to destroy Anu, then I would save what I could. We built it in space, orbiting our world, and I convinced my fellow leaders that it was an experimental colony. They thought I was foolhardy, but allowed me to stock it and to recruit followers.

'It's a good thing I did. We were almost finished when Qataka carried out her promise. You see, we had not known about the computer back-up mind when she had been captured and executed. She, of course, made no mention of it. But this computer-thing was *her* — down to every last detail, every final thought. And it hated us, with a bitter depth of passion. Slowly, it had built up the linkages in the minds it controlled. Some it put to work to house a body for the mind. The rest it put to work building a lethal weapon, one banned from our world for generations without number: a cobalt device.

'I was supervising the stocking of this city-ship when the news came to us. Qataka had emerged from her hiding place, and struck back at our world. She, too, had a ship of sorts, populated by her slaves. Her computer personality went aboard it, and then detonated her cobalt bomb.'

It was several minutes before he could bring himself to speak. Even then, there were tears in his eyes, and a catch in his throat. 'We saw . . . we saw the surface of our lovely world, burning, writhing in the fires of death. The elements themselves turned against it. Everyone still on the planet perished utterly. Anu was ravaged in moments, and left a smouldering, lifeless charred ball in space.

'But Qataka had not known of my plans, as I had been ignorant of hers. She was as surprised by our existence as we were horrified to find her. Then she tried to attack us, too. I had been warned, just before the death of Anu, by my companions on the council, that Qataka still lived as a conputer being. She had not been able to restrain herself from gloating to her victims before she triggered the bomb, and they had a few brief seconds in which to warn me before they perished. But it enabled me to be prepared. I created an electronic organism — a programmed disease that would eat at her mind and destroy it —'

A computer virus?' Ace said.

'A computer virus — yes, exactly, that's just what it was. I managed to use a signal carrier to implant it in her ship.

'It almost worked. If I had had more time to perfect it, perhaps she would have died then. Instead, it simply broke down her linkages with her mind-slaves. Then she attacked us. We fought back. Our battle was one of manoeuvres into and out of hyperspace as we fought and dodged. Eventually, above this planet, we won. Qataka's ship broke apart under our fire, and she was finally extinguished. But it had been too much, too late. My ship, my city, had been damaged, and our fuel supply contaminated and rendered useless. We were forced to make an emergency landing. We selected this site because it is far from the native cities — we had no wish to disturb them. We landed intact, but our power has been draining slowly ever since. Nothing we have been able to do has helped at all. It will not be long before we must leave this craft forever.

'Sadly, our only choice is to try and take this world from the human race. To this end, I posted the Guardian robots to watch the approach. If we had the power, we have enough of them in storage to conquer this planet alone. But we cannot use them with so little energy available to us. We will have to fight, using the primitive weapons of this day, and our technological skills. What else can we do?' He looked up at Ace in sorrow. 'It is a terrible dilemma that we find ourselves in.'

'It's worse than you think,' she told him, grimly. 'You didn't destroy this Qataka you told me about. She's alive and well, and living in Kish as the goddess Ishtar.'

Utnapishtim almost fainted with the shock. 'You're lying!' he finally insisted, wildly.

'No, I'm not. She's there, taking over new slaves and getting ready to take over a new world. Face it, mate — pretty soon it'll be academic whether you or the human race gets control of the Earth. If she's left unchecked, she'll control *everything*.'

After a long slience the colour returned to Utnapishtim's cheeks. Ace urged him to take more of the fruit juice, but he declined. 'I'm as well as I can be,' he assured her. 'After such terrible news.'

'Well,' she challenged him, 'what are you going to do about it?'

'Do?' he echoed bleakly. 'What can I do?' He gestured about him. 'When my ship was at full strength, we barely managed to stop her. Now, we would be lucky to even make her notice us. There is nothing that we can do to stop her now.'

'No!' Ace insisted angrily. 'You can't just give up! She's still weak.' Casting about for ideas, she grabbed his tunic. 'Those Guardian robots of yours. Whey not send them after her? They'd be able to dissect her in seconds, right?'

He shook his head. 'Ace, it's not possible. She'd be able to override their circuitry and turn them on us if she knew they were here. I dare not send them to her. And we cannot take this ship so far — our energy levels are far too low for that. Besides, even if we could get to this Kish you speak of, then what could we do? Throw rocks at her? Or talk her to death?'

'That computer virus,' Ace said, grinning. She felt inspired. 'You said that it might have defeated her if you had a chance to work on it.'

Utnapishtim hesitated a moment, and then shook his head once more. 'No, Ace. I can't do it. Even if I could somehow re-work the virus. I have to get it into her system. That would need doing face to face, because she's bound to have some protection against any such interference again.'

'Then get off your backside, and start working,' Ace yelled. 'You can't just give up. Not with the fate of my species in your hands. I won't let you. This is my world she's threatening now, and my future. I won't let her destroy it just because you've lost the courage to fight for what you believe in.'

With a sigh and a shrug, Utnapishtim clambered to his feet, slowly. 'Very well,' he agreed. 'I'll look into that computer virus. But even assuming I can come up with one that will do what we want, how do we get it to Qataka?'

'I'll figure something out,' promised Ace. 'You get the weapon we can use, and I'll make certain Ishtar gets it right where it will hurt the most.' Grimly, she closed her eyes and knotted her fists. For the sake of the human race, she couldn't afford to mess this one up. She could only pray that the Doctor would have some idea what they could do with the virus...

# 18: Escape

Ninani eyed the vase of ointment she held in both hands, and regretted that it was the only large container that she had. She hadn't even opened it yet, and it was supposed to be a rare and beautiful fragrance, imported from the Indus region. Still, she needed it for a purpose more urgent than scenting herself. Freeing her left hand she eased the door open until she could see through the crack in the frame.

There was just the one sentry, and not particularly alert. Her father didn't really expect her to try going anywhere, and the sentry knew he was on an easy assignment, not to be taken seriously. More fool him. Taking a better grip on the neck of the vase, Ninani used her foot quietly to ease the door far enough open for her to slip through. Her bare feet made no sound on the floor, and she tiptoed to within striking distance.

As she had feared the fragile container shattered when she slammed it down on the man's head. He fell, covered in sticky, odorous ointment, amidst the shards of the pottery. Ninani bent to make certain that he was breathing regularly. She had no wish permanently to injure the man, who was simply following orders. With relief, she noted that he was merely unconscious. Her sensitive fingers found swelling and bruising on his scalp, but the bone did not appear damaged.

She returned to her room for her sandals, and then quickly ran down the corridor, staying in the shadows. She saw no one at all as she made her way down the stone stairs. There was no guard on the cell door: there was no need for one, since it was impossible to open from within, and who would dare disobey the edicts of the king by releasing the prisoners?

Ninani reflected that a few days ago not even she would have dared. But with the menace that was Ishtar growing stronger and more evil day after day, she had no other option. She eased the restraining bar out of its sockets. Quietly, she opened the door.

All three of them were within. Enkidu and En-Gula were sleeping, but the Doctor was still trying to free himself. He had eased off a shoe and sock, and was trying to remember what Harry Houdini had taught him about compressing his foot to get it through a narrow gap. Seeing the light from the door, he glanced up in surprise.

'Princess,' he murmured. 'Is it visiting hour already?'

'Quietly,' she cautioned him. 'I've come to set you free.'

'Are you sure that's wise?' he asked, watching her pick up the mallet and a wedge of wood. 'I don't think your father will be very happy.'

'My father is generally a very wise man,' Ninani answered. 'But in this instance, he is allowing his fears to outvoice his reason.' Dropping to one knee, she placed the wedge she carried underneath the wedge holding shut the stocks. Then, with careful taps, she knocked it free.

The noise woke the two sleepers. Their questions were cut off by the Doctor hissing for silence. As silently as possible Ninani knocked out the second of the wedges, allowing Enkidu to haul the top half of the stocks away from his and the Doctor's feet. The warrior then took the hammer and wedge from Ninani, and set about freeing the priestess. The Doctor hopped about on one foot, replacing his shoe and sock. As soon as En-Gula was free the Doctor beckoned everyone to him.

'Right,' he told them in a low voice, 'we have to move quickly. We don't know when somebody might come along to check up on us, so let's make the most of whatever time we have. En-Gula, can you lead us to the temple of Ishtar by a route that keeps us out of public view?'

'Of course, lord,' she agreed. 'Follow me.'

As she led the way out of the dungeon, the others fell in behind her. Enkidu had kept the mallet he'd used, since it was the only think they had that could serve as a weapon in case of trouble.

Bringing up the rear, the Doctor allowed himself a little indulgence in hope. 'I knew I'd think of a way out of this,' he congratulated himself. A little more luck like this, and Ishtar would be finished.

Agga sat in his throne, drinking new wine from a silver goblet. He had no idea what it tasted like, since his occasional mouthfuls of the liquid were swallowed swiftly. He knew that it was a mistake to drown his fears in strong drink, but since it was the only plan he'd been able to come up with, he was grimly carrying it out.

If he was honest with himself, he knew Ninani was quite correct: Ishtar would enslave them all before she was done. But what could he do? Taking another swallow, he reflected that Ishtar was quite capable of killing Ninani if the whim took her, and he couldn't risk that. And, besides, there was that magical box of hers that could destroy all of creation should Ishtar be killed. Having looked into her eyes, he knew that this was no idle threat.

The whole situation was hopeless. On the whole, he knew that he was a capable and possibly even a good king. But in such extremities as this . . .? The gods mocked him, making him a king of nothing. What could he do? He took another swallow of wine, and realized his goblet was empty. Reaching for the pitcher, he poured himself another drink. Slamming the pitcher back onto the table, he saw a slow movement in the shadows.

'Who's there?' he growled, glaring at the darkness. 'Show yourself, like an honest man.'

Dumuzi moved into the circles thrown by the blazing torches. In the flickering light he looked inhuman. His thin features, his white beard, his heavy nose, and above all those glassy eyes. 'Greetings, lord,' he murmured. 'Taking your ease?'

'Nergal take you, slinker in shadows,' the king replied, his words slurred by wine. 'Why do you creep through the darkness?'

'Because if I did not, then I would be seen as I spied on you, O king.'

'So,' Agga snarled, 'you're keeping an eye on me for Ishtar, eh?'

'Fool,' the high priest snapped. 'I am Ishtar. These eyes are my eyes, this tongue my tongue. I am here, just as certainly as I would be if my body were present.'

'You make my skin crawl,' he told the priest, stumbling to his feet. 'I believe what you say, Ishtar. I've seen you taking possession of men's bodies before. So why do you have Dumuzi's eyes spying on me?'

'I was waiting,' was the priest's reply. 'I wanted to have you in this sorry, bedraggled state when you came before me. It amuses me to see the king of Kish act like a common drunkard.'

'Amuses you?' He laughed. 'A human emotion, surely? Not one fit for a goddess.'

Dumuzi's body shrugged. 'There may not be much that is human within me,' he said for Ishtar. 'But my emotions remain. I enjoy laughter — and, at times, revenge.' The smile on Dumuzi's face was like the rictus on the face of a corpse. 'Now it is time for revenge.'

Staggering down from the dais, Agga moved towards the old priest. Glaring through an alcoholic haze, he tried to suppress his fears. 'Revenge? What are you prattling on about?'

'What?' asked Dumuzi, in amused tones. 'Don't tell me that you have no idea what your dear, beautiful daughter is doing?'

A cold wave of shock washed over Agga, almost sobering him. 'She's in her room, under guard,' he replied. 'She can be of no interest —'

'On the contrary!' roared Dumuzi, voicing Ishtar's pleasure. 'Even now, she has freed the three prisoners that you took and hid from me. Did you not think I would find out about them? And who they are? Fool! She and they are heading to my temple. Agga, I warned you that if she interfered with me, she would become my slave or my feast. Now you will see how I keep my word.'

With a curse, Agga threw the dregs of wine into Dumuzi's face. Pushing the old man aside the king rushed from the throne room. As the wine dripped untouched down his face, Dumuzi watched the king stagger out into the corridor. 'Yes,' he murmured, satisfied, echoing Ishtar's thoughts, 'I thought that would get you moving. Another one on his way to me. I do so love parties ... And what a gathering and a feast this one is going to be!' And throwing back his head the old priest laughed inhumanly into the empty room.

'I don't like this,' Enkidu muttered.

Stifling an urge to scream, the Doctor said with strained patience: 'While I appreciate realism, haven't you ever heard of the power of positive thinking? You've done nothing since our escape but complain about things.'

'That's because I'm naturally cautious,' replied Enkidu. He peered out from behind the pillar that concealed them both. Ahead of them, the main room of the temple of Ishtar stretched out. 'And I tell you, I don't like this.'

'Then I promise we'll speak to the decorators when we're finished, and we'll have them repaint the place for you.'

The ape-man glared at him. 'I mean that it's too quiet.'

'He may be correct, lord,' En-Gula interposed before the Doctor could say anything. 'At this hour, there are usually about twenty priests here, offering sacrifice.'

The Doctor took another quick look. He could see only six or seven of the robed figures, although about twenty worshippers were bearing animals to the slaughter. 'Maybe it's the lunch break,' he suggested. 'Everything looks fine to me.' He stared at them both in annoyance. 'Why can't you be like Ninani, and stop arguing with all of my decisions?'

The princess, still looking apprehensive, was watching their rear. She was quite astonished at her own bravery and skill, and feeling pleased that the lord Ea approved of both what she had done and the attitude she was showing.

'All right,' Enkidu said, reluctantly. 'Then how do we get across the temple without being seen?'

'Must I think of everything?' The Doctor glanced round the pillar again. The only other people in sight were the priestesses, sitting or moving about in their alcoves. From time to time one of the male worshippers would cross to one of them, and throw down an offering coin. The priestess would then lead him to one of the side rooms to commune with the gods. 'Hmmm ... En-Gula, I think it's time you rejoined the priesthood.' She looked blankly at him, so he explained. 'The rooms we want are behind the altar. The rooms the temple priestesses use are between between here and there. We can make the extra little hop, skip and jump before we're spotted.'

En-Gula grinned, catching on. With a nod she quickly rearranged her costume to expose her breasts, thus marking herself as one of the temple staff. The Doctor, meanwhile, managed to use his umbrella to snag and draw to him two of the cloaks from the table where the visitors placed them while they were in the temple courts. He handed one to Enkidu and struggled into the other himself.

Ninani regarded him, a firm look in her eye. 'I am not going to bare myself for this masquerade,' she told him. 'It would not be seemly for a princess to display herself in such a fashion.'

*Don't let the fact that it might save all our lives influence you*, the Doctor thought. Aloud, he simply said: 'Well, let's hope that En-Gula's efforts are enough. Enkidu, you escort her to the communing chambers, then slip into the inner sanctum. I'll be right behind you, with Ninani.'

The Neanderthal soldier nodded. Throwing his cloak about the princess as well as himself, the Doctor suggested: 'At least try and pretend that you're about to offer me heavenly bliss ...'

Every inch of the journey was torture for them. En-Gula managed more than passably to act as if she was back at her old job, teasing and enticing a client to the back rooms. Ninani tried her best to emulate her companion, but to the Doctor's apprehensive ears it sounded as convincing as an amateur vocalist working on Wagner's *Ring* without either a score or an ear for music. Still, no one in the temple spared the group a second glance, so he could only assume that their little act was either completely convincing or utterly boring.

Passing by the entrance to the boudoirs, they slipped into the back rooms behind the altar. The Doctor took one last look over his shoulder, and then let out a sigh of relief. He hadn't been certain that they could make it unchallenged. Throwing his cloak aside, he peered into the gloom. 'Power failure?' he asked. It had been dark like this the last time he had been in here.

En-Gula shrugged. 'Ishtar likes the gloom.'

'Hmmm ... I wonder if it means she can't stand the light,

or that she's got exceptional eyesight and likes her visitors at a disadvantage?'

'Either way,' Enkidu hissed, 'we are in the worst position while it remains dark. It's difficult to see much, which restricts our ability to fight. Or spy.'

'Well, standing here talking all day won't help matters much,' the Doctor answered. 'I can see perfectly well, so follow my lead. 'Without waiting to ascertain that they had agreed, he led the way through the room to the inner door. Thankfully, his eyes were much more sensitive than those of his human companions. If Ishtar made a few more miscalculations like that, he'd be happy.

These rooms were clearly where Ishtar did most of her public work. The stench of ether was much stronger here. He could see several jars by one wall, all carefully sealed. Obviously her stockpile of knockout drops. The room was ornately laid out, and he spotted — with a wry grin — two small alcoves in the wall, one on either side of the doorway. A priestess in each of those, and anyone coming through the door would be grabbed, forced to their knees, and drugged, if the need should arise. That was how they had surprised him on his previous visit.

So why was the room empty? Maybe Ishtar had a pressing engagement somewhere else? Gesturing for the others to stand still, the Doctor crept to the far doorway. He realized, belatedly, that the other three hadn't been able to see his gesture in the darkness, and were still right behind him. 'Stay here a minute,' he hissed. When he was certain that they would, he stepped through the door, and into Ishtar's inner sanctum.

This room was brighter, simply because of all of the machinery in operation. Two walls were filled with computers, both with programmes running continuously. Monitoring equipment filled the rest of the space. There was only one gap in the machinery, some sort of recharging chamber he assumed. If Ishtar was, as he suspected a cybernetic organism, then this was where she plugged herself in for a battery charge. Time to work that out later.

At the end of the room was a throne of sorts, and directly in front of it a small, square box. He hurried over and examined it through his glasses. He whistled, softly, to himself. 'Cobalt bomb — and wired into brain patterns, by the look of things.' He pursed his lips. 'Could make turning her off a bit dangerous. So she wasn't lying to King Agga about being able to wipe Mesopotamia off the face of the Earth.'

Ignoring this complication for the moment, he moved to examine the computers. They were not of a familiar pattern, but he estimated he could get the hang of them quickly enough. A bit of reprogramming might do them all the world of good. Ishtar clearly used a built-in radio somewhere in this lot to stay in communication with the minds she had Touched. If that was ever linked to the immense circuits she had designed for the walls of Kish, her signal might be able to fill the known world of this period. And with the right power source, and enough of the implanted electrodes, she could probably rule the Earth.

A frightening thought, since she would change the whole course of human history and evolution. The Doctor doubted it would be for the better, given what he had been told about her so far. If she felt the need to implant mind-controlling devices in people's heads, it suggested that she had both an incredible disregard for individual personalities and also an overwhelming urge to control others. Neither trait was admirable.

'Time for a little subtle sabotage, Doctor,' he told himself. 'First of all, a monitor . . .' He walked over to the screens on the next wall. Tapping thoughtfully on the buttons below one of them, he started to reroute the command paths of the computer to show on the screen. Without his touching the controls, though, the screen sprang to life.

He found himself looking at the back of his own head. Slowly he turned round, as his image on the screen repeated his actions.

In the doorway to the room, watching him with gleaming red eyes, was Ishtar. Slinking forward slightly, she purred: 'Doctor — so nice to meet you at last.'

# 19: The Feast of Ishtar

Ishtar insinuated herself completely into the room. Like the snake she resembled she glided about the floor, studying the Doctor intently. In return he studied her just as closely. Finally she cocked her head to one side. 'Do you like what you see, Doctor?' she asked.

'Brilliant, quite brilliant,' he replied, enthusiastically. 'Platinum alloy skin, I'd guess. Amazingly complex and yet so supple. Humanoid features are a hangover from the old days, I'd say — perhaps a hint of vanity, eh? — but the snake half of you is good for movement. And durable, too, I'd think. Built-in sensors that seem to be very resilient and adaptable. Some kind of positronic brain in there, too, with human brain cell analogs ... Utterly brilliant.' Then he added: 'Shame you use such skills for such a depraved purpose.'

'Ah,' she purred, amused, 'morality. The weakness that marks the fool from the genius.'

'The strength that marks the wise man from the criminal,' the Doctor countered.

'The *weakness*,' she insisted, 'that marks the dead from the living.' One metal hand touched the Doctor's face and stroked it almost fondly. 'I have no weaknesses at all, you see. And nobody can withstand my strengths.' She smiled again, and he was amazed at how human her expressions could be. And at how terribly beautiful she was. Still, he thought, working with the perfection of platinum helps. It doesn't get acne, or moles, or even laughter lines.

'What have you done with my companions?' the Doctor

demanded.

'The humans?' she sneered. 'Don't try to tell me that you care — or that you are indeed one of that miserable, fragile species.' She tapped on one red eye. 'I am not deceived by appearances, Doctor. I know that you are not human. What I do not yet know is what you are. But you will tell me or ...' She made a slight gesture. Guards pushed Enkidu, En-Gula and Ninani into the room.

'I'm sorry,' the Neanderthal managed to say. His jaw was swollen, and blood trickled down the side of his face. He had not surrendered easily. Bright red marks on the arms and throats of the girls showed how they had been taken and kept silent, so as not to alert the Doctor.

'Don't be,' he replied. 'You did your best.' Turning back to Ishtar, the Doctor asked: 'And now what?'

'Now, the inevitable,' she replied. 'I win. But there are still a few players missing. So I shall be generous, Doctor. Come, let us talk together, shall we? It will be nice for a change to speak with someone whose mind is almost the equal of my own.' She looked down at the humans in disgust. 'Their pitifully tiny brains barely nourish me — but yours ... Ah, that will be a feast I shall remember for a long time.'

'I'd most likely give you indigestion,' the Doctor said, quickly. 'My mind's very cluttered and disorganized. Really not worth the bother.'

Ishtar laughed, delightedly. 'Ah, you are an amusing one! I really will enjoy this. So, tell me — of what race are you? What is your home world?' Seeing him hesitate, she stroked his face again. 'Come, little one. I will know the answers soon enough, either if you tell me now — or while I feast. And, as long as you amuse me, I may hold back my hunger.'

Reluctantly, he told her: 'Gallifrey.'

'*Gallifrey*?' she echoed, her every metal sinew tense. 'Gallifrey, you say?' Her face came down onto a level with his. 'You are a Time Lord?' When he nodded, slowly, she threw back her head and laughed with undisguised pleasure. 'Finally! I knew that one day I should find one of your species! I knew that your people were no mere myth. And I knew that I would find one, no matter how long it took.'

'Or that we should find you,' he corrected her. 'This interference with the development of the human race cannot be allowed, Ishtar. Stop it now.'

'Or what?' she snapped contemptuously. 'Doctor, you live only as long as I choose to let you. Do not try and intimidate me. As for my interfering with the humans — look at them!' She gestured across the room. 'Pitiful, petty little pond scum. Insignificant nothings to beings such as you or I, Doctor!'

Sadly, he looked back at her. 'There we must agree to differ,' he replied. 'True, they are short-lived, and true, at this stage in their evolution they haven't accomplished much. But they have invented civilization from the ground up. And remember: I am a Time Lord. I know they have the potential for much greatness even now, and I won't allow you to destroy this by enslaving them to your depraved lusts.'

'Have a care, Doctor,' Ishtar warned him. 'I need your mind, but not your tongue. If you annoy me enough, I shall remove it. Without anesthetics — which seem not to work on you, anyway.'

'Respiratory bypass,' he smiled. 'Comes in handy when dropping in on hosts like you.'

'That and all of your other intimate secrets will soon be mine, Doctor.' Again, she smiled. 'Such as the manipulation of time, and the ability to live forever. With your somewhat reluctant aid, Doctor, I shall become immortal, and enthroned within the fabric of time.'

'You'll be nothing,' he informed her. 'I cannot allow you to interfere more than you already have. It's over.'

Ishtar stroked his face again. 'I do hope that your brain has not been damaged by all of the foolishness you continually talk,' she told him. 'Otherwise I shall be most upset. I would so like my first taste of a Time Lord to be unsullied and enjoyable to the extreme.'

'I'd stick in your throat like a chicken bone,' the Doctor promised. 'If you ever got the chance to try me.' Privately, he was nowhere near as confident as he tried to sound — and he could see that she knew it. He refused to surrender in despair. Where there's life, there's hope, he reminded himself. But the only hope he could summon was the thought of Ace arriving on the scene with a rucksack full of nitro-nine — and he had sent Ace on a wild goose chase to a range of mountains that were a week's trek away.

The Doctor's attention was jerked back to the room as another figure burst through the doorway and skidded to a halt. He was fighting off the effects of intoxication and panting for breath, having run as fast as he could to get here.

'King Agga,' said Ishtar, relishing her amusement. 'How kind of you to pay us this visit.'

The king ignored her, and ran to Ninani's side. He clubbed down the soldier holding his daughter, and made to scoop her into his arms. Instead he felt a shock of pain as another of the guards slammed the butt of a spear into his back. Spasms of pain racking him, Agga collapsed to the cold floor. With a scream Ninani threw herself across his fallen form to protect him.

'How touching,' sneered Ishtar. 'What a sweet family reunion. Such a shame it must end.' She sent a mental signal to her controlled guards. One savagely wrenched Ninani off her father. He ignored her screams and blows. A second guard hauled the shaken king to his unsteady feet. Ishtar slithered across to him, and held her face almost touching his.

'I warned you what would happen, Agga, if you couldn't control this stupid offspring of yours. You should have believed me, and worked harder at it.' She spun about, and began to move in on the girl.

'Ishtar, don't do it,' the Doctor called. 'Stop all of this, now.'

'No, Doctor,' the snake-woman answered. He felt his arms gripped by two more of the controlled guards. 'You cannot tell me what I must and must not do. No one can. This has gone far beyond your puny powers to correct. Be silent, and see what happens to those who interfere with me.'

She reached Ninani. The princess was shaking, partly with fear, and partly from the crushing grip of the guard. the mind-slave forced her to her knees in front of the goddess. Ishtar reached out her hands, cupping Ninani's beautiful, terrified face.

'Beg for your life,' she purred. 'Who knows — perhaps I shall feel generous if you amuse me.'

'I am a princess of Uruk,' Ninani said, as bravely as she could, determined not to faint. 'I will not disgrace myself or my father by begging for favours from the likes of you.' Then, gathering all the moisture she had left in her mouth, she spat in Ishtar's metallic face.

Ishtar's face twitched She dragged Ninani closer. En-Gula, watching in horror, cried out: 'No! Spare her! Take me, instead!'

'What?' Curiously, Ishtar rotated her head to stare at the young priestess. 'What generosity! And most unexpected.' She glanced at the Doctor in amusement. 'You are correct, Time Lord. This race has a good deal of potential — for the same stupid morality that you espouse.' Turning her back on them both, she cupped Ninani's trembling head. 'Normally, little one, I administer anesthetic first. But you have angered me, and so I will spare you nothing of your agonies. We will experience the pain together.'

The probe in her right palm hissed out. Ninani's terrified eyes were riveted to it as it dilated, showing the metallic point within. 'Say farewell to your mind, princess.' Gripping the girl by the temples, Ishtar sent a signal to her palm.

Ninani screamed as the probe bored into her head. In the background, Agga howled in anguish and fury. En-Gula fainted. The Doctor forced down his anger, seeing Enkidu struggling to keep his own temper in check. There was nothing any of them could do. An expression of ecstasy suffused Ishtar's writhing features.

Fire consumed Ninani's mind. She fell backwards as Ishtar released her. Blood trickled from a cauterized spot on her temple, which was already showing signs of massive bruising. Her eyes opened again, and the pain was gone, along with everything else that had belonged to Ninani. Ishtar looked out from within the princess's skull, and laughed in delight. Shakily at first, the princess rose to her feet, and then crossed to face her father.

'Agga,' she said, with Ninani's clear tones but Ishtar's venom, 'my compliments on raising such a pretty child.' She looked down, stroking the princess's soft robes. 'It's been a long, long time since I was last this far into a humanoid form.' She pirouetted about the room, and laughed. 'It really is quite wonderful, isn't it?' She returned to stand in front of Agga, to torture him. 'I will enjoy the experience. It will be interesting to eat again, and to drink. Intoxication! Something I've not felt for a while. Or perhaps a little sexual amusement — this body seems to be built well to enjoy that sport.' She cocked her head to one side. 'I haven't intruded myself this much into the mind and soul of one of my slaves for centuries. It really is most exhilarating!' She laughed as Agga turned his face against his shoulder, whimpering. 'What's wrong, Agga? Don't you want your daughter to get any fun? Shame on you! Girls need their little amusements.'

'Stop torturing him,' the Doctor broke in, with cold fury. 'Haven't you done enough?'

'*No, I haven't!*' Ishtar hissed, turning her metal snake-form on him. 'I will extract every last ounce of pleasure I can from the agonies of all that oppose me. For now, it is Agga; Ninani's turn will come.'

Agga caught that last implication. 'She is not dead?' he asked, in unwilling hope.

'Dead?' Ishtar laughed. Her voice moved to the princess's throat: 'Not yet, king. She is still here —' Ninani's body tapped its head '— but in the background. Believe me, I am enjoying every second of her fear and disgust. She is powerless to stop me. She will not die until I allow it.' Ninani's body smiled again. 'Until then, she will experience every degradation that I care to inflict upon her. And, trust me, they will be many.'

Ace laughed aloud in pleasure as the small flitter carrying her, Avram and Urshanabi whipped in low across the plains. Close behind them came Utnapishtim's craft, bearing him and an impatient Gilgamesh. They had made good time back from the mountains — less than a day's flight to cover over a week's trek. They had lost a little time stopping at Uruk, where they discovered that the Doctor had already left for Kish. Typical,

Ace thought; just like the Doctor to hog all the excitement while her back was turned.

Urshanabi grinned at her. 'I'd forgotten how exhilarating this can be,' he admitted. 'But powering up these two flitters took most of our remaining energy. I can only pray that you're right in thinking this Doctor of yours can help us with a fresh supply.'

'Trust him,' Ace said, mentally crossing her fingers. 'He's always on top of the situation.' She glanced at Avram, who was watching the landscape below them whip past at tremendous speed, 'Isn't this wicked?'

He raised an eyebrow. 'A strange word to use,' he said. 'It is fascinating. I only wish I had the chance to write a song about it.'

'Songs later!' Gilgamesh called, a wide smile on his own face. 'Battles first! My axe is very thirsty.'

Ace rolled her eyes. Talk about one-track minds. Still, he'd probably enjoy the next part. It was unlikely that Ishtar would have left the temple door open and the red carpet out.

The walls of Kish suddenly sprang up on the horizon. Ace was concerned to see that the copper traces on the walls were far more extensive. Had they managed to arrive in time to prevent Ishtar from finishing her plans?

Urshanabi adjusted the controls slightly. The flitter nosed up and flew across the main guard tower. Ace barely caught a glimpse of a half-dozen startled faces as they shot over them. Behind her Gilgamesh roared with pleasure, swinging his axe as Utnapishtim's flitter zipped across the walls. Ace prudently didn't look back to see if the king had managed any success with the blow.

Then the flitters dropped down to about eight feet above the crowded streets. The townspeople screamed and dived for cover as the two small craft whipped through the streets and towards the temple of Ishtar.

The great stone walls appeared in front of them, and Urshanabi slowed down. Ace saw why. The huge double doors were closed, and a body of the town's soldiers was ranged in front of them, ready for action.

'We'll not get in that way,' the pilot muttered.

'There is no other access large enough for us that I know of,' Avram commented.

'Now what?' Ace asked.

Gilgamesh raised his axe high. Blood was dripping from it. 'Now,' he said, with great satisfaction, 'we fight!' And with a loud war-cry he threw himself from the flitter to the ground. 'Come!' he cried to the massed troops. 'It is time for you to die!'

Ace sighed, and hauled out one of her precious cans. 'Once more unto the breach,' she said softly, and leapt down to join him.

'You really are a pitiful little worm,' the Doctor said loudly, hoping to distract Ishtar's attention from taunting Agga. 'Such pointless cruelty is hardly worthy of your powers.'

Slithering her snake-body across the floor, Ishtar caught the Doctor's chin in her vice-like grip. 'Have a care, Time Lord,' she advised him. 'I enjoy the torments of lesser creatures. It comforts me to know that I shall never experience them. But perhaps I shall be merciful. Who knows how generous I shall feel once I have fed off your mind? Or what knowledge I shall gain.' She smiled down at him. 'You do not think I can be merciful?' she asked. 'Oh, it's true, you know. Allow me to demonstrate ...'

Ninani moved over to En-Gula, who had come to her senses and was in the grip of her guard. The man let her drop to the floor. Warily, scared almost out of her mind, the girl started to clamber to her feet. Ninani moved quickly, lashing out with her foot and catching En-Gula behind the knee and slamming her painfully to the floor. As she cried out Ninani jumped on top of her, her fingers gripping the temple prostitute's throat, squeezing. En-Gula struggled, but to no avail. Ishtar's metal face was only inches from the Doctor's. 'Shall I kill her now? It would save her much pain later, and that would be a mercy.'

'Stop it,' the Doctor asked her. 'Don't do this to them.'

'Doctor,' the snake-woman laughed, 'you claim to have compassion for these pitiful creatures. Yet you ask me to let the harlot live, so I may inflict further cruelties on her later. How insensitive of you. But very well — have it your way.'

Ninani let En-Gula's neck go. Red marks were burned into the young girl's throat. Hacking and straining, she managed to take in a coughing breath, and then another. As soon as she was breathing normally again, the guard grabbed her and hauled her to her feet once more.

'Why are you doing this?' the Doctor demanded. 'Isn't it enough for you to win?'

'No,' Ishtar said icily. 'Winning is never enough. You must also savour the defeat of those who opposed you. They must acknowledge that you have won and they have lost.' She didn't look around as Dumuzi entered the room. The high priest was blankly under her control once again. 'Take Dumuzi there. He was kind enough to find me in the hills, and to give me the initial energies I needed to reach this dung-hill of a city. But he has struggled against me all the time I have been in his mind. If he had been kinder, perhaps I would have been generous to him.'

'Perhaps,' said Ninani, in Ishtar's tones, 'I would have let him use this pretty body for his pleasures. But it's too late for that.'

'It's not enough simply to have power, Doctor,' continued Ishtar, grimly. 'One must also use that power. And when you hold the power of life and death as I do, then sometimes I grant life. And other times . . .'

'No,' he contradicted her. 'One must decide that there are times where it is wrong to use all the powers one possesses. A person must learn restraint.'

'Perhaps you have had to,' she agreed, perceptively. 'You with your powers of temporal travel and that brain of yours — you could easily have ruled this pitiful world instead of protecting it.'

'Maybe,' the Doctor said cautiously. He remembered others of his race who had tried to accomplish exactly that. 'But it never works. Power engenders a thirst that some insist on attempting to slake. But it becomes an insatiable master.'

'Quaint moralizing,' sneered Ishtar. 'I have the power to do as I will. And my will is — to free Dumuzi.'

Puzzled by this apparently aberrant behaviour, the Doctor stared at the high priest. As Ishtar spoke he convulsed, and gave a loud scream. Then, finally, the intelligence seemed to awaken within him. his eyes met those of Ishtar, and he scowled. For the first time in weeks, his mind was entirely his own, the link with Ishtar quiescent.

'You lied to me and used me,' he said in a little more than a whisper.

'Yes,' Ishtar agreed calmly. 'And you still have one further use, priest.' She turned her back on him, and coiled to face the Doctor. 'His mind is his own again, for all the good it will do him. I have already drunk from him all the knowledge that I desire. But there is one more way in which he can serve me, one more thing he had that I want — his life.' She clutched her metal hand into a ball.

Dumuzi felt the fire pour through the link that had so long controlled him. Screaming, he fell onto his knees, pounding at his temples, fighting the waves of agony that thundered through his entire body. With one final, drawn-out scream, his mind dissolved, and his limp body fell to the floor.

The Doctor dragged his appalled gaze from the wreckage of what had been a human being, and stared at Ishtar. Her face showed delight, sickeningly mirrored in that of the princess. With a long, satisfied sigh, the metal face turned back to look into the Doctor's.

'Most enjoyable,' she crooned. 'And utterly delicious.'

'There was no need for that,' the Doctor replied.

'Oh, but there was,' Ishtar said. 'As a demonstration for the rest of you. And simply because I wished to do it. My will is all that counts here, Doctor. But enough of this.' She started to slither across the floor. 'Prepare yourself, Doctor. Your mind is next.' Her right palm came up, and with a whirr the probe extended and dilated, ready to consume his mind.

A muffled boom broke the silence.

## 20: Ace's High

The temple shook; dust and fragments of stone fell into Ishtar's chambers. The electronics faltered for a second, then sprang to life again. From outside came the sound of another dull explosion.

Ishtar swivelled to face the source of sound. 'What was that?' she hissed furiously.

'Sounds like a friend of mine,' the Doctor replied. 'It has all of Ace's subtle undertones.'

'Stop them,' Ishtar commanded her guards. Glaring at the Doctor, she added: 'This is at best a temporary reprieve.'

'I'll take what I can get,' he assured her. His eyes scanned the room, seeking any advantage. With the guards despatched to stop Ace, there were left only two holding Enkidu, and one each for himself, En-Gula and Agga. The odds were improving slightly.

Another explosion rocked the room. Enkidu seized his own chance as the blast put his captors off-balance. A quick throw flung one of them across the room. Enkidu turned, raking his fingers across the face of the second guard. As the man screamed, Enkidu grabbed the guard's sword, reversed it and gutted him. Kicking the body aside, he attacked the guard holding Agga.

'Incompetents!' screamed Ishtar, momentarily distracted by the fighting. Her mental hold over the remaining guards faltered slightly. The Doctor, feeling the grip of his arm loosen a little, jammed his umbrella down hard on his captor's foot.

The soldier yelped, and the Doctor reversed his umbrella,

196

hooked the handle about the man's ankle, and then jerked. The guard topped over, and the Doctor was free. He launched himself across the room at the computers.

Enkidu was in his element now. The guard pinioning Agga had no chance of matching the fury of the Neanderthal fighting demon. Enkidu hacked him down, then threw the dead man's sword to Agga. The king stared into two burning eyes. 'For the moment,' Enkidu told him, 'we fight a common foe.'

Nodding, Agga joined him to attack the two surviving guards.

Seeing her plans crumbling, Ishtar sent a mental command for more troops to come to her aid. This was irritating, but hardly fatal. The guards might be susceptible to the edge of a sword, but primitive weapons could not harm her metallic form. She twisted and saw the Doctor fiddling with the control panels. That was more dangerous! Hissing, she coiled and sprang.

The Doctor was still trying to get the hang of the alien programming when the metal fury smacked him aside. The coils of Ishtar's tail wrapped round him. Her face suddenly appeared in front of his and grinned wickedly down at him. 'That was a pointless attempt,' she whispered, and began to tighten her grip. The Doctor could feel his body being crushed in the metallic embrace. He shut out the pain and began to close down areas of consciousness.

There was a sudden smell of ozone, and an explosion from the panels behind him. A bolt of light had glanced off Ishtar's left arm, leaving a trail of liquid metal. For the first time, uncertainty and pain appeared on Ishtar's face.

'Back off, bitch!' Ace yelled, doing her best Sigourney Weaver impression. She was hefting a needle gun cannibalized from an unused Guardian robot. She fired again. Worried about a ricochet from the metal body hitting the Doctor, she was aiming high. Another of the computer panels behind Ishtar exploded, showering fragments of circuits and tape everywhere.

'No, Ace, don't!' the Doctor yelled, prising himself free from the metal coils. Ishtar reared up, ready to spring at this new interloper. Ace dropped to one knee to fire again. The Doctor had no option but to use his umbrella. He flung it as hard as he could.

It hit Ace in the stomach, and she doubled over with a yell. The needle gun clattered to the floor. Ishtar sprang over Ace's prone form, and the Doctor managed to grab his companion's arm and pull her towards him.

'Why'd you do that?' Ace gasped, fighting to get her breath back. 'I could have ended it right then!'

'You'd have ended more than you thought,' the Doctor told her grimly. He pointed to the cobalt bomb. 'That's the grandfather of all atomic bombs there, and it will be triggered by Ishtar's death.'

Realizing what she had almost done, Ace paled. 'Then what can we do?' she asked.

'Think!'

Urshanabi brought the flitter in low again. This time he cut the restraining field. Gilgamesh leapt from the back with a howl of joy, swinging his battle axe as he dropped towards the waiting troops. The weapon cut a bloody pathway through the men. Screams of agony joined Gilgamesh's wild war chant. Urshanabi flew on, deeper into the temple. Ace had gone ahead of them, worried for the safety of her friend the Time Lord.

Utnapishtim and Avram followed on the second sky scooter. The two small flyers zipped through the vast doorway and into the temple building. Inside, it was chaos. The priests and worshippers alike had given up any attempts at devotions, and were cowering in whatever safety they could find. Ishtar's guards were kicking aside anyone in their way as they hurried towards the back rooms to aid their mistress. Urshanabi, infected by the fighting spirit, yelled out wordlessly and drove the flitter into them. Men flew aside and many of them didn't get up again.

'A glorious fight!' Avram howled over the noise. Utnapishtim snorted.

'And senseless! These men fight because they are forced to, not because this is their battle. But that was ever Qataka's way.'

Within her holy of holies, Ishtar once again held sway. Enough of her fighting men had piled in to wear down Enkidu at last. Struggling, he was held and forced to his knees, a sword at his throat. Agga, dispatching what had once been one of his loyal guards, spun to help his one-time enemy.

Standing between them was Ninani. With an evil smile on her face she leapt at her father. Though he knew she was possessed by Ishtar, he could not bring himself to strike at his favourite child. As he fell backwards, powerless to defend himself, his head hit the metal of the monitoring stations, and he collapsed. Ninani snatched the sword from his nerveless fingers and held it over his heart.

'Weakness,' she hissed. 'Compassion!' But she did not drive the weapon home. Agga, stunned by the blow, simply stared up into the face he had always loved, his heart broken.

The fighting was over. Ishtar slithered from behind a pillar and approached the Doctor. 'It was wise of you to stop this child from attacking me,' she told him, glaring venomously at Ace. 'But, as you see, her futile gesture has won you nothing.'

'Not nothing.' Utnapishtim's voice came from behind her. 'She has gained us time.'

Ishtar hissed in disbelief and fury as her old foe walked through the doorway, flanked by Urshanabi and Avram. Utnapishtim moved grimly towards the computers.

'Stop!' yelled Ishtar. 'You can accomplish nothing!' Despite her words, there was panic in her voice.

Utnapishtim withdrew a small device from his tunic. It was a box a few inches across, and flat. Two mandible-like prongs projected from the front. He smiled thinly. 'My computer virus,' he told her. 'And your doom!' He thrust the device towards the closest panel.

Ishtar didn't hesitate. Even with her superhuman reflexes she could not reach him in time. Instead she raised her right hand, and the linkage she had readied for the Doctor's mind flew towards her enemy. The needle sharp implant slashed across Utnapishtim's wrist in a spray of blood. Screaming, he dropped the software insert. As it hit the floor, Ishtar pounced and slammed her tail down on it. Stunned by her speed, the others could do nothing but watch as she crushed the device into twisted metal fragments.

'So much for your virus!' she sneered, backhanding

Utnapishtim across the room. He lay groaning where he fell, his face bruised, his wrist still bleeding. Avram jumped to his aid, tearing a strip from his own tunic to bind the gash.

Ishtar looked triumphantly about the room. More of her guards had arrived, and the day was clearly hers. 'What stupidity!' she snarled. 'You were all doomed to failure before you began. Accept your fate.'

'Get stuffed,' Ace said. She was held by two of the guards, her arms behind her back, twisted painfully. 'There's still Gilgamesh.'

'Yes,' agreed Ishtar, licking her lips in anticipation. 'There's still Gilgamesh. And I have a score to settle with that one!' She gestured at the doorway, through which the struggling king of Uruk was dragged to join the rest of the captives.

He was red with blood, but it seemed to be mostly that of his opponents. He had several cuts from blows he had taken, but none were serious. It took three guards to drag him into the room and kick his legs from under him, forcing him into a position of respect before Ishtar. With hatred in his eyes, he looked up at her, and spat.

Ishtar laughed. 'Poor Gilgamesh — is that the only weapon you have left?' She reached out to stroke his matted beard. 'Once, you refused my embrace, O king. But this time, you will have no choice in the matter. This time, you will feel my arms about you — crushing the life out of you.' But instead of carrying out her threat she turned to survey the room, a smug smile on her face. 'Well, Doctor, I owe you a debt of gratitude.'

'Why?' he asked, struggling helplessly in the grip of two impassive guards.

She gestured at the captives. 'Why? Because you have assembled all of my enemies for me to take my slow, slow revenge upon. Utnapishtim, who sought to destroy me. Gilgamesh, who mocked and spurned me. Agga, who fought against me. And you, Doctor, who can provide me with the knowledge of temporal control! How delightful!' She gave a sibilant purr of pleasure. 'Freed from the restraint of time, who knows what I can accomplish?'

'Don't even think about it,' the Doctor warned her. 'You've

got no chance at all.'

'On the contrary!' she replied. 'I cannot be defeated now. Who is there to fight me? Don't be foolish, Doctor. I am the future, and nothing can stop me now. Earth first, and then perhaps all of time and space will become mine. Think about it: there will be no crime, no pain, no dissent. There will be one mind and one aim for the whole human race.'

'Your mind,' the Doctor said. 'Not theirs. Don't try and paint a picture of Utopia, Ishtar — what you envision is slavery and hell.'

'Ah!' Ishtar smiled again, revelling in her glory. 'But your hell is my heaven. My mind will become omnipotent, Doctor, filling the reaches of time and space. I may be posing as a goddess now, but soon I shall become one in fact!'

'She's flipped her metal lid,' Ace said loudly. 'She's completely mad.'

'Mad?' Calmly, the snake-woman considered the point. 'No, not mad, child. I am completely sane. It is you and your friends who are mad, for thinking that you could stop me. Now, I am ready to enter into my glory.' She held up her right hand, extending the probe. The gleam of one of her implants caught Ace's eye. 'And I shall begin with you.' She smiled at the Doctor. 'You will be next, Time Lord. But, before your mind is sucked into nothingness as I feast upon it, I want you to see your final failure — as your companion dies!'

Bringing up her hands, Ishtar caught Ace's head in her metallic grip. Then, with a laugh of cruel pleasure, she injected the implant into Ace's temple.

# 21: Armageddon

Ace screamed in agony, and kept on screaming. The Doctor screwed his eyes tightly shut, appalled. Another of his companions doomed, and nothing that he could do to stop it. Silent accusers, memories of Katarina, Sara Kingdom, Adric and others passed through his mind. And now Ace would be one of their number.

He realized that it wasn't only Ace who was screaming. The arms holding him loosened their grip. He saw that Ishtar, too, was writhing, in pain. So was Ninani, and several of the guards. Other temple soldiers were simply stationary, gazing helplessly.

'It worked!' Utnapishtim breathed, struggling to his feet. 'We tricked her!'

'What worked?' The Doctor rushed over to check on Ace. The entry of the probe into her skull had left a red mark, scarred and bruised, but despite her obvious pain she was alive, and not weakening.

Urshanabi kicked Ishtar's writhing metal coils, and laughed. 'That device she destroyed was just a dummy. We knew she'd attack it. The real virus was overlaid on our minds. As soon as she tried to take over any one of us, she would trigger the real virus and suck it into her intelligence circuits.'

In horror, the Doctor realized what was happening. 'It's attacking her circuitry now?'

'Of course,' Utnapishtim said, extending his good hand. 'She'll be finished soon, and her slaves will be free. You must be the Doctor. I'm Utnapishtim.'

'You're an idiot!' the Doctor yelled back. 'Take a look at

202

what's in front of her throne' He turned away, bent down and, with regret, punched Ace sharply on the jaw. She stopped screaming and rolled over, unconscious.

Utnapishtim had followed the Doctor's instructions. His face paled. 'This is the same kind of bomb she used to destroy Anu!'

'And it's tied into her mental processes,' the Doctor added. He managed to drag Ace to her feet, one arm slung over his shoulders. 'The second your virus kills her, that bomb will go off. And it's the end of human civilization and a good portion of this planet.'

Shaking, Utnapishtim asked: 'What can we do?'

'Only one thing for it.' The Doctor flashed Avram a brief smile as the singer helped him to support Ace. 'I've got to get back to my TARDIS immediately. I take it you have some fast transport lying around somewhere?'

'Two flitters in the temple precincts,' Urshanabi offered.

'Good. Get them both ready. Avram and I will bring Ace. Utnapishtim, you bring that bomb.'

'Me?'

The Doctor sighed. 'If Ace were in her right mind, I'd have her do it; it's right up her street. But you'll have to do for now. Enkidu!'

The Neanderthal rushed over. 'How can I help?' he mumbled.

'You keep things straight here. Stop Gilgamesh from killing everyone while I'm gone. Look after Ninani and King Agga. Hopefully, I'll be back very soon. Right, let's go!'

The ride on the flitters was swift, and within five minutes the small party was standing by the incongruous shape of the TARDIS among the date palms. Fishing in his pocket, the Doctor dragged out his key.

'Are we in time?' Utnapishtim asked, holding the colbalt bomb gingerly. The Doctor nodded towards it.

'As long as that thing hasn't gone off, we've got some time left.' The door opened, and he and Avram dragged the unconscious Ace inside. Utnapishtim and Urshanabi followed them. 'Kindly refrain from any comments on the size of the interior,' the Doctor said. 'I've heard them all before, and it's time to get busy.' Leaving Avram to bring Ace, he hurried over to the central console and began to power up the systems. Instinctively he started to set the force field about the ship, but stayed his hand in time. 'No, that would be a mistake of explosive proportions...'

Urshanabi and Utnapishtim stared at the controls in fascination. 'Interesting technology,' the older man commented.

'Very,' the Doctor agreed brusquely, pushing him out of the way as he set the controls of the telepathic circuits. 'Avram, bring Ace over here, please.'

'What are you going to do?' asked Urshanabi.

'Deceive the bomb. It's tuned to Ishtar's brain patterns, so all I have to do is to keep them going even if she dies. We have a link to Ishtar through Ace, so if I can drain her thoughts into the circuits here, it should help.'

'Can you do that?'

'Oh, yes,' the Doctor assured him, remembering what had happened the last time he had used them, and the effect they had had on Ace. 'I think I can guarantee that it will work.' He stopped what he was doing for a moment, his fingers hovering indecisively over the buttons. 'Well, perhaps I could do with a second opinion,' he said, grudgingly. He wasn't at all certain that this was a good idea, but there was little else he could do.

'Mine?' offered Utnapishtim, curiously.

'No, mine,' the Doctor replied. 'At least, an opinion I used to have.' He hesitated over the telephthic circuits for a moment. 'I don't like this part,' he admitted.

'What are you going to do?'

Eyeing the contacts nervously, the Doctor explained: 'We Time Lords achieve the near-immortality that Ishtar so desired by a process of bodily regeneration. I've undertaken it a few times myself. But each time we do it, our personalities undergo a certain amount of change. We almost develop new personalities, new skills, new methods. My third self was the one most capable with the technology I really need.' Taking a deep breath, he slammed his hands down on the contact pads. 'So I have to bring him back.'

'Physically?' Utnapishtim asked, astounded.

'No. That's impossible. Mentally.'

The Doctor's body arced in a spasm of pain. He had to submerge his current personality, and use the TARDIS's capabilities to augment the traits, knowledge and skills that his third self had once possessed. It wasn't going to be an easy task, because the memories were buried deep in the recesses of his mind and his present personality would try to reject the overlays imposed by the TARDIS. But it had to be done. He lacked the certainty that he could do the job as he now was.

The silvery snake-form of Ishtar writhed in agony on the floor of her holy of holies. Gilgamesh had wanted to bury his war axe into her metal form, but Enkidu had convinced him to wait. Grudgingly the king had taken his temper out on the remaining dazed guards, clubbing them into line and setting them to work cleaning the dead bodies out of the room.

Agga and En-Gula were bent over the convulsed form of Ninani. The priestess could see tears of pain and despair in the eyes of her king as he watched his daughter being racked by the spasms. She laid a daring, gentle hand on his hairy arm.

'Trust the Doctor,' she said. 'He is wise. He will help her.'

Agga nodded, but he could not accept it. His daughter, his favourite, seemed to be dying. And perhaps in moments, they would all die if Ishtar perished.

'Well, it's about time.'

The Doctor straightened up from the panel, and looked about himself in amazement. Then he looked down at his clothing. 'Jumping Jehosephat! Is this what I've become? A scarecrow?' Without waiting for an answer, he looked down at Ace. 'Ah, I see the problem. Quite right of me to come to me for help.'

Hesitantly, Utnapishtim touched the Doctor's arm. 'Doctor? What has happened? You sound different.'

'That's because I am different.' He rubbed his chin. 'Look, we Time Lords have many personalities over the centuries. But they are all linked. Like the different faces of a multi-coloured cube. What he — I — did was to sort of mentally invert the cube to show a different face.' He touched his nose. 'Well, the same outward face, but a different inward one. I'm far more capable with the telepathic circuits than he could ever be.' A brief shadow passed over his face, as his old self seemed to flash back. 'Showoff!' he accused himself.

Deeply worried now, Utnapishtim stared at the strange figure. 'And you think you can stop Ishtar from destroying this world?'

'If I can't, no one can.'

'God help us,' Utnapishtim sighed, convinced he was faced with a maniac.

'Right,' the Doctor ordered. 'Brigadier, you bring Jo over here, please.' Then, realizing what he had said, he rubbed his brow. 'Avram, bring Ace over here, please,' he corrected himself.

Urshanabi dragged at his mentor's sleeve. 'He's schizophrenic,' he breathed. 'Dare we trust that he knows what he's doing?'

'What option do we have?' Both of them stared at the bomb, knowing that it could explode at any second.

Avram accepted what was happening with simple trust. This box they were in was no more magical than any of the sights he had witnessed since running into Ace. If this odd Doctor had a new personality, what difference did it make? He helped the Doctor to place Ace on the floor beside the console.

Kneeling, the Doctor gently slapped Ace's face. 'Wake up, Sarah Jane,' he smiled. 'Come on, there's a good girl.'

'Ace,' prompted Avram.

Glancing up crossly, the Doctor snapped: 'I knew that! Ace, Ace, come on.' He slapped her slightly harder.

Ace's eyes flashed open, and she started to struggle and howl again.

'Ishtar's still alive and kicking,' the Doctor gasped. 'Come on, you two. Give me a hand to connect Ace to the telepathic circuits.' Together they managed to get Ace erect and her hands, clenched into tight fists, into direct contact with the telepathic inputs. Leaving the other three to hold her in place, the Doctor returned to the controls.

'Maybe I should reverse the polarity of the neuron flow?' he mused to himself. Then, with a touch of the seventh Doctor's fire, he shook his head. 'That'll never work! Just get on with it.' Blinking, he surveyed the controls again. Utnapishtim and Urshanabi exchanged very worried glances over Ace's writhing body. Trusting that the Doctor really knew what he was doing was getting harder and harder.

It wasn't much easier for him, if he was willing to tell the truth. Dredging up his past self was an incredible strain on both his bodily and mental processes. The personality clashed with the form it was in, and was being held in place only by an almost overwhelming effort on his part. Concentrating through this fog was difficult. It was hardly surprising that he was making a few minor mistakes. But at least he knew now what he had to do. Plunging down on the controls, the Doctor grimaced. 'Here we go!'

The central rotor started to rise and fall, and a terrible grinding sound filled the room. It was all they could do not to let Ace go and jam their fingers into their ears. Ace shook again, but her spasms seemed to be dying down.

'I need a good deal of precision here, Sergeant Benton!' the Doctor yelled at Avram. 'Try and keep her steady.' He manipulated the controls, and the rotor stopped moving vertically, and started spinning, faster and faster. 'Right, just a touch of the old sleight of hand...' Gingerly he moved the controls, all the time watching the telepathic circuits like a hawk. A single slip at this point might doom them all.

In a brief flash of light, the metal probe that had been implanted in Ace's head fell out and lay on the input panel. With a final scream, Ace went limp over the controls.

'You've freed her, Doctor!' Utnaspishtim called. 'Well done!'

'Not now, Brigadier. It's still very tricky.' He bent down, watching the implant intently. Ace was going to recover now, but the link between Ishtar and the bomb was being maintained only through the TARDIS's telepathic circuit and the sliver of metal resting on it. If the link was lost, the cobalt bomb just inside the doors would explode — which might save the Earth, but wouldn't do the interior of the TARDIS the slightest bit of good. Boosting the signal and tapping in command codes, the Doctor began to transfer the mental link into the TARDIS's circuitry. This was the tricky bit. If he lost the mental signal linking the implant to Ishtar for even a nanosecond, it would all be over.

The implant vanished.

For a second the Doctor expected to be dead. Then he realized that the bomb hadn't detonated. Somehow, whatever had happened had not triggered the bomb. Hardly able to believe his luck, the Doctor grinned. The instruments showed that the line to Ishtar was still open. He wasn't sure what had just happened, but there wasn't any need to admit this to the others as long as everything was still working.

'We seem to be doing fine,' he said, crossing to his tool chest. Dragging out his electronic pack, he hurried over to the bomb. 'Now, all I need to do is disconnect the detonator here, and we should be set.' He waved over his shoulder. 'I'll need total silence for this, so please don't applaud.' Bending to his task he selected one of his instruments, and began to work on opening the outer casing.

Ishtar was still writhing in the throes of agony when her body suddenly went rigid from her platinum hair to the point of her silver tail. With a final scream she slowly faded away, till there was no trace of her left in the room.

Agga looked at Enkidu, unable to comprehend what was happening. 'Is it — over?'

The ape-man shrugged. 'Who can say? We must do as we were told, and wait for word from the Doctor.'

The Doctor was busy reassembling the casing of the bomb. 'Right,' he said briskly, getting to his feet. 'That should do it.' With a smile, he tossed the bomb at Urshanabi, who caught it out of reflex. 'We can erase Ishtar from the telepathic circuits now. I've disarmed the mechanism, Sergeant Benton.'

'What should I do with it?' the nervous ferryman asked.

'I should think it might come in handy to help repower your wrecked ship,' the Doctor told him, patting him on the shoulder. 'Along with the rest of the circuitry and equipment from Ishtar's inner sanctum, I think you could get your ship ready for lift-off again. With my help, of course. That should solve that little problem, too. I do love a tidy solution, don't you?'

With a groan, Ace awoke. 'Who kicked my head?' she muttered, rubbing at her temples. Struggling, she was glad to accept Utnapishtim's help to sit up. Then she realized where she was. 'What's going on. Professor?'

'Professor?' The Doctor glared down at her in a haughty fashion. 'My dear Liz, please call me the Doctor.'

'Liz?' Ace stared up at him in bewilderment. 'What's happened to you? You don't sound quite right in the head.'

'I'm perfectly fine, thank you, Jo. I've just had to regress to one of my former incarnations to solve the problems we faced, that's all.' He rubbed his hands together, studying the odd readings flickering across the console's registers.

'The name's Ace, Professor.' Remembering the apparition she had seen at the TARDIS console before all of this nightmare began, she asked: 'Are you that bloke we saw who was all hair and teeth?'

'That buffoon? Certainly not.' With all the dignity he could muster, the Doctor gripped his coat lapels. 'I've reverted to my third incarnation. Which I always thought was the best — I think. Certainly the most competent, at any rate.'

Ace's head had stopped spinning now, and she made it fully upright at last. 'So, what did I miss?'

'Just about everything,' he replied. 'I've managed to defuse the bomb, and I'm about to erase Ishtar's mental patterns from the telepathic circuits.'

'You put her in there?' Ace was shocked. 'Professor, you know you've been having trouble with them!'

'Nonsense, Sarah Jane. There's nothing wrong with either my memory or my ship.' He patted the console, lovingly. 'She's a good girl — which is more than I can say about some people.'

'You managed to lose my memories in it,' she pointed out.

'A slight miscalculation, nothing more.' With a sigh, the Doctor turned to the controls. 'Look, I'll get rid of her right this — Jumping Jehosephat!'

'What's wrong now?' Ace asked, dreading the reply.

'I can't seem to find a trace of her...' He bent over the

readout, indexing through. 'She doesn't seem to be where I put her.'

It didn't sound good. 'You've screwed up,' Ace said, feeling icicles slipping down the inside of her spine. 'You've really done it this time.'

'Don't be silly. I know exactly what I'm —'

There was a sharp burning smell, and an arc of electricity snapped at his fingers from the panel. He sucked at his fingers, staring at the instrument readings. 'That shouldn't have happened,' he complained. 'I'll just —' As soon as he tried to move in again, another huge spark crackled across the controls.

'That doesn't look good, Professor,' said Ace, grimly. 'What's going on?'

'Probably nothing,' the Doctor replied, sounding far from certain about this. 'The old girl is getting on in years, and probably just needs a good overhaul to set her right.'

There was the sound of an explosion from deeper within the TARDIS, and the ship shook. Struggling to keep her feet, Ace pointed as the viewer screen came to life.

Ishtar's silver face smiled down at them, triumphantly. 'Doctor! I really must thank you. This is an intriguing little device, isn't it!'

'What's happened?' Utnapishtim called out, waving about in an attempt to regain his balance as another spasm seemed to shake the ship about them.

Swallowing, the Doctor stared in horror at the central console. 'It looks as if I've made a terrible blunder,' he admitted. 'Somehow, Ishtar is still with us — a bit too literally. She's inside the TARDIS control circuitry...'

## 22: Apotheosis

Ace was flung against the large chair, which she clutched at for support. 'Why is it so difficult to stand?' she yelled.

The Doctor clutched at the hat-stand. 'She's varying the internal gravity,' he explained. 'Flexing her mental muscles, so to speak. Creating pockets of positive and negative gravitic waves. Makes things very unstable.'

Urshanabi slid across the floor, slamming into one of the walls. Grabbing at the roundels there, he managed to stabilize himself. 'Doctor, what has gone wrong?'

Reluctantly, the Doctor admitted: 'I made a small mistake. I thought I was transferring just the brain patterns of Ishtar into the telepathic circuitry. Somehow, she must have used that link to physically transfer herself. It's theoretically impossible, but so is the flight of the bumblebee, and he manages well enough.'

Hanging onto another portion of the wall, Utnapishtim called out: 'But what about the virus I set to destroy her?'

'Offhand, I'd say it didn't entirely work.' The Doctor had more important things on his mind than talk. Somehow, he had to regain control of his TARDIS. But how, when touching the controls might be enough to kill him?

Looking down at them all from the screen, Ishtar laughed. 'You fools! Thinking you could destroy me!'

'We almost did!' Ace yelled back, fighting the nausea that came from the fluctuating gravity.

'No,' Ishtar replied. 'That virus of Utnapishtim's did not destroy me — it made me stronger! I was not to be taken by such a simple trick a second time. My pathways are guarded against such intrusion. All that it did was to lock my mechanical attributes for a while. Now I am free, and have a delightful new form to take on.'

With a laugh, Ishtar started to play with the controls on the console. Levers and switches moved, dials registered and fell back. Lights pulsed, and the rotor began to spin.

'With this device in my control,' she boasted, 'I shall be restrained no longer to one space or time. I shall be free to roam the reaches of the Universe! Soon the entire created order will know one mind, one will — one true goddess!

The Doctor, ignoring all possible repercussions, threw himself onto the console, and tried to wrest control from her. For a second, nothing happened. Then, coupled with an evil echoing laugh from the screen, a tremendous jolt of electricity passed through him. With a cry, he staggered back from the panels.

'No, Doctor,' Ishtar snarled. 'You cannot have your ship back. It is mine, now and forever!'

Inside the temple, everything was still. Gilgamesh and Enkidu were moodily prowling about the room. En-Gula and Agga maintained their vigil over the stricken princess.

With a moan, Ninani opened her eyes. Staring weakly upwards, she asked: 'Father?'

He pressed his lips to her cold hand. 'Daughter. You are well again?'

'I am — myself again.' She struggled to move, but fell back. 'Yet I am so weak.' She stared at En-Gula, averting her eyes from the marks that were still visible on her friend's neck. 'I am sorry,' she whispered. 'Ishtar was too strong for me. I couldn't fight it.'

'Hush,' En-Gula told her. 'Rest. It's over now.'

'Yes,' Agga agreed happily. 'You are whole, and Ishtar is gone. Everything will be fine.'

The room was still shaking. Ace managed to stagger drunkenly to where the Doctor had fallen. Thankfully he was still alive, and merely dazed. 'Come on,' she told him. 'Get with it! Come on...'

His eyes finally managed to focus. 'Are we at sea?' he asked, disoriented.

'Permanently,' she replied, trying to help him up.

'First-class cabins, I hope,' he muttered, regaining his feet. Swaying, he looked about the room. 'That's better. It's good to be back in control again. For a while there, I was lost.'

Ace stared at him, understanding dawning. 'That other one of you — he's gone.'

'Hopefully,' he agreed. 'I was getting heartily sick of him and my smug ways. It's hard to believe I was ever that arrogant, isn't it?' When Ace didn't answer, he pulled a face. 'You don't know when you're well off, my girl.'

'We're not well off,' she complained. 'Ishtar still has the TARDIS under her control, remember?'

'Oh yes,' He paused to think. 'I wish she'd stop this playing about. I'm getting quite giddy.' Then he gave a grin, and added loudly: 'I don't think she *can* stop this gravitic fluctuation. She's not as much in control as she thinks she is.' He winked at Ace. 'Brer Rabbit and the Tar Baby.'

'The what?'

The floor suddenly became firm once more, and the Doctor managed to straighten up to his full five foot six. 'It's about time,' he grumbled, eyeing Ishtar's image on the scanner. 'Taken you this long to work out something simple like the internal gravity?'

'Bait me all you wish, Doctor,' Ishtar smiled. 'I am in control here, not you. And you will never have your craft back again.'

'Fat lot of good it'll do you,' he sneered, tapping his head. 'You need what's up here to make the TARDIS work.'

With a scornful laugh, Ishtar's image vanished from the viewer. 'You forget, Doctor,' came a whisper all about the room, echoing inside all of their heads. 'I can *be* in there. I control the telepathic circuitry as well as everything else in the TARDIS. Anything that you know, I can absorb from their data banks.'

'Try it,' the Doctor said, softly. 'It'll give you a bigger headache than you ever bargained for.'

'You taunt me, Doctor!' Ishtar's voice was filled with fury.

'I could slay you in a moment! All I need to do is turn off the life support systems inside this ship, and you and your friends will perish in agony! Slowly, achingly, despairingly.'

'Can she do that, Doctor?' called Urshanabi. Even though gravity was back to normal, he was still sitting by the wall. Ace realized that he was nursing a broken and swollen wrist.

'Not from here,' the Doctor replied. 'I routed all the life supports through the secondary control room long ago.'

'The what?' Ace had no idea what he was talking about.

'Secondary control room' he explained. 'It's a rather nice wooden affair. About half a mile off thataway.' He pointed beyond the interior doors. 'I used it for a while, but this old place has grown on me. Anyway, I never bothered to reroute the life supports from there, so we're safe for now, whatever she threatens.'

There was a sighing, like a wind through their minds. 'Fool!' came Ishtar's whispering voice. 'I am here, within your puny ship, and I can be there also. Now we shall see if you can live without air.'

The voice was gone, and the Doctor jumped quickly to his feet. 'What an idiot!' he crowed. 'She fell for it, hook, line and sucker.' Dancing about the central panels, he snapped quickly at several switches, and then grinned at their mystified faces. 'Got her where I want her.'

Ace voiced what was in all of their minds. 'What are you talking about?'

'Haven't you ever read Brer Rabbit?' he asked her, scornfully, carefully working on the now-safe controls. 'He was once trapped by Brer Fox, who was going to kill him. Brer Rabbit begged for anything but to be thrown into the minefield, or hawthorn bush, or something. Anyway, he begged so long and loud that eventually that's where the fox threw him. Which was precisely what Brer Rabbit wanted, of course, and he hopped off to freedom.'

Ace said: 'You're not making much sense.'

'Look,' he said, patiently. 'I told Ishtar she could control the life supports only from the other control room. Thinking I didn't want that, she naturally rerouted herself into the circuits there.

214

Which was exactly what I *did* want, and closed off the rest of the systems. She's trapped inside the other room now.'

'But won't she turn off the air?' asked Utnapishtim.

'Let her,' the Doctor answered. 'By the time it affects us, I'll have the circuits purged of her. There's nothing she can do to us now.'

'The last time you said that,' Ace observed, 'the TARDIS went —'

The TARDIS gave a shudder, and the lights started to dim. It felt as if they were trapped at the epicentre of an earthquake. The craft was bucking and twisting.

'You were wrong again!' Ace yelled, furious.

'She put in a couple of buffers of her own,' the Doctor admitted ruefully, studying the panel. 'She's really remarkably adaptable, I'll say that for her. Thanks to these, she'll be back in the main circuits again soon. Unless...' He eyed the power levels, worriedly.

'Unless what?'

'Well,' he told her, slowly, 'there's the architectural configuration. Only it's a chancy game.'

'And dying isn't?' she yelled.

'True.' The Doctor's fingers hesitated over the panel. 'All right.' He started the programme running, explaining as he worked. 'I need a lot of power to wrench her drastically out of the circuits — more than the TARDIS can normally offer. So what I'm doing is reconfiguring the interior dimensions, losing some of the TARDIS's mass, which gets converted into energy for us.'

'You mean you're using up a bit of the TARDIS to give us power?'

'Basically. E equals MC squared, or something like that. Or was it cubed? Anyway, with that power, I'm going to jettison the bits of the TARDIS circuitry that Ishtar has taken over into the Vortex. That will fix her, once and for all.'

'Vortex?' Utnapishtim asked, puzzled.

'It's a sort of whirlpool of energy and so on that underlies the body of time and space,' Ace explained to him. 'Tremendously destructive, if you don't have the right sort of equipment to control the flux.' She glanced at the Doctor. 'but if we jettison these bits of the circuits — won't we be up the creek, too?'

'No. Plenty of redundant areas in the circuits. She's mostly in the secondary mechanism for now, and I won't miss any of that. The other bits I could soon replace, I'm sure. Trust me, ejecting her into the Vortex is the best answer.'

'And it will destroy Qataka?' asked Utnapishtim.

'It will destroy anything,' the Doctor assured him. 'It's raw, primeval starstuff. Uncontrolled and uncontrollable forces, tugging in all directions simultaneously. We can only enter it within the protection of the TARDIS. It'll snuff her out like a candle in a hurricane.' With a wild grin, he shot home the final levers. 'Now!'

The TARDIS gave another lurch and settled down. The lights flickered, went out, and then returned. The time rotor spun, and a deep, roaring noise filled the room. The fabric of the ship seemed to tear, and for a second Ace felt as if she, too, were being wrenched apart. The ship gave a final shudder and then everything was normal once again.

'That's it?' Ace asked, hardly able to believe it.

'That's it,' the Doctor beamed, checking the readouts. 'She's out of the ship, and gone forever. Snuffed out of existence in the cosmic winds. Extinct as a hoodoo, Ace.'

'Dodo,' corrected Ace, automatically.

The Doctor frowned, and stared at her. 'Are you sure?' he asked. 'I was certain your name is Ace. Or is it Jo?' He shook his head. 'I'm still not quite the person I was and will be. But it'll come to me in time. All things usually do.'

Shaking her head, Ace grinned at Utnapishtim. 'Well, I think it's all over at last.'

The old man nodded, thankfully. 'I hope so. I had thought Qataka dead once before, though. She's very tough.'

'Not this tough,' the Doctor retorted, reconfiguring the controls. 'Right, let's tie up a few loose ends, shall we? Who's for a quick walk? The air will do us good. And maybe we can have a feast with the kings, eh?'

\* \* \*

The Doctor studied the horizon from the walls of Kish. 'About there, I think,' he announced, pointing off towards the southeast. 'Utnapishtim and his technicians should be about ready to leave now.'

Avram started off into the distance, shading his eyes against the glare. 'They are going back to the heavens?' He had an arm draped with obvious pleasure about En-Gula's waist.

'Something like that.' The Doctor grinned down at Ace. 'I knew they'd manage it with my help.' The two of them had spent the past few days working on Utnapishtim's ship. The Doctor had been forced to restrain himself from improving on the original design, and settle for just repowering the craft. As one last gift, he had accessed the TARDIS memory banks and selected a destination for the survivors of Anu — a world where there was currently no life.

'Will they make it, do you think?' Ace asked him. He grinned back at her.

'I don't need to think,' he replied smugly. 'I know. According to the data bank, they will settle the planet they're heading for. An expedition from Earth will contact them sometime in the thirty-second century. When I help people out, I do it properly.'

'Right,' Ace retorted. 'And I did nothing, eh?'

'You helped a little.' The Doctor winced in mock pain as she punched his arm. 'Perhaps more than a little. You did fine.'

'I'm not the only one.' Ace nodded to where Gilgamesh, Enkidu, Agga and Ninani were all conversing. 'They all seem to be getting along well, I think —'

Whatever she was going to say was lost. 'Look!' En-Gula cried, with delight, pointing into the distance. The Doctor looked at his pocket watch, and smirked.

'Right on time, too.'

On the horizon a bright plume of light shone, rising from the ground. As it moved upwards, the predominant yellow of the glare started to change, flashing purples, reds and oranges. Still signalling maniacally, the light rose until it had shrunk to nothingness.

Turning back to the Doctor, Ace laughed. 'Well, they're on their way to that planet you suggested. Utnapishtim doesn't have to worry about war with the human race now.'

'No,' the Doctor agreed, pensively. 'Just about restarting his own race. Well, we all thrive on challenge. He'll be right.' He glanced down at Ace. 'You're looking insufferably smug about something.'

She grinned, pointing at Avram and En-Gula. Now that they had seen Utnapishtim's ship return to the skies, they were slipping off together. 'Isn't it great? If it wasn't for us, they'd never even have met up.'

'Oh, I don't know about that.' He stared at some inner reaches of his mind. 'Fate and time have their ways of working things out, you know.'

'And what about that?' Ace nodded to where Agga and Gilgamesh were clasping hands and slapping one another on the back. Ninani — looking somewhat embarrassed — and Enkidu were looking on. 'Those two old enemies are friends now. I love happy endings.'

The Doctor looked at her sharply. 'Have you never paid attention to me, Ace?' he sighed. 'I thought you'd progressed beyond seeing only the surface by now.'

'Oh, you're just still bad-tempered because I yelled at you.' She refused to allow him to destroy the warm glow she was feeling.

'Happy endings!' he replied scornfully. He gestured towards the two kings. 'Agga's basically sold his daughter to Gilgamesh to cement an alliance. Nobody cares whether she wants to marry that lout. And it won't work, anyway. Gilgamesh will throw over the treaty, invade Kish and enslave the lot of them in a couple of years. Just as soon as he gets tired of Ninani. He's very changeable. Happy endings!'

Her smile wiped away now, Ace looked at him. 'What about the rest of them, then?'

'Enkidu? He's going to die shortly of some wasting disease, which is what prompts Gilgamesh's bad behaviour, but doesn't excuse it. Avram — well, he's going to go into Gilgamesh's employ as the court musician. He's going to write down his version of this adventure — and it'll become the oldest known story in your world. Of course, no one will remember that he wrote it, but you could pick up a copy of it in a good bookshop in Perivale.' He smiled. 'If there are any good bookshops in Perivale. Mind you, since Gilgamesh is paying him for it, I'll give you three guesses who ends up the hero.'

'It figures,' Ace said glumly. 'And what about Avram and En-Gula?'

'History doesn't say. In the grand scheme of things, a musician and his wife aren't considered very important. You can imagine a happy ending there, if you like.'

'Thanks a lot.' She surveyed the horizon again. 'Well, I guess we should be going.'

'Bored so soon?'

'Not exactly. I just want a more varied diet. I'm getting really sick of baked pheasant. And that barley beer makes me want to puke.'

The Doctor smiled again. 'Back to the TARDIS and the food machine, eh?' He looked back at the conversing kings. 'I think it's high time we slipped away, too. Off we go.'

To Ace's disappointment nobody seemed to notice their departure. She had rather enjoyed the attention that she'd been getting during the past few days. Still, the Kishites had a lot of cleaning up to do, so she couldn't blame them. She and the Doctor briskly strode back across the fields towards the oasis where the TARDIS waited. They were almost there when something occurred to her.

'Oi, Professor. What about this Timewyrm thingy? We've not seen hide nor hair of it.'

'Yes, I'd wondered about that myself. The only thing I can conclude is that the message I triggered was for some other time. When I was fiddling about with the telepathic circuits I must have started it up early.'

Ace shrugged. 'It makes as much sense as anything else about you.'

'Cheeky!' The Doctor unlocked the TARDIS and ushered her in. 'I've a good mind to leave you here, you ungrateful wretch.'

'But then who'd tell you how brillant you are?' she said. 'And speaking of having a good mind, are you back to normal now? When you were your old self, you kept getting things muddled.'

'It's hardly surprising,' he replied, crossing to the time controls. As he began to set the co-ordinates, he added: 'There are physical aspects of personality too, you know. My third persona was a bit annoyed at what he was stuck with for an exterior. I was always very vain back then. It must have caused him some grief. But now I'm whole and complete again. He's back in the closets of my mind where he belongs, and I'm the captain of my own mind once more.'

'Which reminds me,' Ace said. 'I don't remember that you ever apologized to me for mucking about with my memories. I still haven't forgiven you for that, you know.'

He regarded her through the glass column of the time rotor. A puckish grin twitched at the corners of his mouth. 'Ah, but how do you know that I didn't apologize, and that you've just forgotten about it?'

'Don't start that,' she begged. 'My memories are important to me, you know.' She shuddered. 'It was horrible, when I woke up and didn't know who I was.'

'Yes,' he agreed. 'Memories are a very important part of ourselves. Without them, we're just flotsam and jetsam in the seas of time.' He seemed haunted by his thoughts, and patted the console. 'I sometimes wonder if it's a good idea to ever wipe out my old memories. I lose enough when I regenerate as it is.' He eyed her again. 'I'd advise you never to take up that business. The price you pay for it is perhaps a shade too high for most beings. It might have been difficult for you to maintain a sense of your own identity without your memories, but think for a moment how I must feel — when the only memories I have really belonged to some other, distinct personality who once shared this body with me.'

'A bit rough, eh?'

'But endurable,' he added. 'Still, with great power comes great responsibility.'

Ace grinned. 'Is that from that Hegel bloke again?

'No. Marvel Comics, I think.' He smiled, impishly. 'I don't quite remember.'

Ace laughed. It was impossible to stay angry with him for long. His quixotic nature was too infectious. Besides, as she had told Enkidu, the Doctor was one of the few people she'd ever met whose purposes she almost fully agreed with. When he bothered to share them with her. 'So,' she asked, 'now where are we off to?'

His fingers began to dance across the controls. 'Oh, I thought we deserved a little vacation after all of that. I was thinking of — ' He broke off, and looked at her. 'No. You did a good job back there, Ace. You choose. Any where, any time.'

She thought for a moment. 'Well, there is one place... But you'd probably find it boring.'

'Never!' he replied. 'There's always something fascinating to see and do.'

'Well, I've always had this dream of travelling in a paddle boat on the Mississippi River.' She sighed. 'With all of the gamblers, and the ladies in their posh dresses, and the fella at the honky-tonk piano, playing —'

'*Waiting for the Robert E. Lee*?' he suggested, eyes twinkling. 'Well, why not?' He finished setting the destination. 'I've always wanted to try a mint julep myself.' With a flourish, he set the time rotor in motion. Accompanied by the usual cacophony, the TARDIS slipped out of phase with the Earth and back into the maelstrom of the Vortex.

'Well, that's a relief.' Ace frowned, and pointed. 'Hey, your pocket's bleeping.'

The Doctor stared down at the pocket in question. 'Odd. I wonder why it's doing that?' He stuck in his hand, and pulled out a small device. A red light on it was flashing in time with the electronic noises. 'The time path indicator...'

Ace had virtually forgotten about his little device. 'Didn't you say that it only registered when there was something moving through time straight at us?'

'Yes.' He began feverishly connecting it back into the main console.

'Then it has to be the Timewyrm, doesn't it?'

He nodded, and she could see an excited gleam in his eye. 'At last!'

# 23: Timewyrm!

The bleeping sound from the time path indicator was getting louder and higher in pitch. The red light was flashing like a strobe at a disco, hurting Ace's eyes. Glancing away, she asked: 'Presumably we're in trouble?'

'I should think that's a fair guess, yes.' He completed the work of rewiring the device back into the main controls. 'Right, let's see what we can find out about this beastie, shall we?' Without waiting for an answer, he began to manipulate the controls. The time path indicator continued to register, however, and the Doctor frowned. 'That's very odd.'

'Now what's wrong?'

The Doctor bit his lower lip thoughtfully. 'Well, taking off from the Earth should have gained us a bit of time. But this Timewyrm thingy — or whatever it is — seems to have compensated for the move almost instantaneously. Which is theoretically impossible.' Then he grinned. 'Still, you know how unreliable theories can be.'

'I know how unreliable *your* theories can be,' Ace agreed. 'So we're still in dead lumber then?'

'You have a colourful way of phrasing it, but you're essentially correct.' He began scanning the signal he was picking up. 'It's most perplexing. This reading says that it's the TARDIS coming towards us.'

Ace tried to work that one out. 'You mean it's another Time Lord after us? The Master, maybe?'

'Ace,' the Doctor said, exasperated, 'I didn't say *another* TARDIS — I said *the* TARDIS. This one.'

'But that doesn't make sense, Professor. Does it?'

'Everything makes sense when you have enough information. I just don't have enough information, that's all.' He tapped at the readings, but they refused to change. 'Maybe it's something time-reflective, bouncing our own signal back to us?'

'Or maybe it's on the fritz, and is tracking itself?'

He glared hard at her. 'I can tell the difference between an internal fault and an external puzzle. This is definitely the latter. But we should find out what it is in about sixteen seconds.'

'How can you be so sure?'

'Because,' he replied, smugly, 'the other TARDIS is going to materialize then.'

'Wait a minute,' Ace said. 'I thought we had a force field about the ship to stop that sort of thing from happening.'

'We do,' the Doctor agreed. 'But in this case it will do us no good at all. The other object is moving on precisely our own frequency. It can slip through the field like a hot knife through butter.'

None of this sounded at all reassuring to Ace. 'So what can we do?'

'Wait!'

Within seconds, they could hear the same off-key wailing, crashing sound that the TARDIS itself made on materializations. Between the console and the door, something began to take shape. Something seven feet tall, metallic, and vaguely female in form.

'Ishtar!' yelled Ace. 'It's Ishtar! I thought you'd destroyed her!'

'So did I,' the Doctor agreed, showing as little surprise as he could. It never helped if the enemy saw you looking uncertain.

With a final curl of her lips in contempt, Ishtar's form was complete. Delightedly, she threw back her head and laughed. Then she looked down at them both. 'So,' she purred, inching towards them, 'you thought that you had destroyed me, didn't you?'

'That idea had crossed my mind, yes,' the Doctor agreed. 'But I must admit you appear to be very fit for a corpse.'

'I am fit, Doctor!' Ishtar slithered closer to them, her red eyes burning down on them both. 'I've never felt better in my lives. You thought you'd trapped me when you cast me off into the Vortex, didn't you? That I would be torn apart by the forces there?'

'So — why weren't you, scumbag?' Ace growled.

'Because I am infinitely adaptable. And now, I have become virtually infinite in power, also.' She smiled down at them, confident that they could not escape her. 'When I was in the Vortex, I could hear voices speaking to me. It is not some great, raging inferno of chaos out there, Doctor! It may seem like that to your narrow, petty minds, but there is order, and there is a grim beauty in the time winds. And there are creatures that live there. I could hear them feeding.'

'The Chronovores,' the Doctor murmured, mostly to himself. Seeing Ace's look of bafflement, he explained: 'They are creatures that live outside time and space as we know it. Somehow, they devour time, growing stronger. Rather like the Third Law of Thermodynamics incarnate. I met one once.' He shuddered at the memory. 'And I hope never to meet them again. They're very strange, very mysterious and very powerful beings.'

'And very logical, in their own way, Doctor,' Ishtar informed him. 'I, too, being mostly mechanical, am very logical. When I could feel the forces of the time winds ripping at my fabric, I applied my mind to adapting to the forces within the Vortex. Thanks to the portions of the TARDIS that you cast off with me, I could begin to control the fluxes. And, ironically, that old fool Utnapishtim even helped me. That computer virus he attempted to destroy me with proved to be flexible and adaptable. Instead of it destroying me, I merged with it.'

'Ishtar —' the Doctor began, but she cut him short with a slice of her hand through the air.

'No, Doctor — I am Ishtar no longer. Just as I was once Qataka and then grew to become Ishtar, now I have gone beyond the entity that was once Ishtar. Now I am more than humanoid, more than computer programme — more, even, than the elemental forces of the Vortex itself. I heard the Chronovores whispering in the time-winds. They gave me a new name. *Timewyrm*.'

Ace tried to grin. 'Bit late, aren't you?' she joked. 'We've been waiting for you since we first arrived on the Earth.'

'Indeed?' That interested her. 'And how did you know of my becoming?'

'I warned myself a long time in advance,' the Doctor replied. 'Now I know why. Because in my meddling, I've created you, haven't I?'

'You, Doctor?' The Timewyrm laughed. 'No, you merely created my possibility. The Vortex made me. I am no longer restricted to one small segment of time and space. Now I can roam wherever I please, and act as I wish. There is no one in all of creation who is powerful enough to stop my will from becoming reality.'

'You do go on, don't you?' the Doctor complained. 'Why don't you just tell us what you're here for, and then shut up?'

If he was hoping to irritate her, it failed. The Timewyrm smiled that slow, infuriating grin again. 'Doctor, surely you have not forgotten? I promised to devour you, and so I shall. All that you have done to me has not destroyed me. It has made me stronger. Now, when I taste all of those thoughts within your mind, I shall know all that you know, absorb all that you are.' She licked her metal lips in anticipation. 'You should be happy, Doctor. You will become a part of what I am — though a very small part.'

'No thanks,' he answered, skipping back behind the console, keeping it between them. 'I've other things to do with my life. I don't intend to end as an hors d'oeuvre for a jumped-up tin goddess.' He began to reset the controls as quickly as he could.

'Doctor, do something,' Ace hissed, edging around to join him without taking her eyes off the Timewyrm for a second. 'Is she really as dangerous as she thinks?'

'No,' he replied, working feverishly. 'She's probably far worse than she even knows herself. So — forgive me for what I have to do. It's been nice knowing you — most of the time, anyway.'

Suspecting the worst Ace tried to turn to face him, but at that moment the Timewyrm made her move. Fading slightly until almost transparent, the shimmering snake-woman shot into the space occupied by the rotor. She extended her ghostly right arm; the hand disappeared into Ace's chest. Ace felt needles of ice passing into her skin, and gave a cry of shock and fear.

'I am not tied to the dimensions you are chained by,' the Timewyrm gloated. 'I can be incorporeal — or dangerously solid ...' As she spoke her arm began to regain colour and body. Pain grew within Ace's chest as she felt the fingers of ice becoming fingers of steel. The agony expanded, flowers of flame bursting within her. She tried to scream, but nothing would come. It felt as if her chest was being torn out from the inside.

It stopped. The Timewyrm screamed, fading almost completely to a barely-visible spectre. Ace collapsed on the floor, sobbing. Her chest heaved as she sucked breath after welcome breath into her tortured lungs. The Doctor, a look as pale as death on his haggard face, pressed the final buttons in the pattern.

From somewhere deep within the TARDIS the cloister bell began to sound a death knell. *Boom ... Booom ... Boooom ...*

'What is happening?' the shadowy Timewyrm screamed, clutching at her head in agony.

'Time ram,' the Doctor said, with finality. 'You chose the weapons, Timewyrm. You've incorporated parts of the TARDIS within you to give you your powers. Now you will experience the peril of playing with time. I've set my TARDIS to materialize in exactly the same coordinates that you have chosen. As the power builds up, the dimensions will overlap exactly. And then — BOOM!' He clapped his hands together. 'Mutual annihilation.' He looked down at Ace. 'I'm sorry, but there's no other way. I created this abomination, and it's the only way to destroy it.'

Ace managed to drag herself onto one elbow. She stared at the snake-woman. 'As long as it takes her with us, Professor, it'll be worth it.'

The walls seemed to be losing their shapes, flowing and

melting into that of the Timewyrm. Ace could no longer hear the tolling of the cloister bell. The whine from the central console was far too loud. It seemed to be getting very warm, too. Or was that just her imagination? The floor began to buckle as the TARDIS moved on its inexorable pathway to destruction.

'No!' the Timewyrm screamed. 'No, I cannot be destroyed like that. I can't! Not by a feeble little creature like yourself. I am the Timewyrm —'

The sinuous shape and hissing voice faded simultaneously into nothingness.

Suddenly, everything returned to normal. The TARDIS was whole again. Ace breathed a sigh of relief, but the Doctor leapt to the controls.

'No!' he howled, beating his fist on the instruments in frustration. 'Come back and fight! You hear me?'

Ace gingerly clambered to her feet, levering herself up using the edge of the console. When the room stopped spinning inside her head, she grabbed the Doctor's arm and shook it hard. 'Cool it, Professor!' she yelled. 'The Timewyrm's gone. It's over. We're safe.'

# Epilogue

The colours and shapes of the Vortex whirled about her. Voices rustled through her mind as she began to analyze herself and her capabilities. The Time Lord had not won, not at all. He had been lucky to escape with his life.

The Timewyrm basked in self-satisfaction. So much had been gained! This wonderful power to pass through the portals of time, to dip into any epoch, any mind that she might choose. And there were other gifts, still to be explored. No, the Doctor had not won. The first round of their fight was over. The Doctor had freed Kish and its people, but the Timewyrm had gained far more than she had lost. Mentally, she could see the vast ranges of time and space open to her gaze.

Where to go first? There was so much to do! So many possibilities! And she knew that the Doctor would cross her path again. Those moral scruples of his would compel him to try to take up the fight again. Well, the next time, he would not find the Timewyrm so unprepared ...

Meanwhile, a little trial of the powers she now possessed. Somewhere not too far off, an easy target, ready and ripe for the taking...'

Ah, yes...

'Safe?' The Doctor turned guilt-racked eyes towards Ace. 'The Timewyrm isn't dead. It's grown. It's learnt how to change frequencies. It's using the controls it's inherited from the TARDIS. It's escaped!' He massaged his forehead with his fingers. 'How can anyone in the Universe be safe when I've unleashed that abomination? It's a virus in the lifeblood of time, Ace. It can lurk and strike anywhere and anywhen it pleases. We'll never be safe again until I can destroy it.'

With another of his bursts of feverish activity he began to work on the panels again. The coordinates started to change, and the TARDIS lurched in flight as he fought the controls to move along a new setting. Gripping the rim of the console to steady herself, Ace managed to ask: 'What are you doing?'

'The Timewyrm still has parts of the TARDIS within itself. And I now have part of one of its implants — the one I took from your head — lodged inside the telepathic circuits. I've aligned the circuits to lock into its wake through the Vortex. Now, wherever it's heading, we can follow.'

'And?'

'Haven't you been listening? Destroy it, of course. We've loosed this horror on the multiverse. It's up to us to destroy it.'

'What's with this *we* stuff?' Ace demanded. 'You never bothered to tell me what you're up to, so how can you blame me for —'

'Quiet!' the Doctor snapped, pointing at the time path indicator. It had turned a solid green and was whining urgently, like a dog desperate to be let out. 'It's landed somewhere, somewhen.'

'Where? When?'

He shrugged. 'What's the difference? We have to follow — now!' He threw home the controls, and with a groan of protest, the TARDIS locked in on the signal and bore onwards through the Vortex.

Ace had barely had time to find her way to her room when she heard the Doctor's voice echoing through the TARDIS corridors, calling her back. She retraced her steps to the control room, and immediately saw the answer to her unspoken question: the time rotor had stopped moving; the TARDIS had landed.

'Let's see where we are, shall we?' the Doctor said, flicking the switch that turned on the scanner. The screen glowed, faded, and cleared — to display a grey vista of mist and drizzling rain.

Ace recognized it instantly. 'Oh no!' she said. 'It's a wet weekend in Wigan — or somewhere like that.'

'London,' the Doctor said. 'That dirty-looking stretch of water is the Thames. I think. The natives look as cheerful as ever, don't they?'

Ace glumly watched a few overcoated figures tramping stolidly through the downpour. 'Professor — what's that tower in the background?'

The Doctor peered at the screen. 'Oh yes,' he said, with a self-satisfied smile. 'We are in London, then. It looks as though I'll need my brolly out there.'

The next book in this series is *Timewyrm: Exodus* by Terrance Dicks.